Times and Places

Julie,

I very much hope you will enjoy reading my book.

With best wishes

Keith Anthony

——— 9/4/18.

Times
and
Places

Keith Anthony

The Book Guild Ltd

First published in Great Britain in 2018 by
The Book Guild Ltd
9 Priory Business Park
Wistow Road, Kibworth
Leicestershire, LE8 0RX
Freephone: 0800 999 2982
www.bookguild.co.uk
Email: info@bookguild.co.uk
Twitter: @bookguild

This work is entirely fictitious and bears no resemblance to any persons living or dead.

Typeset in Minion Pro

Printed and bound in Great Britain by CPI Group (UK) Ltd, Croydon, CR0 4YY

ISBN 978 1912362 141

British Library Cataloguing in Publication Data.
A catalogue record for this book is available from the British Library.

For Mum, Dad and Sally

Contents

Acknowledgements

I am very grateful to my mother for her enthusiasm and painstaking work, editing earlier versions of this my first book, and to my father, who had his own poignant, humour-full flair for writing. Both your influences permeate my story. Thank you for having been my loving, inspiring, fun, hardworking parents.

Thank you as well to Georgina, who first read my manuscript through the night (and still went to work the next day!) and then re-read it more slowly, providing many thoughtful suggestions.

While my main character, Fergus, goes on retreat in Lancashire, I went to St Beuno's in North Wales and the seeds for "Times and Places" were sown there, over four years ago. He and I were lucky to find such special locations. Similarly, I don't know what meditation app Fergus uses, but thank you to "Headspace" which has served me well.

Finally, I took a cruise and it inspired the setting for my book, but the *Magdalena* is not that ship and the bizarre goings on I describe on board did not happen in real life! I hope, therefore, nobody misrecognises themselves or is hurt by anything I have written: it is fiction. Thank you to the officers, entertainers and entire crew of that real ship for their hard work, often a very long way from home, giving others holidays to remember.

Keith Anthony
Autumn 2017

He himself fixed beforehand the exact times and the limits of the places they would live. He did this so they would look for him, and perhaps find him…

Good News Bible, Acts 17 26–27

Prologue

London – August 2001

"Excuse me…"

The woman who had rushed up to the police officer must have been about eighteen years old – just a year in the job and it was already automatic for the newly recruited constable to make assessments of those she encountered on her busy central London beat – yes, about eighteen, around five foot six, white, brunette, pretty rather than beautiful, bright rather than academic… middle class, fit, arty maybe.

"… I think the gentleman over there is in some sort of trouble, he says he's lost something, or someone, he seems to be very upset."

The officer, only six or so years older herself, followed the pointing finger and saw an elderly man, sitting on the kerb and crying uncontrollably, while passers-by stared, mocked or gave him a wide berth.

For a moment, she turned back from the distressed man and looked the young woman straight in the face. In the Metropolitan Police you quickly learned that urban life could be grim, but also that goodness was out there, sometimes hidden, sometimes shining conspicuously against the sprawling cityscape. Such felt the case today: the young face appeared to belong to someone naive and caring; though not yet confident enough to intervene personally herself. It was the face of someone in town for the day before retreating back somewhere less harsh. It was the face of someone lucky.

"Thank you miss, that's kind of you. Leave him to me, I'll make sure he's OK."

And with that the police officer headed across to the sobbing gentleman, while the young woman disappeared back into the crowds.

1

Southampton – Saturday 19th November 2016

It all ended with Fergus in his pyjamas being escorted off the ship in Southampton, with a port security official either side, but how had it begun?

It seemed both an age and but the blinking of an eye since he and his wife, Sylvie, had left their Chiltern home, a seventeenth century house set like an island on a sea of green lawns, which sloped up to woodland on three sides and to a hedge and the road on the fourth. This was their idyll, where they had lived for approaching forty years, where between them they had accumulated almost two lifetimes of memories and where a third entire life had played out, that of their daughter Justine.

It was hard for them to leave, even for a three week holiday, but now the car was packed, weighed heavily with suitcases and bags. Fergus checked his small holdall one final time for wallet, tickets, passports – yes, all still there. As they set off down the drive, it was as if the house were clinging to them, until finally, once they pulled out into the lane, it was forced to let go and watch them disappear, wondering how long it would have to wait, once so full of life but now entirely empty, for their return.

Sylvie drove through the village and on towards the main road, feeling relieved that all the preparations were finally complete. Next to her, however, she sensed a certain restlessness increasing in her husband until, at the roundabout where they were to join the motorway, he suddenly confessed:

"It's no good... I can't remember switching off the boiler!"

Sylvie had grown used to this sort of thing and, knowing he would otherwise spend their entire holiday worrying about returning to the smouldering, blackened shell of their beloved home, she was keen to set his mind at rest.

"Don't worry, we're in good time, I'll turn round."

Ten minutes later, it seemed a little surreal to arrive back at the house when they should already have been twenty miles away. They were seeing it as they had not been meant to see it, looking a little abandoned and rather sad, though unsurprised by their premature homecoming – there had almost bound to be a false start. Fergus disappeared inside.

"So?" she gently enquired as he got back into the car.

"Yes, it was off." He wondered whether this was a good or bad answer in the circumstances, but then another thought came to mind.

"Just a moment..."

He suddenly climbed out again, leaving Sylvie bemused as to what was going on. She watched him hurry back up to the house, fiddle around with his keys and then give the front door a good final push, just to be sure.

"Sorry, I thought I might have forgotten to double lock it as I came out."

"And had you?"

"No."

"And, while you were in there, you didn't turn any lights back on, fire up the wood burner, leave the freezer door open, start running a bath perhaps?"

It was meant as a kindly tease and he wasn't in the least

bit worried about the latter three possibilities, though he did fleetingly wonder about the lights. However, even for him, enough was finally enough. He plugged his seat-belt in with a decisive click:

"Everything is definitely off, everything is definitely locked!"

She released the handbrake and they headed back down the drive, the house again receding behind them in the rear view mirror, eventually disappearing for good behind a hedge as she turned back into the lane.

They travelled mostly in silence. The traffic was light and, despite the thirty minutes their return home had added to the journey, they made good progress. Fergus hypnotically watched the motorway unveil itself in front of him, relaxing before what he suspected might be fairly chaotic scenes of handing over luggage and car keys; not to mention all the queuing he feared would be involved with check-in. Still, the cruise had been booked months previously and now they were finally on their way. The fact that the weather had turned cold was perversely satisfying: they were heading south to the sun!

This was a proper holiday and one that was long overdue, a treatment prescribed by his wife to counter the anxiety she had seen creep up on him since... well, since their world had dramatically changed. Somehow, it had not felt right to go before now, or he at least had not felt ready. He struggled to remember the last time they had actually gone away. There had been his eight day silent retreat in Lancashire three and a half years earlier, but that had been on his own and hardly a holiday. And there had been their week together in Slovenia six months after that, to celebrate his sixtieth – yes, that should definitely count. Otherwise though, he had to go all the way back to when the three of them had visited the Lake District in the autumn of 2005, striking lucky with sunshine in that beautiful but notoriously rainy corner of England. Yet, more than the fine weather, he remembered how fortunate they had felt that their twenty-three year old daughter had still wanted to come away with her parents. Things had looked so good for her then, none of them could have guessed her own luck was about to run out.

Fergus sighed involuntarily.

"Nearly there!" Sylvie said, resting her hand a moment on his thigh.

With only twenty miles to go, they still had over an hour to reach the docks. This should have been plenty of time, but just a few minutes later they saw an ominous motorway sign, shimmering amber in the distance: '*Slow Down – Carriageway Blocked*'. Fergus felt his stomach tighten: this didn't look good.

The warning was unnecessary, the traffic had no choice but to reduce speed and, all too soon, it came to a complete standstill. Feeling a familiar panic begin to surge within him, Fergus sought to remember the calming mindfulness techniques he had been learning – another Sylvie prescription for his nerves – but somehow he couldn't focus. He cursed his constant need to check things. He had known he had switched the boiler off, why had he not trusted himself? In going back to the house, they had thrown away the advantage of leaving early, thereby allowing misfortune a foot in the door. Fergus feared they were going to '*miss the boat*', or at least be involved in a '*will we or won't we make it?*' cliff-hanger all the way to the port: the prospect exhausted him. It did not escape him, either, that he had slipped from a relative calm into this intense anxiety in a matter of minutes: his inability to control his own mind annoyed him every bit as much as the congestion which now held them captive – all they could do was wait.

Looking ahead about half a mile, he could see flashing blue lights: someone was clearly having a worse day than him. Nevertheless, it was with relief that, after a short while, he noticed the vehicles far in front seemed to be inching forward and, slowly but surely, this ripple of movement drew ever closer, until before long they too began to move. A few minutes later, they drove past the scene of the accident, which was on the other side of the carriageway and involved a burnt-out car.

Fergus couldn't help but wonder whether unknown lives had come to an abrupt end, certainly there must have been injuries. He pictured how, later in the day, relatives would be reeling with shock as they learned of the tragedy, even as he and Sylvie were perhaps sitting down to their first ship board dinner. He was familiar with that sensation of horror and disbelief and how, over time, it gave way to grief, an uninvited companion to whom you eventually grew so accustomed that you actually became scared it might go away, though it never really did. With the accident behind them, they picked up speed again, continuing south down the motorway, while the northbound traffic queued stationary for several miles as (Fergus imagined) paramedics fought to save those precious but unknown lives.

The respite was brief as Southampton itself was completely snarled up with what the radio described as *'football traffic'*. They crawled through the city's suburbs, growing ever more concerned that, not having seen a sign to the docks for several miles, they may have taken a wrong turn. Suddenly, Fergus saw one, an image of a ship on an arrow, directing them left:

"There!"

He pointed it out to Sylvie just in time for her to swerve across two lanes of furiously hooting traffic, escaping the worst of the congestion as they dived down an anonymous side road towards the port. So close and yet, even then, the journey still felt interminable, with painfully slow progress through road works and repeated traffic lights, all conspiring to turn red as they approached.

By the time they finally arrived shipside they were late, but the well-practised machinery of the cruise line swung into action, reassuringly indifferent to the fact that they should have been there thirty minutes earlier. Before they knew it, Fergus and Sylvie's luggage had been whisked away, they had handed over their car and they were in a long but steadily moving line of passengers zigzagging across the departure hall.

Looking around, it was clear that this was not a cruise for the younger generations. The predominant hair colour was grey and the accessories of choice appeared to be walking sticks, zimmer frames and wheelchairs, with a handful of mobility scooters into the bargain. None of this worried either Fergus or Sylvie. They were both retired themselves and, if they were to be below the average passenger age, then they would enjoy being the youngsters again. Anyway, they knew what they wanted from this cruise and it did not involve nightlife and parties, but rather relaxing in warmer weather and experiencing the wonder of being out on the ocean, the beauty and vastness of which Fergus hoped would re-invigorate his spirits, and perhaps even his faith.

They passed through security and checked-in. Painless. Furthermore, because they were late, they were able to board straightaway, clanging their way across the gangway onto the ship and receiving a warm:

"Welcome aboard the *Magdalena* Mr and Mrs Fredricks!"

The smiling steward directed them to their cabin two decks below and Fergus tried his key card in the lock, hearing a soft click as he did so and seeing a little light flash green. He pushed down on the handle and opened the door. They were on deck four, the second lowest on which passengers could reside, the areas beneath deck three being reserved for crew quarters and the working parts of the *Magdalena* which were out of bounds. They had wondered whether, being so far down in the ship, they would find themselves in some sort of modern steerage, but in fact what greeted them, as they tentatively peered inside, was a very pleasant surprise. Two single bunks, with plump green quilts, stretched invitingly lengthways against either side wall. Above the bed heads a big picture window looked out onto the docks, while between them was a table, with a softly glowing lamp reachable from both sides. Although their accommodation was small, it was very homely, and big enough if they were organised with their storage strategy. They were on the port side and well towards the bow. Fergus hoped this meant they would feel the pitching and rolling of the ship as they roamed the Atlantic. Sylvie was more cautious and checked her handbag for the seasickness tablets she had purchased, just as a precaution, though she did wonder, should they hit bad weather, how long Fergus' seafaring enthusiasm would last.

They entered the cabin and found their luggage already waiting for them inside. Fergus finally relaxed again. His wife, well attuned to him after thirty-eight years of marriage, kissed him. She also felt relieved the journey was over.

"We deserve this," she smiled.

"Yes, I think we do," he replied, his tension almost visibly evaporating above him, like morning dew rising from a hedge.

"Explore or unpack?" Sylvie asked, but she was already opening the bags and assigning him cupboard space, so Fergus simply joined in. Soon both were busy emptying their cases and putting their clothes away, either hanging garments in wardrobes or tucking them away in drawers, he half wondering if they would ever find anything again.

They finished just in time to attend a muster drill, which simultaneously instilled both confidence and nervousness: the former because the crew clearly knew what they were doing, the latter because many of the passengers evidently did not. With their broken English, the staff had difficulty explaining the intricacies of lifejackets and escape routes to pensioners who appeared unsteady enough on their feet while mustering in the stability of a port, let alone while going down in a storm. Fergus and Sylvie, however, simply noted where their lifeboat was situated and how they should fasten their own vests, laughing as they practised putting them on, until they were both sure they would know what to do in the unlikely event of disaster. Thereafter, they put the exercise out of their minds, even he understanding that there were some things it did no good to worry about.

By the time they had done all this, the ship was just getting underway. It was already dark, but both felt they should go out on deck for departure. In truth, there was not a great deal to see, no bands playing rousing tunes and no excited crowds waving them off with cheers and ticker tape. Instead, the ship manoeuvred quietly out of its berth and made its way slowly through the gloom of the Solent towards the flickering lights of the Isle of Wight. A low key departure maybe, but, despite its modesty, the beginning of an adventure that would take them deep into the Atlantic, to the Azores, south to Cape Verde and then back home via the Canaries and Madeira... some six thousand miles over twenty-one full days, eleven of which would – and here was the highlight for both husband and wife – be entirely at sea.

"Happy holiday Fergus," said Sylvie reaching for her husband's hand.

"Happy holiday," he replied, gazing dreamily into the distance.

Nearby, a crew member emerged from below and took down the red and green striped flag of the cruise line which had been flying from the stern, packing it away neatly in a large storage box, before disappearing again down a chained-off stairway. Clearly there was nothing further to see.

"Come on, you're getting cold." Fergus led his wife to the door leading back into the ship and heaved it open against the wind for her to step through.

"Let's explore!"

2

London – Late June 2006

Justine had been conceived outdoors on a balmy evening, amidst the beauty and risk of an only half hidden nook on a Cornish headland, to the accompaniment of the Atlantic waves crashing on the rocks below... she was the welcome result of an expression of love.

If her creation had been idyllic, her demise, almost exactly twenty-five years later, was tragically mundane. As so often is the case with sudden deaths, the day had begun without hint of the horror to follow and, leaving the house to a slightly fumbled paternal embrace and to her mother's promise of vegetable lasagne for supper, Justine was surprised only by the unfamiliar freshness in the air, after what, until then, had been an oppressively hot week. And so, at half past seven, she was waiting at the station, shivering slightly in the unexpected chill and unknowingly entering the last hour of her life at the same time as her train entered the platform, its headlight shining brightly, but unnecessarily, on this Midsummer's morning.

Justine was new to commuting and still took a secret pride in feeling different from her fellow travellers. They huddled in groups in the places where decades of experience had taught them the train doors would open and where, like hatchlings scrabbling over food, they would discreetly jostle for the chance of a seat. She had been amazed the first time she had witnessed this. It had reminded her of childhood days when the village boys had fought each morning to get the best seats on their school bus, a heaving mass of struggling bodies by the door, with the driver usually appearing bored, gazing wearily out of the windscreen until this daily 'survival of the fittest' was finally over and he could pull away. Justine had always felt relieved to be a girl as she watched this little battle, while waiting for her own lift to school. Commuting had echoes of this, though here the women were just as determined as the men, and Justine was resolved not to be a part of it.

So, as usual, she was last to board the train. Normally there were seats left, though only those difficult to reach ones: the place by the window the other side of someone reading or sleeping by the aisle; or else the seat taken up by bags belonging to someone looking the other way, making it awkward for Justine to ask they be removed. If she did, nevertheless, approach such people, they would immediately let her sit down, as if they had all the time been willing and had only needed to be asked. Occasionally she did have to stand, but she preferred that to joining the daily edging for position on the station platform. She wondered if she would still feel that way if, like many on board the train, she commuted for years and years, decades even... She hoped she wouldn't have to. She didn't.

Justine was untypical for her age in never making or receiving calls on public transport and quickly feeling impatient and intolerant of those who did. The so-called 'quiet coach' had at first seemed the obvious answer, but she had soon learned that there were almost as many phone calls there – tedious, self important, one way discussions about presentations, sales pitches and meetings – only here they were all the more annoying for taking place in a part of the train where there should have been peace and quiet.

'People couldn't care less,' she had concluded to herself with an irritation untypical of her usual good nature, before chuckling at the echoes of her father's grumpiness in her own thoughts. She rapidly adapted and, after a few days, accepted that trains were rarely now the havens of calm from the outside world that once they had seemed. Instead, she learned to while away her journeys listening softly to music in her earphones, daydreaming and perfecting the art of letting any intruding chatter pass her by. If she could not avoid the loudest conversations (and she noted volume of speech was almost always in direct proportion to dullness of content), she could, at least, be grateful that her working world – dance – seemed so much more interesting and colourful than theirs.

Today she had found a seat and, unusually, everyone sat in silence, some dozing, some reading, the only noise the quiet tap tapping of a woman across the way on her laptop, and of course the train itself rattling down the track. As she looked around, Justine quite unexpectedly felt a surge of compassion for her fellow travellers and a certain warmth in their commute shared. She smiled to herself, remembering a happy trip to Penzance she had taken with her father some thirteen years earlier, it felt in another lifetime, which had begun with the run down this very line. She loved the Chilterns and wondered whether she would ever grow tired of the scenery on this route as, the occasional station rushing past, the train shot across fields, through woodland and tunnels, passed over viaducts and raced on towards London.

She switched on her music and a song began to play in her headphones, 'Roam' by Summer Martins:

"*It's just one year ago since she went away,*
It feels like forever and like yesterday,

She was so full of colour, the world has turned grey,
And feels small when it once seemed so vast.
No it doesn't ring true but her absence is real,
You're still wanting to call her to say how you feel,
But she's no longer with you and you can't conceal
How she haunts you, this ghost from your past."

Justine had actually met Summer eight months previously because she had been selected to dance in the video accompanying this very song. Even though she had only been performing in the background, it had still been a big break and she had been thrilled when it had gone on to be a hit. Justine the commuter danced out the routine again in her mind, as the familiar words and tune played into her ears against the competing rhythms of the train.

Looking out of the window at the next station, she noticed a young man and woman standing facing each other, both holding on to one cup of coffee between them, allowing it to heat their hands on this first, fresher morning, each releasing it occasionally to enable the other to take a sip. She smiled to herself again, warmed by this intimacy, and, as she did so, the man caught a glimpse of her and smiled back, prompting his girlfriend also to look. She didn't appear resentful of her partner's interaction with an unknown woman through a train window… quite the contrary, she seemed at ease and content. Justine was pleased for her, for them both.

Lost in these thoughts as the train pulled away, Justine twisted a lock of her hair, appreciating how lucky she too was to be so content. More than content, she was happy. On the day she was to die, she felt vibrantly alive: she was dancing for a career, practising for a London show, and, in the first seven days of rehearsal, she had easily held her own amongst her colleagues, even gaining the praise of the director. More importantly, she had Jones. Yes, she was twenty-four and back living at home, but that did not matter: she loved her mother and father and adored the old house in which she had grown up. She always pitied those who bemoaned their parents. Had they all been as awful as claimed? She remembered once meeting a woman who had ferociously criticised her mother whilst simultaneously eulogising about her toddler son playing with a toy lorry just a few feet away. Justine had wondered how hurt this woman would be if, one day, he disparaged her the same way.

Yes, marriage, children, parenthood… at twenty-four these thoughts were beginning to bubble to the front of Justine's mind: she felt sure Jones was the right man for her and was quietly confident the feeling was reciprocated, though she didn't allow the fantasy to run away with itself. However, as the train reached the suburbs, life was certainly looking and feeling good and she was grateful.

Just after twenty past eight the train pulled into Marylebone station. Justine, as always, allowed those who wanted to hurry to do so, before she herself gathered her belongings and stepped off the train. She strode down the platform to the automatic barriers, where she put her season ticket to a gate. It rudely snatched it from her fingers, spitting it out a second later and opening just long enough to allow a begrudging exit, before closing fiercely behind her. Remembering to post a small package in an old fashioned red pillar-box on her way, she crossed the main concourse to the echo of announcements bouncing off the station walls, either detailing the next train services or pleading for passengers to keep their belongings with them at all times. All the while, her fellow commuters swarmed around her, the majority diving down into the Underground and on to offices across the Capital, while a few queued for coffees first, to take with them. She held her breath as she passed through the huddled group of smokers at the station entrance, then spluttered because, misjudging when it was safe to breathe again, she inhaled a cloud of smoke blown out by a man lighting up a few paces ahead of her. He briefly turned around, irritated and assuming she was making a point with her coughing. Justine recomposed herself and finally reached the bus stop where she waited, sniffing for any lingering smell of nicotine in her clothes and dimly aware that the usual crowd of people was not waiting there with her.

She preferred taking buses to the tube – true, there was always someone having a loud mobile phone conversation on board them too, in English or in one of the many other languages spoken in London, the common factor always its volume. Nevertheless, the bus felt safe while, at rush hour, the Underground heaved and lurched like a threatening beast, with immense crowds filling the platforms and squeezing on to the trains. Anyway, there still felt something special about riding the top floor of a London double-decker bus; at least there did for Justine.

All of our lives are quietly counting down to their ends and, as the final minutes of hers ticked away, Justine wondered why no buses were coming and why nobody else was waiting there. Eventually, she looked up and noticed the little yellow sack with black writing which had been placed over the top of the post. It read:

"Bus Stop Out Of Use."

For a moment she felt foolish, standing there all on her own, and she looked around to see if anyone was watching, but the world was uninterested in her embarrassment. She briefly wondered what to do, before picking up her bag and deciding to walk the short distance to another stop, on a different route, just around the corner.

No sooner had she set off than it started to rain. She had got used to the recent fine June weather and was only wearing a blouse and a light jacket. She certainly had not thought to bring an umbrella. Still, her aversion to the tube was stronger than her dislike of a summer shower, so she put her head down, quickened her pace and kept going. All she needed to do was walk a hundred yards, turn left at the junction, then another fifty and she would be there.

As she approached that next street, she noticed a woman walking towards her, from the left, pushing a double buggy – twins perhaps? Stepping out from the corner, Justine looked closer to see if she could glimpse the babies she was already imagining, tucked up safely behind their rain covering. She never saw them. Instead, a cyclist, swerving to overtake the pushchair, rode into her at speed. Justine didn't know what had hit her, spinning round for a moment as she hopelessly sought to keep her balance, before falling and striking her head with great force on the pavement.

The improbability of the accident only added to the sense of disbelief felt by those she left behind: it would not have occurred had the bus stop been open, had she taken the Underground, had she not had her head down against the rain, had the woman with the twins been moments earlier or later, had the cyclist not been on the pavement. These and so many other things had needed to align. How could it have happened? It seemed so unlikely – and yet somehow it had.

Such questions were to torture her parents over coming years, and Jones too, but they were not to distress Justine herself, as she was no longer there. Perhaps she had returned to wherever she had come from that balmy evening some twenty-five years previously, on that headland against which, even as her spirit departed from a coldly indifferent London street, the waves continued to wash timelessly, and for whom Justine's lifespan had been but a fleeting moment.

3

English Channel – Sunday 20th November 2016

Their first full day at sea started with both Fergus and Sylvie waking slowly, gradually becoming aware of the motion of the ship, gently rising and falling, as it approached the mouth of the English Channel and the beginning of the Atlantic. Above them, shining through a gap in the curtains, a light reflection from the sea danced playfully on the ceiling. They had slept soundly, perhaps the combination of this rocking motion, a bottle of Merlot with their evening meal and a late night, having attended the 'Welcome Show' in the Poseidon Theatre.

The show had begun with the 'Cruise Director', a professionally jolly woman in her thirties, presenting various members of the ship's company to the passengers. Noticing the large number of crew on stage, each eagerly anticipating their own turn to step forward, Sylvie had wondered grimly quite how long this process might take.

"And this, ladies and gentlemen, is Jennifer," the Cruise Director announced, making a sweeping gesture stage left towards an awkward-looking young woman wearing black-framed spectacles near, but not quite in, the shadows. "Jennifer is a very hard worker, she is responsible for the library and she also hosts the quizzes and... and... and what else do you do Jennifer?"

There was a brief pause while the self-conscious young woman said something out of range of a microphone – the thick lenses of her glasses occasionally flashing brightly in the spotlight – so the audience was obliged to wait in suspense for her answer, which was subsequently passed on with a flourish:

"Ahhhh yes, of course, she also teaches crafts at ten o'clock every day in the art room on deck three. Jennifer won't mind me telling you, ladies and gentlemen, that she is a real chatterbox and that there is nothing, absolutely nothing, that she likes more than to talk away those long sea days. So when you see her about the ship, please do stop and introduce yourself, she'd love to hear your news and, of course, she'll let you in on all the crew gossip too."

Jennifer seemed to squirm and to inch a little further into the stage left gloom, removing her glasses, perhaps hoping she might not subsequently be recognised. It was hard to tell in the dim lighting there, but Sylvie thought she looked horrified at the prospect of finding herself cornered in such inescapable conversations... but she couldn't be sure. In fact, on the whole cruise, Sylvie was never to see Jennifer again and Fergus was only to encounter her fleetingly once, which made them both think that, as well as being a very hard worker, Jennifer also kept a very low profile.

Meanwhile, the next crew member was already being introduced with a similarly extravagant arm gesture, this time stage right towards a neatly dressed man in his early thirties, smiling a grin so broad that Fergus worried it might actually hurt:

"And this, ladies and gentlemen, is Gavin... he is also a very hard worker..." It transpired that Gavin was the manager of the Tours Office and, as he jumped enthusiastically into the spotlight, waving both arms high above his perfectly coiffured head, it was clear he had none of Jennifer's inhibitions. Fergus could not help but conclude that Gavin looked the more likely chatterbox and that the timid librarian would probably be much happier left only to the company of her books.

And so it went on for another thirty minutes until, mercifully, a whole group of young men and women were introduced all in one go, as the 'Magdalena Show Troupe'. A few moments later, the music struck up, everyone else melted off stage and they took over the rest of the evening, performing a series of songs and dances around the theme of the sea.

Fergus felt the show was a little lame, but he couldn't help admiring the dancers with their extended arms and their high kicks, twisting their way across the stage, whirling and twirling, performing dramatic lifts and 'quick-changing' between a range of sometimes skimpy, sometimes extravagant costumes. Towards the end, as they raced around with long blue and green ribbons streaming behind them – apparent metaphors for the ocean – Fergus was drawn to one dancer in particular: a slight, rather boyish brunette, with deep brown eyes, who reminded him of his daughter, who herself could very easily have been performing cabaret on a ship, had things worked out differently. At one stage, the dancers came running down the aisles and, as she passed him, he caught her eye and she smiled. Somehow, this left him feeling slightly sad, but perhaps he was just tired after his lengthy day.

It had been after midnight by the time he and Sylvie finally slipped, exhausted, into bed. Now, waking up the next morning, having slept deeply through the night, they both felt relaxed and at peace. They lay resting a few moments longer, enjoying the *Magdalena* gently pitching and rolling them on the swell, before finally getting up on this, the first full day of their holiday, quietly relishing the prospect of spending it at sea.

Passengers were allocated set tables in the evenings but – thank goodness, thought Fergus – breakfasts were free seating, meaning he and Sylvie could sit where they chose and were thus spared another encounter with the woman they had endured two tables away from them at dinner, just twelve hours earlier. Her raucous outbursts had actually made them jump and she had seemed more interested in talking at high volume to the couple on the neighbouring table than to her own husband, who had sat patiently opposite her, perhaps with years of practice behind him. Instead, Fergus and Sylvie were able to eat their breakfast in peace, sharing a table for two and looking out on the Atlantic through the large restaurant windows, as they enjoyed a very full meal, beginning with some fruit, as a sop to healthy living.

"That was lovely," commented Sylvie, as finally she put her cutlery down "... but maybe not every day." Fergus agreed on both counts.

The *Magdalena* was small by cruise ship standards, but this and the plentiful 'sea days' had been the precise reason they had chosen this particular trip. They had no desire to hop between crowded tourist traps in a floating tower block of cabin apartments. There were just nine hundred passengers on board, compared to the several thousand on the largest modern vessels, and a little over three hundred crew. Of the ten decks, the upper eight housed passengers, the long corridors becoming more ornate with every level until, on deck ten – which they dubbed 'Millionaire's Row' – each cabin had a large pot plant guarding its door. Fergus and Sylvie, however, were very happy with their own more simple accommodation, down on deck four, with their picture window and the ocean its other side, just a few feet below.

Despite their good night's rest, they spent the morning sleepily digesting their breakfasts on a sheltered part of deck, enjoying the sea air. At noon, they were stirred by a brief fanfare over the public address system, heralding the first of the Captain's daily progress updates:

"Good afterrrnoon, ladies and gentlemen. An update from the brrridge. We are currrently steaming west south west and apprrroaching the entrrrance to the Bay of Beazcay."

Sylvie tried to place his accent, but struggled.

"The weather is parrrtly cloudy with wind force 6, an air tem-Per-ature of 7 degrrrees and a sea tem-Per-ature of 13 degrrrees. We are scheduled to arrrive at Praia da Vitoria, Azores, on Wednesday at seven thirrrty in the morrrning. Our speed is 14.5 knots."

Fergus sought to take in the technical detail, listening attentively and oblivious to the wild guesses as to the Captain's nationality – "Bulgarian? Italian? Croatian maybe?" – emanating from his wife.

"As therrre is some swell, please hold on to the hand rrrails as you move about the ship, in orrrder to avoid acc-Sea-dents."

"Russian do you think?" Sylvie said, vainly demanding an opinion in response.

"A few hygiene advices, please wash yourrr hands frrre-Quent-ly for twenty seconds in hot soapy water, as well as using the hand sanitisers you see about the ship and at the entrrrance to the restaurrrants. That's it forrr now, I wish you a very pleasant afterrrnoon."

"Well, whatever his nationality, he was a little dull!" Sylvie concluded.

"He's probably fed up," answered Fergus, now mentally back with her. "It's his official party tonight, he has to have his photo taken shaking hands with every passenger!"

"Not with us he won't!" Sylvie responded, appalled at the prospect.

"So that just leaves 898 others… I'm sure he'll be relieved!"

Both had brought e-readers and, skipping lunch on account of their earlier feast, they spent the afternoon further exploring the ship and moving between sheltered spots on deck, where they could read and relax, out of the wind. They did have to wrap up a little – a day out of Southampton in November is no guarantee of sunshine – but both felt exhilarated looking across the sparkling sea, with no land in sight. Sylvie even thought she glimpsed a pair of dolphins leaping out of the water, though they vanished again beneath the surface the very moment she saw them and Fergus, who had briefly strayed off on his own, missed them entirely. Still, this boded well.

Most people had remained indoors but, besides them, amongst the few exceptions were three young men who managed to spend the whole afternoon in the hot tub on the rear deck, steam and bubbles rising around them, as they lounged and sipped at a regular supply of cocktails brought to them from the bar. They seemed out of place on a ship where the average age must have been considerably over twice their own, and well over three times in many instances. Every now and then an elderly couple in dressing gowns trundled out to see if the bath was free, each time retreating back uncomplainingly when, even after a couple of hours, it still wasn't.

By around four o'clock and beginning to feel the chill, Fergus and Sylvie returned inside. They immediately found themselves in a very different world, one of quizzes, bingo, karaoke and various presentations on the islands where the ship would dock. For some obscure reason, there were also lectures on criminality, given by a jovial man with a ruddy complexion, a whisky glass permanently in hand and an infectious enthusiasm for his subject, advertised today throughout the ship as '*Rigor Mortis and the science of body decomposition*'. Of course there were also the numerous bars. Neither Fergus nor Sylvie really understood why anyone would want to do any of these things when there was a spectacular ocean outside, and they both had the feeling that there were going to be some elements of cruising they loved and others that felt very alien to them. At the same time, they had to admit that all this activity gave the interior of the ship a real buzz – the electricity of people having a good time – and for a moment they wondered whether they were missing out:

"We're a grumpy old couple of codgers!" laughed Sylvie, as they ambled to the Midships Lounge for a warming cup of tea.

"That's probably true," he replied, "but each to their own."

Fergus had spent much of his youth unenthusiastically doing things other people felt he should enjoy, but he had long since learned that sometimes you need to be faithful to what you want to do, even if it did make you feel different, and Sylvie agreed. They were to rely on this approach later that evening.

It was indeed the Captain's Party and the first of three 'formal nights' that would be held during the cruise. On these occasions, passengers and crew dressed up in their best attire: the men in black tie, the women in long evening gowns and accompanying finery, the staff themselves in their smartest white uniforms. This appealed to neither Fergus nor Sylvie and they were very willing to forsake their restaurant to avoid it. Instead, they ate early in the buffet, where a few other like-minded passengers did the same: perhaps the Captain would be spared quite so many photos after all. However, wandering the ship afterwards, they came across a long line of fancily dressed passengers, all patiently waiting to meet him. The queue snaked from the lounge where the party was being held, across a lobby, past the shops and the ship's gallery and, from there, over half the way back down a corridor towards the stern.

"Poor man!" Fergus muttered, sympathetically.

"I'm going to take a closer look," Sylvie whispered, as if setting out on a mission.

"No, no you can't, don't..."

But it was too late, she had gone, feigning a visit to the 'Ladies' near the entrance to the lounge, where the Captain was being berated by an elderly woman in a lurid blue dress and dripping gold jewellery. She appeared extremely upset that he didn't remember her from a previous cruise and his ever more profuse apologies seemed to cut little ice. He was beginning to look increasingly desperate, until the photographer finally intervened:

"Smile please!"

They both turned to look at the camera and there was an enormous flash, after which, before she could recover, the elderly lady was ushered away into the lounge. The Captain took a deep breath and turned courageously to the next in his line of guests, subtly trying to peek down the ship as he did so in order to see how much of the queue remained, his face briefly dropping as he realised it still stretched out of sight.

"Was it as bad as we feared?" Fergus asked, as his wife returned.

"Worse... far worse! Drink?"

Feeling like rebellious teenagers, they fought their way through the well dressed crowds and took the lift to deck ten, where earlier they had discovered what would prove to be their favourite evening haunt. 'The Conservatory' bar had windows looking out over the port and starboard sides of the ship, as well as forwards over the bow, and in the day time these provided beautiful ocean views. Now, at night, the reflections in the windows, combined with the slightly subdued lighting and the mellow music, created the most soothing of atmospheres. With so many at the party, the bar was almost deserted and the pianist played to just a handful of people. Fergus and Sylvie clapped encouragingly every time he completed a number, to the extent that he looked across at them and gave them an appreciative but slightly bemused nod, as if his musical skills had never before received quite such an enthusiastic response.

"Cheers!" Fergus lifted up his Pimm's to his wife as an elaborate upwards scale rang out from the pianist, presaging the start of a new tune. They clinked glasses and sat in a comfortable silence, eventually broken by Sylvie:

"Happy?"

"Yes," he nodded and they both let out a short laugh of relief at being back somewhere quiet, a contentment radiating within them as they savoured the prospect of this long holiday in each other's company.

"I bought you this… in the boutique… this afternoon," Fergus said, pulling a jewellery box out of his jacket pocket, "a souvenir from the ship, to say thank you, and that I love you."

Sylvie's eyes widened with surprise. "But you already say you love me in so many ways."

"I want to say I love you in every way."

Sylvie looked across at her husband and he appeared tired. Tired, and for the first time a little old. They had both been through so much, but what broke some couples had from the start brought them closer together. Their love was no longer passionate, but it was deeply rooted and, despite everything, there were many times when Sylvie felt blessed.

"Thank you," she said, kissing him on the cheek. She opened the box to find a lapis lazuli stone on a silver chain. She stared at it for a few moments in silence.

"It's beautiful," she wondered.

"I know," he answered cheekily, "and it's deep blue like the sea."

"Deep blue like the sea," she echoed. "You couldn't have chosen better!"

They sat again in silence, she contentedly, simply enjoying the moment with her husband, he seeking to do the same, but deep in the background disturbed by an insidious fear, that of living a life without her. She was precious to him beyond anyone's comprehension: he had no other close family, no friends whom he came close to loving, there was now only Sylvie. He had already learned once the hard lesson of how quickly something fragile and priceless could be lost. The prospect of a repeat terrified him.

4

London – Late June 2006

The scene of the accident was not promising, not promising at all. Police tape cordoned off the pavement twenty-five metres either side of the street corner, but there was nothing within that cordon other than a street sign, wet paving stones and a few manhole covers. There were no skid marks, no drops of blood, no torn bits of clothing, just the unforgiving, miserable surface against which some poor girl had contrived to fall and hit her head hard enough to send her directly to the morgue at St Mary's.

Katie – that's to say Detective Sergeant Katie Brady of Paddington Green Police Station – didn't think this was going to be a quick case to solve, unless a witness or CCTV gave them some sort of amazing break, but, unlike the victim, she wasn't holding her breath. The Scenes of Crime Officer shrugged his shoulders at her, it didn't look as though he were going to be providing any answers either.

"Not nothing!" he said, and in this instance Katie knew that the two negatives didn't make a plus. By this stage, the accident had taken place two hours earlier. An ambulance had been called promptly, but there had been nothing the paramedics could do except rush the already deceased victim to hospital, where she had quickly been formally pronounced as such. The scene had briefly been a hive of activity, as a number of officers secured it and identified those few witnesses who had lingered. They agreed on the following: a swerving cyclist, riding on the pavement, had hit the girl as she walked round the corner; the cyclist had been a woman and she had been riding too fast, if indeed any speed wasn't too fast when on the pavement. Beyond this, there was no consistent response as to her likely age, what she had been wearing, the type of bike she had been riding or where she had gone. The only constant was that "it all happened so quickly."

A police photographer took some photos, and an officer erected a yellow sign giving the time of the accident and appealing for witnesses before, after conferring with Katie, he took down the tape. She tried not to feel too despondent, there were still things they could do. She called the office for an update their end: the victim, a twenty-four year old, had been identified as Justine Fredricks and Thames Valley Police were on their way to her address to notify the next of kin. They had also volunteered to drive them up to the hospital, where PC Wendy Jackson – a family liaison officer from the Met – would take over. Eventually, they would be driven home again to pick up the pieces of their shattered lives. Katie sighed at the thought of the family receiving such news – perhaps at that very moment – and she didn't envy the officers who had to give it.

The plan proceeded as smoothly as it could under the circumstances: the girl's father and mother were brought to Casualty and a doctor escorted them on to see their daughter; meanwhile, Katie and Wendy met up at Reception where a nurse directed them on to an airless side room, explaining that the parents would be with them shortly. They sat down and waited, Katie feeling uncomfortably hot and nervously running her fingers around the inside of her collar, as if to help her breathe. A few minutes later, the door was suddenly thrown open and a doctor ushered a middle aged man and woman through, the hubbub from outside briefly intruding until it closed again behind them. He gestured that they should take a seat and gave them time to settle. The extra bodies quickly added further heat to the already oppressive atmosphere of the room and Katie felt her heart pounding in her chest as the doctor introduced them.

"These ladies are from the Metropolitan Police. They will look after you from here and talk you through the next steps. I am so sorry." With that he disappeared, leaving the parents sitting there, grey with shock and grief: an unmistakable, unfeignable look. Wendy waited a moment and then spoke softly, commiserating with their tragedy and explaining that, while she would do her best to support them, her colleague DS Brady would lead the actual investigation. Katie knew this was her cue and she felt a determination that she should sound sympathetic but also businesslike, it was important the parents had confidence the investigation was in good hands.

"Mr and Mrs Fredricks, I too am very sorry for your loss. As PC Jackson said, it is my job to ensure we investigate what happened, to do so as thoroughly as we possibly can, so that you have answers and that anyone who caused or contributed to your daughter's death can be called to account." She paused for a moment, then continued:

"What we believe so far, from witness statements, is that your daughter walked around the corner of Great Central Street and was hit by a cyclist who was riding along the pavement of the Marylebone Road."

Mrs Fredricks gasped. Katie paused again.

"We believe she fell and hit her head. She may have passed away instantly, the post mortem might tell us that, but we do know that she was immediately knocked out by the fall. I am sure she didn't suffer at all." Katie was aware this was a lot to take in, but she could also see that the father, at least, was listening intently, the mother appeared to be more obviously struggling to hold herself together.

"I'm sorry, I know this is hard for you…" she paused a third time. "The cyclist did not stop. We know she was a woman and we will do everything we can to find her." Katie momentarily pondered whether to say what they would do, but she decided that she had already given enough detail.

"Would you like to ask me any questions at this stage?" The parents shook their heads in unison, both looking downwards and holding each other tightly. "Wendy will take care of you now, you can stay here as long as you like and, when you are ready, she will ensure you get home safely. After that, she will stay in close touch with you, keeping you posted with the investigation, and I will do the same. And you can reach me too, either through Wendy, or by contacting me direct." Katie handed Mr Fredricks her card. "I cannot promise what the result will be, or that we will find the person involved, but I commit personally to running a professional investigation, to the very best of my abilities, to give us the best chance possible."

"Thank you," said Mrs Fredricks, quietly but genuinely, despite the words being better suited to receiving a cup of tea or a gift than to their actual situation. "It won't bring her back though, will it?"

"No, I'm afraid it won't. I'm so sorry."

Katie felt relieved to escape the hot, intensity of the room and, leaving her colleague behind, she sucked in deep lungfuls of fresh air as she returned to the police station, where she quickly received approval for her plan. First she would seek to trace the cyclist as far back and forward along her route as possible, using CCTV, and then, the next day, she would deploy officers to look for witnesses, or even a potential suspect. They would do this both at the spot where the calamity had happened and at strategic locations half a mile back and half a mile forward, as the perpetrator might seek to avoid the accident site itself. If they had no luck, they would interview female cyclists again a week or so later in the same places, in case the offender had by then regained her nerve.

In this manner, they were quickly able to trace the cyclist's route back towards the Tufnell Park area and on as far as Sussex Gardens, but any hopes they would follow her all the way back to her front door, or all the way on to wherever she was headed, were forlorn. The street enquiries the next day, and again just over a week later, led nowhere and Katie had to watch as police officers took vitriolic abuse from a number of women cyclists who found themselves being stopped for a second time in ten days.

Katie wasn't immune to such comments, they both stung and grated, but she had heard the like a thousand times before and knew they were made in both the heat of the moment and in ignorance of the tragedy. She was also experienced enough to realise that these women were venting frustration and that the last thing they really wanted was a good explanation. She hoped, therefore, that the officers on the receiving end of their fury would neither take the bait by arguing back, nor seek to justify themselves by providing anything beyond a brief but sufficient background to the case... they deserved better, of course, but sometimes you just had to roll with the punches and Katie briefly felt a sense of pride, even affection, as she watched her team at work.

A few women, including several who had been stopped the previous week, looked genuinely shocked to hear about the accident. They restored Katie's faith but, ultimately, it was all for nothing. She could see the investigation was going nowhere and indeed had nowhere left to go.

Wendy had been keeping Mr and Mrs Fredricks up to speed over this period, supporting them as best she could. She learned that Justine had been their only child and, furthermore, they seemed to have few friends and family to whom they could turn, though their daughter had had a boyfriend, who clearly shared their grief, and with whom they were obviously close. Katie had spoken to them on the phone twice, providing updates as to what she was doing, but there were never any real developments to tell them. Anyway, there was no hope of good news that mattered since (as Mrs Fredricks had observed at the hospital) the only thing they wanted – their daughter back – was not going to happen. A fortnight after the accident, a funeral took place as if to prove that point.

After asking first, Wendy and Katie both attended. It was a beautiful setting of a small church in a pretty village, surrounded by fields and rolling hills. The sun shone high in a blue sky traced with the occasional vapour trail of a jet heading from A to B without any knowledge of the personal disasters and dramas over which it flew. Pearl white cumulus clouds passed lazily across the valley, defying gravity as they cast their equally slow-moving shadows over the countryside below. Despite the occasion, Katie felt momentarily euphoric to be out of the city and, as ever more mourners passed through the lych-gate and along the path across the graveyard, she watched in fascination as no fewer than five red kites rode the thermals above the hillside.

They sat down in the last two remaining seats at the back of the church, which by now was also hot and sticky, on account of the hundred or more young people cramming its pews, interspersed with a handful of elderly relatives. All had come to celebrate a beautiful life and to mourn its early passing. Wendy had to ask a lone young woman if she wouldn't mind moving up. *"No problem,"* she had replied with a soft German accent, and Katie couldn't help but wonder what her connection might be. Mr and Mrs Fredricks entered and made their way down the aisle – an echo of a happier day – smiling encouragingly as they passed Justine's boyfriend sitting amongst his friends, but actually stopping just the once, for her to embrace an old man. His fragile arms held Mrs Fredricks tightly, as if it were too painful to let her go. Whoever he was, they seemed to be extraordinarily close. Eventually, he released her and she and her husband took their places, the sole occupants of the front pew and, despite the love around them, somehow alone in the crowd as their daughter's life was commemorated.

Every now and then, the mourners would be bathed in brightness, as shafts of light broke through the stained glass windows like dust filled laser beams; then, a few minutes later, these would fade as the sun slipped back behind a cloud, returning the congregation to the chapel's gloomy natural light. The effect added to the atmosphere of alternating grief and hope while prayers were said, hymns sung and friends recounted their memories of a young woman neither Wendy nor Katie had known, at least when she had been alive. Eventually, the service drew to an end and Mr and Mrs Fredricks were driven, along with the boyfriend and the old man, behind the hearse to the crematorium for a final private farewell.

"I think I need to update them personally, I mean there's not much to say, but perhaps I should find a way at least to say that," mused Katie, hesitating on the way back up the church path. "What do you think?"

"Give it a couple of days and I'll arrange something," Wendy replied, but Katie's attention was already taken again by the kites as they continued to circle effortlessly over the hillsides, as innocent of the tragedy beneath them as the distant aeroplanes higher still above.

5

North East Atlantic –

Monday 21ˢᵗ and Tuesday 22ⁿᵈ November 2016

By the second and third days of their cruise, Fergus and Sylvie were already slipping into routines which would hold them in good stead for the next three weeks. Once or twice a day, Fergus would practise his mindfulness with the help of an app that he had been using on his phone for a year or so, every day progressing to a fresh twenty minute session. The ship could be an idyllic place for this, with the sea air, the relaxing hum of the motors and the wash of the water breaking against the hull. The only time to avoid was noon when, on the Monday, Fergus was jolted out of his meditations by the loud fanfare heralding the Captain's daily report. Throughout the cruise, this regular update was never to vary, except in some minor weather and scheduling details, always concluding with the same *'hygiene advices'* and signing off with *'have a very pleasant afterrrnoon'*.

These were days Fergus and Sylvie both loved: surrounded by sea, their whole holiday ahead of them and nothing much to do but relax, read and (in Fergus' case) meditate in the strengthening sunshine. Other passengers found their own preferred ways to amuse themselves, or to be amused by the entertainments team, and the lifts were the places where all lives met. They had asked one man they encountered this way, somewhere between the fourth and tenth decks, how he spent his time and he had replied:

"Eating… what else is there to do?!"

The man had an endearing manner – along with an expanding waistline – and Fergus and Sylvie laughed genuinely, along with everyone else, but, once they were alone again, she couldn't help but comment:

"He'll put on a ton by the time we get home!"

And he wasn't alone, while Fergus and Sylvie ate well at breakfast and usually at dinner, they continued to skip lunch or just to take a salad. Others, meanwhile, seemed to spend most of their time eating, ingesting as much as possible at every opportunity, as if they feared the food would be taken away from them at any moment. You could almost see them visibly growing out of their clothes as they whiled away time in one of the lounges, waiting impatiently for the next feast.

"All the better for us," hailed Fergus, savouring the empty deck space.

Not being naturally gregarious, they rarely got involved in conversations with others at this stage, except that Fergus, whenever leaving or returning to his cabin alone, seemed to bump into Mrs Huffington, an elderly lady with a zimmer frame, whose quarters were even further up the corridor towards the bow. He never seemed to meet her when he was with Sylvie, to whom she became increasingly mythical as her husband related yet another encounter:

"She's always there!" he bemoaned. In fact, Mrs Huffington was perfectly pleasant. She just liked to talk, there was never an easy escape and Fergus was far too polite and, to his credit, caring to make an exit that risked causing offence.

"Ah, hello again Fergus! I'm beginning to wonder if you are stalking me!"

"No, no, Mrs Huffington, just coincidence," Fergus mumbled guiltily, cursing to himself as he emerged from the cabin at just the wrong moment.

"The swell's going to get up… you can tell from the air," she said, looking him earnestly in the eye, daring him to disagree, though how she could predict the weather from the air deep inside the ship he was not sure.

"Do you really think so Mrs Huffington?"

"Yes, it was just like this in May when I cruised to Iceland and Greenland, oh it was terrible it was. Soon people were being ill everywhere and you couldn't walk around it was so rough." She gripped her zimmer firmly, reliving the storm in her mind.

"Could you not?" said Fergus, desperately trying to sound interested while fighting a greater desire to get back to his book, out on deck with Sylvie.

"Oh, no… people were falling around all over the place. There again, I blame the Captain, he could have taken a more southerly route, but he wanted to make up time."

"Do you know much about navigation Mrs Huffington?" He hadn't meant his question to sound sarcastic, but evidently she wasn't sure and she fixed him in the eyes again:

"I have been cruising for forty years Fergus. I went on my first in 1976, a few years after my Lawrence died…"

Fergus suddenly felt compassion for this old woman who had lost her husband relatively young and had apparently been wandering the oceans alone, ever since. It felt to him as though she were in the gilded cage of a modern day Flying Dutchman: a ship which provided its captives with lectures, line dancing, pub quizzes and never ending games of bingo, along with inexhaustible supplies of food and alcohol, but never took them home.

"Oh, I'm sorry to hear that…"

"Well, it's a long time ago now," she replied and paused.

Fergus didn't want to be mean, but he didn't want to lose the opportunity afforded by the break in conversation either.

"I'd better get back to my wife, she'll be wondering where I am."

"Oh, she should know you can't get far away on a ship!" Mrs Huffington responded, not unreasonably.

Fergus and Sylvie felt a quiet admiration for the numerous very elderly passengers walking around, like Mrs Huffington, with their zimmer frames and sticks, or manoeuvring unpredictably on their mobility scooters. How much easier it would have been for them to stay safely at home, yet here they were, venturing out on the high seas, destined for exotic locations. They were travelling in luxury, that's certainly true, but they somehow still looked vulnerable and when one elderly woman slipped awkwardly to the floor, a concerned Fergus rushed across to help. Unsure quite what he would actually do, he was relieved to be beaten to it by a crew member who appeared well practised and adept at recovering such situations by standing in front of her, holding her hands and rocking her steadily to her feet.

Sylvie had known her own heartbreak with the old: she had been thirty when she had lost her mother and her relationship with her father had grown very close in the subsequent two and a half decades, with his slow deterioration painful for her to witness. He had died around four years earlier and, in the end, had been so confused that he couldn't even remember Sylvie's mother, his own wife:

"Was she pretty?" had been his last words.

"Very," Sylvie had replied holding his hand, "and you loved each other very much." She watched him smile and moments later slip away. It had felt both a very sad and a very happy way to end a long life.

If Sylvie had been good to her father, well, it was clear there were also other saints on board: Fergus had noticed them and looked on in admiration. Often it would be elderly husbands or their wives tenderly taking care of each other, especially when one was clearly much the older or frailer. One woman particularly caught his eye as daily she assisted her husband into the restaurant, helping him into his dining chair, cutting his food up for him and occasionally dabbing at his mouth with a napkin, before eventually heaving him back out of the chair and supporting him, as they threaded their way slowly back out again between the tables. Fergus was aware that he only witnessed these few kindnesses, in this one small section of their routine, and he pondered the many other things this lady would be doing for her husband throughout the day. It struck him as a deep love and he wondered whether he and Sylvie would be as patient with each other. He hoped so, but it was the sort of thing you could not be sure of until you were in the situation, though Sylvie had certainly been devoted to her father.

That same day, Monday, Fergus felt proud that, as far as he could tell, he was the first passenger to use the pool. It was filled with warm salt water and he could float effortlessly on his back, watching the clouds go by, rising and falling on the swells created by the gentle pitching and rolling of the ship, and disturbed only by the noise from the three Caballeros (as Sylvie had christened the trio of young men) laughing and joking from the nearby hot tub to which, once again, they had retreated. A number of passengers approached, asking Fergus what it was like and he assured them it was lovely. Sure enough, a short while after he had climbed out, he noticed several of them tentatively lowering themselves in. It was, however, the getting out that was the more painful: still very much in the North Atlantic, the winds whipped across the deck, encouraging a shivering Fergus to dash for a sheltered spot, where he fumbled to get dry and dressed as quickly as possible, while preserving his dignity as best he could.

He swam the next day too and, while half asleep on his back, he heard a voice calling to him.

"Hello there!" He lifted his head out of the water, it was the brown haired dancer to whom he had felt drawn at the cabaret.

"You are quite the little mermaid, I've been watching you!" she teased, as she crouched at the side of the pool.

"It's wonderful in here," he called back, while treading water, "but not so wonderful getting out!"

"Treat yourself to a brandy afterwards, doctor's orders!" She replied.

"Except you're not a doctor…"

"Oh, we all have to muck in when out at sea!" She stood back up, gave him a little smile and headed off.

Though his body was in the pool, it was his mind that was swimming: he hadn't just noticed the girl, he had been noticed too! He knew it meant nothing of course, but it still felt good. It wasn't a romantic attraction either, although he could see she was pretty, rather it was some deeper chord she had struck in him, and he had a good idea what that was. He decided such distinctions were probably best not shared with Sylvie, not yet at any rate, it was (he had to admit) a little complicated.

They both felt slightly uncomfortable about the staff more generally. The passengers, officers and the show team were almost all white, but the waiters, waitresses, bar staff, cabin maids and other crew were all from Thailand, the Philippines, China, Indonesia or India. It felt a little too close to some sort of apartheid for comfort, and the staff all seemed to work (and be worked) like Trojans. If they felt any kind of resentment they hid it with consummate professionalism, always being friendly, always immaculately turned out. Often Fergus and Sylvie would chat briefly with the waiters at their table or with the bar staff who brought them creamy coffees to enjoy on deck. Through these conversations, they gleaned that the crew worked every single day, often starting early and finishing late, with just a few short hours off in the middle, and that they had a total of two months' holiday a year, which initially sounded a lot, until Fergus calculated:

"That only adds up to one and a bit days off a week... not even equivalent to weekends, let alone having any actual leave!" The only time the mask slipped from a staff member, however, it did so briefly and with a heartbreaking honesty:

"I'm homesick madam," one barmaid admitted, when Sylvie asked her how she was, and they both felt a surge of compassion for this young woman, who was working on the Atlantic but whose heart was clearly some ten thousand miles further to the east.

"I guess," said Fergus, trying to see the positives, "they don't spend much while they are on board, so, even if their wages aren't great by our standards, they must save up money that will go a long way back home." Sylvie suspected this was true and, after all, nobody was forcing anyone to work on the ship, but somehow this logic didn't entirely relieve her conscience.

Despite this slight unease, they began to feel ever more at home on board and in their private little cabin, the only hint of annoyance continued to be at dinner in the restaurant, where the food was good, but the loud lady a couple of tables away was starting to fray their nerves. On the brighter side, they were also beginning to get to know their waiter, a Filipino called Angelo. At first they had thought he was uninterested, but they came to realise that in fact he was just kept very busy indeed. When he did have a moment, he would often come and talk to them, and they were keen to hear about his wife and young son and daughter back home in their small town, two hours north of Manila. He was counting down the days, even the meals, until he could return to see them in September:

"283 more breakfasts, 283 more lunches, 283 more dinners!"

It felt to Fergus and Sylvie that this was an awfully long countdown. Even then, it turned out his leave would not be much of a holiday as, when home, he described how he helped his parents on their farm. His priority was seeing and helping his family, not relaxing, which he explained (without meaning any criticism of the passengers) only left him bored.

As for the noisy lady, they had managed to control their irritation on the Monday evening, but by the Tuesday Fergus found himself getting edgy, watching her out of the corner of his eye as he ate. She would lean forward and sideways, her head angled, to hear what the smartly dressed couple at the next table were saying. As soon as there was an opportunity, she would jump in, embarking on a loud anecdote of her own, always concluding with a booming guffaw:

"… and then I said to him 'you can feel my buns anytime!' Hahahahahahah!"

Fergus winced and Sylvie looked at him sympathetically and conspiratorially. Worse, the couple's waiter seemed to be encouraging her, even bringing out a guitar to sing her a ballad, over which she loudly enthused, while her husband sat there, silent and superfluous.

"The restaurant's lovely…" Fergus said, as they strolled back to their cabin, "but I don't think I can stand that woman for three weeks! We may have to eat more often back in the buffet."

"It's bad luck, but don't let it spoil things, let's see how we go," Sylvie replied soothingly.

They had avoided the Poseidon Theatre on the Monday night because a comedian had been performing and, for both of them, the reward of being entertained by a good comic wasn't worth the risk of the forced laughter required by a bad one, or the embarrassment if he were crude. Instead, after dinner, they had relaxed back in the Conservatory Bar, sipping Pimm's and listening to the pianist. However, on the Tuesday night, the singers and dancers were scheduled to be performing again and Fergus and Sylvie were both keen to go. Sure enough, the troupe put on another good effort, given they were performing on a small stage rolling around in the middle of the Atlantic. Fergus tried hard not to stare at the dancer who had spoken to him from the side of the pool, making a point of spending time looking at the others in order to justify fleeting glimpses towards her. If she saw him she didn't show it, but he wasn't naive, he knew that to her he was just one of hundreds of much older men on board, to be replaced by hundreds more in a couple of weeks or so. He brought back no memories in her, but to him the resemblance was definitely there. It wasn't precise, in fact it was subtle, but still somehow haunting: she was a dancer; not dissimilar in size, hair and eyes; she was even about the age his daughter had been when she had died. The similarity was by no means uncanny, yet it was enough to provide a glimpse back through time.

After the show, the entire cast had somehow made their way from backstage and were waiting in the foyer as people left the theatre. Fergus saw his dancer there, relaxed, chatting and oblivious to the deep impression she had made on him. She noticed him approaching and, teasingly, mimed doing the breast stroke in his direction. He felt awkward and slow witted, not sure what to do or say, finally settling on a smile and a simple:

"It was a great show."

He and Sylvie walked a lap of the serenely quiet deck, drawing in deep breaths of Atlantic oxygen. He cursed to himself how, even in his early sixties, an attractive young woman could so destabilise his equilibrium, though he knew there was more to it than that. They ambled back to the cabin, Sylvie unaware of this mental wrestling going on in her husband's mind. Had she been alert to it, she would not have been annoyed, still less jealous, but would have immediately recognised her husband's feelings as rather typical of the grieving man she loved, someone adept at tormenting himself and who rarely made his own life easy.

6

Ljubljana – August 2004

Jones stepped out of the Hotel Kristina at about ten o'clock. It had been a long, hot, very full few days in which he, his best friend Ben, along with their other two friends, Andreas and Jack, had pooled their funds, hired a car and driven a grand tour of Slovenia. The adage that the best things come in small packages had proved accurate and, to Jones, the country seemed to be a little known haven of forests, lakes, mountains, rivers, hills and villages, along with a few small cities and just twenty-seven miles of north eastern Adriatic coast. He had been a little cautious not to sound too sensitive about Slovenia in front of his friends, but nevertheless it had made a deep impression.

They had flown in on Thursday afternoon, staying in Ljubljana that night, getting their first feel for this little capital city, nestled in the foothills of the Julian Alps. They arrived in time to witness a brief surge of activity as locals returned home from work, after which a relaxed calm descended on a town centre busy only with friends and families wandering the streets, taking in the atmosphere and enjoying the restaurants and bars. This was how Jones and his friends had spent their evening too, exploring lazily and conserving their energies for the more demanding days ahead.

On the Friday morning their tour had started in earnest. They hired the car and made the short drive to Bled, passing numerous wooden hayracks dotted around the countryside, like wall bars from a gym placed randomly in fields, but upon which the local farmers dried their crops. Some were simple structures, but others had sides and roofs, small buildings even constructed on top of them, almost as if they were somebody's home, though Jones didn't suppose they were. At the time, he wasn't even sure what purpose they served, but they added to a traditional charm which left him jealous that his own country's rural culture was rather less valued, ever increasingly squeezed by expanding cities, and scarred by the transport links between them.

Lake Bled itself was exquisitely pretty with its island church, to and from which a tiny ferry shuttled visitors without worrying about the need for a timetable. From a cliff top high above, a castle hung precariously over the water, offering those with the energy for a climb the reward of panoramic vistas and a refreshing mountain breeze. The friends scrambled up and gazed out across the lake, the island church and the Slovenian countryside beyond. Jones felt blissful, as if he could easily have remained there all day, drawing the air deep into his lungs and imprinting the scene on his mind. All too soon though, their planned itinerary demanded they scrambled back down, in order to walk the two hour circuit of the shoreline. Half way round and looking back across the water – between the island church to their right and the cliff top castle high to their left – they could see straight through to the Alps, which appeared to be brooding as dark clouds gathered moodily around their peaks, a portent of a stormy end to another day.

By the time the rain began falling on the lake, they were

already back in Bled itself, relaxing in the warm glow of an inn, drinking from pitchers of beer and taking lucky dip from a menu they couldn't understand. They suspected English versions would have been available had they asked, but somehow that would have detracted from their sense of adventure and of being somewhere new and wonderfully foreign.

The following morning they had driven on to Slovenia's largest lake, Bohinj, which Jones had found altogether wilder, further off the beaten track than Bled and more ruggedly beautiful, set deep in its mountain surrounds. They had walked around it, meeting only a handful of other hikers in the four hours it took them to complete the circuit. Those they did meet were invariably better equipped than them and much fitter, striding forward at speed, even the older ones, planting their hiking sticks with each step and exchanging a cheerful "dober dan!" with the boys as they passed, before quickly receding into the distance behind them. By comparison, Jones and his friends progressed slowly, but it did not matter and there was no rush. All the same, they greeted the reappearance of their car with relief, finally removing their boots and able to nurse their aching ankles and feet.

Satisfied with their efforts, they recovered for a short while in a nearby guesthouse, over coffee and slices of a layered pastry, a local delicacy containing ricotta, apples, raisins and walnuts. Jones pondered how even the cakes were nutritious in this healthy corner of the world. Energies restored, they drove on to Nova Gorica by the Italian border where, that evening, they straddled the frontier, not physically, but through their choice of hearty Slovenian foods and cold Italian beers, before collapsing into bed.

The next day, Sunday, had been spent on the Adriatic coast, wandering the cliffs and stony beaches of Strunjan and eating at the buffet in the local spa hotel. From the shore, it was possible for Jones to look right across the Adriatic to the coastline the other side of the bay. So close to Italy – he thought – and yet in its language, food and culture, Slovenia felt less western European and more a gateway to the mysterious Balkans beyond.

They spent the evening exploring the narrow streets and piazzas of the nearby Venetian styled town of Piran. Had it been located on the coasts of Italy or France, it would no doubt have been bustling with tourists, its lanes clogged up with their buses. It would certainly also have been the backdrop to countless magazine covers of skinny supermodels sulking and skulking around its dark, lazy interior, the Adriatic shimmering behind them in the distance. However, tucked away as it was here, Piran remained a hidden gem, familiar only to those in the know or who, through good fortune, stumbled upon its charms.

On their way back to Ljubljana the next day, they visited the caves in Postojna, marvelling at the light railway that wended through the stalactites and stalagmites to a cavernous chamber deep underground. For half an hour or so, they explored this subterranean world which, for millennia before the first little train arrived, must have remained undisturbed, home only to the blind Salamander living in its cold waters, and to its small, invertebrate prey. Suddenly, the lights went out – a standard surprise for the tourists – swallowing them in a blackness that was pitch and complete: hands could not be seen even as they brushed the lashes in front of eyes which, as the Salamander had found aeons ago, served no purpose here. Ears were barely more useful and, in the darkness, Jones became aware of the total silence, punctuated only by the sound of irregular dripping, each drop sending a slightly different tone ringing through the amplifying acoustics of the caves, an eerie soundtrack to this alien world.

Without thinking, Jones stretched out his arms and waved them in front of him, as if to explore the darkness, and, to his horror, his left fist knocked weightily into someone, provoking a short cry of shock or pain. A moment later, the lights came back on, revealing a young woman to his left, grimacing slightly as she rubbed the side of her head.

"Oprostite!" Jones said, mortified at his clumsiness, but also with a hint of pride at his recently learned ability to apologise in Slovene. The woman did not reply, instead she smiled stoically from beneath the peak of an old baseball cap, thereby reassuring him no serious harm had been done. For an instant, as her gaze lingered, he was struck by how attractive she seemed, though much of her face was shaded and she quickly turned away. Meanwhile, laughs of relief echoed through the chamber as, able to see once more, the four friends and their fellow visitors continued their exploration, eventually coming back to the little train which, once all were aboard, meandered back up to the surface. They were briefly blinded again as they emerged, this time by the bright daylight of their own world, one the Salamander could not have begun to imagine. Jones briefly wondered whether such an unimagined world might exist for humans too, one of still greater light and colour perhaps, if only they had the senses to detect it, but this was no more than a passing thought.

On arrival back in Ljubljana that evening, they had returned their hire car and checked into the hotel, before heading straight back out to enjoy the city.

And so, standing outside his hotel on Tuesday morning, Jones looked back at their itinerary with some satisfaction: they had made the most of their short stay, striking that difficult balance between seeing as much as possible but without ever rushing. Now back in the small but modern Capital – the road in front of him busy at the start of a new working day – Jones felt that the Slovenians had, despite an occasionally traumatic history, also maintained a balance: that of developing their country successfully whilst safeguarding and valuing the countryside, culture and traditions which were at its soul.

The plan for today was to explore Ljubljana and then

to enjoy a final night out, before flying home the following morning. One by one, his three friends joined him outside the hotel, all feeling lazy in the building heat. They were, though, to make the most of their last day, exploring the city centre and climbing the hill to the castle, from the turret of which they enjoyed more spectacular views, this time of the city below and of the mountains rising in the distance, separating them from Austria. Late in the afternoon, they finally collapsed in Tivoli Park, spending two hours recovering from their exertions and recalling all the things they had seen and done over the preceding days in a country they were about to leave, but where they were beginning to feel rather at home.

As evening fell, they finally made their way out of the park to where the turquoise Ljubljanica river flows through the heart of the city, closely lined on one side with bustling cafés and restaurants. Although it was a week-day, the fine weather had brought out the crowds and finding an outdoors spot to eat was proving challenging. Finally, Ben spotted a table for six, occupied by a lone, young woman outside a traditional looking bar.

"Er, may we?" asked Jones hesitantly.

"Of course," the girl replied.

"Umm, you sound English?" Jones asked, kicking himself at his latest word fumbling.

"Yes I am," she answered with a smile, "you too?" Jones was confused, both by her slightly knowing look and by an odd feeling that she was faintly familiar. Was he missing something, he wondered? He put the thought out of his mind.

"Yes, we were here for a long weekend, we fly home tomorrow."

"Oh, thank goodness!"

Jones was momentarily offended that the young woman could be so rude, but then, appearing from behind him, a waiter placed a large orange juice in front of her, its ice clinking loudly as he did so. She immediately picked it up and drank insatiably, almost reaching the bottom of the glass.

"Sorry about that," she said, slightly embarrassed, "but I thought it would never arrive. I've been exploring all afternoon, I think I must have got a bit dehydrated in the heat." She looked a little uncertain, fearing that in satisfying her thirst so voraciously she may have appeared ill mannered, but Jones was just relieved.

"It could be an interesting evening if you drink your beers like that!" he joked and the young woman laughed, flashing that smile again.

"I'm Jones," he continued, "and these are my friends: Ben, Andreas and Jack." The three young men all said "Hi", reaching out one by one to shake her hand.

"I'm Justine," she replied, "Justine Fredricks."

She didn't know why she had added her surname, it seemed overly formal, businesslike, and she winced internally as she said it. It hadn't mattered though, as that initial exchange with Jones had opened a new chapter in both their lives: it had crept up on them stealthily, ambushing them in a place far from home, where neither had been before and which neither would visit again. Of course, they were unaware of this significance at the time, instead they simply relaxed, enjoying the moment, chatting easily over a meal, she secretly jealous of the boys' wider adventures around Slovenia, they envious of her rail odyssey across a whole continent.

As they exchanged travel tales, Justine knew she was the outsider, but she was also aware that she had become the centre of interest in their evening and she enjoyed the feeling. More than that though, she sensed a growing rapport with Jones. His friends must have felt it too as, after the meal, they made excuses to leave, while he found a reason to stay. And so they chatted on, two hearts beginning the fall into love, both innocent as to how these moments would be treasured in the one destined to beat out a full lifetime; both innocent also that, in less than two years, the other was fated to stop.

In fact, Justine had recognised Jones instantly as the man who had accidently hit her the previous day; she had found his embarrassment rather charming at the time. Seeing him again here had been a surprise and she had been waiting for him to recognise her too, but until now he hadn't. She rubbed the side of her head and flinched, as if in pain, so as to give him a clue.

"Are you OK?" he asked, suddenly concerned.

"Oh yes, it's just that some clumsy man knocked me on the head yesterday..." She waited in vain for a reaction. "In the caves? When the lights went out?"

The clues fell into place and Jones flushed red, suddenly realising why she had looked so familiar.

"Ah, I think, maybe..." he stammered.

"I think maybe too," she interrupted slightly flirtatiously.

Flustered, Jones launched into a profuse apology, but she insisted she was fine and that she was only teasing him because he had not recognised her. This initially embarrassed him further, until she reminded him that she had been wearing her baseball cap and he remembered how shaded her face had been. It was clear she was not offended and, finishing their drinks, both were able to laugh at their initial rather bruising encounter, oblivious to the fact that it was getting late and that they were now alone amongst the once crowded tables that surrounded them.

Time for one last walk and a final look at the city they would both be leaving the next day, though in different directions. He held out his hand to help her balance as she extricated herself from between bench and table. Even as he did so, he wondered whether it was too old fashioned a gesture, but Justine didn't appear to mind and soon they were strolling along the riverbank.

"Jones is an unusual name... for a first name that is... I mean it's nice, but..." Justine hesitated, realising she had unwittingly tied herself in a verbal knot and didn't know how to complete her sentence.

"It's just what my friends started calling me from primary school," he interjected, sparing her further awkwardness. "My actual name is Casey."

"Ahhh, Casey Jones, all is clear!" Justine laughed and mimed pulling on a steam engine's whistle. "Were your parents into trains?"

"No, in fact I was named after my mother's cat, he died shortly after they married and then, when I came along, well I guess the grief was still pretty raw!"

"You were named after a cat?!"

"Yes, I'm afraid so." They continued in silence while she considered this rather strange news.

"Well, I like cats," she finally pronounced decisively. "I have one… they are very serious animals. Plus, Casey Jones, I happen to like trains, that's why I'm inter-railing across Europe. By myself. None of my friends would come!"

"Hmmm, it's good to hear you have friends though! We were wondering when we saw you there on your own."

She gave him a dig in the ribs, but knew she had deserved this return tease and saw it as a good sign. She had thought Jones liked her, now she felt sure.

"Still, to be named after a cat!" she mused. They headed further along the river in silence for a few minutes, he sinking into thought, she enjoying the cooler evening. Eventually they reached a bar, out of which pumped an oompah style polka of clarinets, tubas, violins and accordions.

"Would you like another drink?" she asked. Jones was silent. "A beer? A glass of wine?" Still silence. In desperation "… a saucer of milk maybe?"

Jones woke up: "Sorry, sorry… I was just thinking. What were the chances of us meeting here again, tonight? I mean what were the odds?"

"You think too much. If you hadn't met me you would have met someone else."

Jones was a little hurt, perhaps this didn't feel as special to her as it was beginning to feel to him.

"But I'm pleased it was me," she added, sensing his disappointment.

The music inside the bar abruptly stopped and, in the sudden silence, as she stood there in the dark with the river glistening in the background, Jones had an overwhelming urge to hold her. He stepped forward, put his arms around her waist and gently pulled until she was against him. He stared down into her eyes for a second or two and then, without fear or forethought, he kissed her, surprising even himself in the process. This was rather startling for Justine too and she caught her breath in shock as he drew her in. His subsequent brief hesitation had however provided her sufficient recovery time and, from that moment, the rest had been inevitable: if he hadn't kissed her, she knew she would have kissed him.

They stood there a few moments and then he said with a smile:

"Ready Freddie?"

"I used to be called that at school," Justine confided, not sure how pleased she was to hear her old nickname revived. Jones looked puzzled and too late she realised his had been an 'off the cuff' remark, unrelated to her name at all.

"What do you mean?"

"My surname? I told you earlier?" She waited for the penny to drop.

He tried to remember, but it was no good.

"Fredricks!" she reminded him with mock impatience. "At one stage there was another Justine in my class and so, for a few years, I became known as 'Freddie', but only in school."

"Freddie, Freddie..." Jones repeated the name to himself, weighing it up as an option, but just then another rousing polka struck up from the bar, so his verdict never came, though Justine imagined she would find out soon enough.

With a gentle tug on her arm, he led her across the river and they headed back to Prešeren Square, with its pink Franciscan church and, nearby, the Three Bridges, marking the centre of the city and over which just a few late night pedestrians now leisurely strolled. Jones and Justine stopped halfway across the first of these, barely noticing that somewhere along the way they had started holding hands. Taking in the scene around them, with the floodlit castle high above and their reflections shimmering in the water below, both privately concluded that it was as magical a place as any for a romance to take its first tentative steps.

7

The Azores –

Wednesday 23rd and Thursday 24th November 2016

Fergus peeked through the curtain and caught his first sight of land in three and a half days: at some stage early in the morning, they had already arrived in the Azores. He got up quietly, hoping not to disturb Sylvie, but then absent mindedly began singing to himself one of the songs from the previous evening's cabaret, as he searched through the wardrobes for his shirts. His wife listened contentedly to him from beneath her duvet, until the impromptu performance was interrupted by a sudden tannoy announcement from the Cruise Director:

"Ladies and gentlemen, welcome to Praia da Vitoria. The gangway today can be found on deck three, forward, port side."

Fergus felt a mixture of excitement at the prospect of exploring this new exotic destination and resentment at the loud, big-brother-like intrusion into their personal space.

"We will be running a shuttle bus service to the town centre and, in order to do so efficiently, we ask you to collect a boarding

card and then to wait in the comfort of the Poseidon Theatre until your bus number is called."

Sylvie placed her pillow over her ears, seeking to preserve the last vestiges of pleasant sleepiness she had been feeling just a minute earlier.

"The ship departs at five o'clock this evening, so please do be back on board by four. We hope you have a wonderful day, ladies and gentlemen, and we look forward to welcoming you back on the Magdalena later this afternoon."

"Let's get going!" said Sylvie, suddenly throwing off her duvet and coming to life, keen to get on with the day, forgetting the fact that her husband was already half dressed and well ahead of her.

During breakfast, they heard on-going announcements for those holding boarding cards for various numbered buses to make their way to the gangway, while urging others to continue waiting "in the comfort of the Poseidon Theatre" until it was their turn.

"She makes it sound like the height of luxury!" remarked Fergus.

By the time, an hour later, they themselves were ready to set off, there was no longer any need to wait, the rush was over and they were able to go straight to the gangway. Placing their feet on dry land again for the first time in approaching four days, they disembarked and boarded the shuttle, which drove them the three miles into town.

They both liked Praia da Vitoria. The weather was warm, but not overly hot, and the houses and buildings were painted in the vivid colours you associate with a sub-tropical climate. It felt good to be back in summer clothes and Fergus pulled the peak of his old blue-grey baseball cap down a little, to protect his eyes from the glare of the sun. They wandered down the long, cobbled high street, both slowly becoming aware of a delicate music floating towards them on the Atlantic air. In the distance, a group of troubadours were walking in their direction, singing and playing folk songs on their guitars and mandolins. As they drew nearer and their music grew louder, it became clear that they weren't even asking for money, but were simply playing for the joy of it and for the love of their culture, the tourists around them being quite incidental. Fergus and Sylvie found them enchanting and the melodies echoed in their ears long after the musicians themselves had passed by, eventually disappearing up the road behind them.

They found a church and spent thirty minutes or so inside, lighting a candle there and saying a prayer in their daughter's memory. Other tourists joined them from time to time, ambling around taking photos, some stopping to pray too, most unintentionally clanging the heavy door behind them as they left. Between these interruptions, the silences when they had the building to themselves were sublime, though frustratingly brief. When eventually it was their turn to leave, Fergus shut the door gently – as if fearing he might bring the whole edifice down around him – and it closed with the softest of clicks, sealing Justine's unflickering flame in the stillness, until the next visitors arrived.

A little further down the street they reached the seafront. It was unspoiled, with just a few quiet bars in the harbour area, next to which a black sandy strand stretched out for half a mile or so. For a few seconds, Fergus wished he had brought his swimming things, but getting changed here would have been problematic, so he didn't regret this long and, instead, enjoyed walking the length of the beach, hand in hand with his wife, looking across to the *Magdalena* moored another mile or so across the bay. It felt good to be somewhere new, somewhere they were unknown, somewhere with no connection to the past.

Back in the restaurant that night, their noisy dining neighbour was perhaps a little quieter than she had been on previous evenings, but she could still easily be heard from two tables away, guffawing to the couple between them and engaging them in tedious, inescapable conversation. If the Maitre D' was aware of their torment, he did not seek to assist them, as he weaved between the tables asking diners if everything was alright, without waiting long enough to hear their replies. Fergus and Sylvie felt grateful they themselves were not next to the woman, that they were just witnesses to her cackling rather than its focus, but she still tested their patience, even on this quieter night. In his imagination, Fergus saw her as somehow spider-like, waving her arms around, and he wondered whether, beneath the tablecloth, her legs were equally skittish and, indeed, quite how many of them there might be.

"Come on, try to enjoy the meal," Sylvie urged him. "Where is all your mindfulness practice?"

Fergus was indeed finding it hard to draw on all the hours of meditation he had put in...

"Yes," he said, "Buddhists would say she might even be my spiritual guide, giving me a wonderful opportunity to practise tolerance... but the test is too advanced."

After dinner, there was a magician performing in the Poseidon Theatre, but neither Fergus nor Sylvie were interested. Instead they played Scrabble in the deserted Card Room, which to Sylvie seemed to be straight out of an Agatha Christie novel, with its dark wooden panelling and green baize covered tables.

"It feels very 'Cluedo' in here," she observed and Fergus looked around with pretend nervousness, as if expecting to find a body slumped in one of the corners or hanging silently from a light fitting, perhaps swaying gently as the *Magdalena* rode the waves, through the night and on to its next island.

Ponta Del Garda, the following day, was much bigger and busier than Praia da Vitoria and it was within walking distance of the ship's berth. Although they both liked it, they missed the quieter charm of the previous town and were horrified to hear Christmas music being piped into the streets, from speakers attached to the lamp posts. It was very late for a summer holiday, but nevertheless that is what they felt they were on, and the music, which could have been atmospheric and festive at a cold Christmas market, sounded cheap and out of place in the heat of a sunny day. The prematurely festive feel descended into further tackiness when they turned a corner to find the dystopian vision of an enormous plastic Mickey Mouse outside a shop, dressed as Father Christmas and pumping out a tinny version of Jingle Bells as, bathed in sunshine, it waved a mechanical arm in greeting to those who passed by.

Fergus and Sylvie escaped up a side street and soon found themselves out of the heat and intensity of the town, wandering uphill, away from the sea, passing a school playground where lucky pupils, to whom the mid Atlantic was home, shouted and played no differently from children anywhere else. The lanes here were narrow and a car hooted as it sped past them, forcing them to jump back, pinning themselves against a wall as it roared by. Eventually, they reached the top of the hill and a small park, where they sat on a bench, recovering in the sunshine from what had proved a less than relaxing morning. A wincing Fergus took off a shoe and sock, revealing a nasty blister on his heel. Sylvie quickly whipped out a plaster from her handbag and, as he stuck it over the wound, he marvelled at how his wife could always be so extraordinarily well prepared.

Batteries recharged, they braced themselves for the return trip, but the afternoon was to prove much more pleasant, and they were able to relax as they descended into the town centre, admiring its distinctive Portuguese architecture as they went. Back at sea level, they stopped for a well-earned iced drink in a café opposite the main church. As they sat there taking in the scene, Fergus noticed his dancer walking across the square.

"Justine could easily have been a dancer on a cruise ship," he mused, remembering how he had felt two evenings previously at the show. Sylvie followed her husband's eyes and watched the young woman disappearing up a side street.

"Justine could have been many things, but for us she was the only thing that matters: she was our daughter. She lived and we loved her and she us. Nothing can change that."

"I'm sorry," he said.

"For what?"

"For having said something sad."

Sylvie gently took her husband's hand:

"Don't ever apologise for talking about our daughter." She held his eye and was rewarded a few seconds later with a rather melancholic smile in return. They walked slowly, hand in hand, back to the ship, enjoying the sun shining on their backs and the unfamiliar cocktail of smells mixing in the sea air as they passed the cafés and restaurants along the way.

Back on board, while Sylvie took a bath, Fergus decided to go for a wander.

"Hello again Fergus!" he heard, as he stepped out of the cabin. Behind him Mrs Huffington was slowly making her way up the corridor, heading to the first sitting of dinner.

"Oh, hello there Mrs Huffington. How are you?"

"It's not easy, you know, when you get to my age. I was telling the ship's doctor earlier… he's Romanian you know?"

"Er, no I didn't," Fergus answered, not quite sure of the relevance.

"He comes from Timisoara…"

"Does he now?"

"I've never been to Romania, but I've been to Croatia… yes, lots of times to Croatia, their coastline is wonderful and I've called at all the ports there." Fergus thought she was making it sound as if she herself were the ship.

"Dubrovnik, Split, Rijeka, Koper…"

"I think Koper is actually Slovenia," interrupted Fergus, remembering his visit to that country with Sylvie just three years earlier, albeit they had not gone to the coast. Mrs Huffington looked at him disapprovingly.

"Well, at my age it is all still Yugoslavia to me. Tito was a very great man you know. He stood up to Stalin."

"Yes I know… that he stood up to Stalin," he quickly added, "not that he was necessarily a very great man."

"He kept Yugoslavia together. Look what happened after he died."

"You make a good point Mrs Huffington," Fergus said, unconvinced but in avoidance of an argument, and then, spying an opportunity, added: "I'll go away and have a think about it."

"You do that Fergus. You do that."

Making his escape, Fergus headed up three levels and out on deck. At certain times of the day it could be like a busy ring road, with people walking round and round, itching to overtake as they came up behind slower passengers. Now in the early evening, however, everyone was already inside, either eating or preparing to do so at second sitting, so Fergus was able to watch the glimmering lights of the Azores fade into the distance all on his own, until eventually they disappeared completely.

"Three sea days ahead," he said to himself, relishing the prospect of the long crossing to Cape Verde. He found a quiet, sheltered corner, plugged in his headphones and started to meditate. After a year of practice, how could he still be so bad at it? He was supposed to be focussing on his breath, but he seemed to be only able to manage a few seconds before his mind wandered: had he given Mrs Huffington enough time? How could he be so affected by the girl from the cabaret? How were they going to manage two and a half more weeks in the dining room with the loud arachnid lady? Each time he realised he was distracted, he tried to note the distraction (as he had been taught) and then gently to bring his attention back to his breathing. But those distractions came thick and fast and Fergus couldn't help but conclude he wasn't turning out to be much of a meditator.

Later, the Maitre D' was as usual standing at the entrance to the restaurant, nonchalantly squirting sanitiser into passengers' palms as they arrived for dinner. Fergus rubbed the liquid into his hands and led Sylvie through the restaurant to their table. The loud woman and her husband were already in their places and Fergus managed to force out a "good evening" as he passed. She ignored him, or perhaps – engrossed as she was in the menu – she did not hear, but Fergus suspected her silence would not last. The grey haired couple on the table between them looked on sympathetically and, as soon as Fergus and Sylvie had sat down, immediately introduced themselves as Richard and Cressida, swiftly engaging them in small talk about Ponta Delgada.

Fergus and Sylvie recognised this for the tactic it was and, while they would have preferred to eat in peace, neither blamed the couple for seeking respite from their noisier neighbour. Richard, they discovered, was a retired diplomat and, to their surprise, they both found themselves genuinely interested in his and Cressida's (probably oft told) stories of various postings to unusual capitals around the world. They both had engagingly mischievous senses of humour, cutting through the froth of the Diplomatic Service and telling tales on the all too human ambassadors, consuls, (often aptly titled) vice-consuls and even Foreign Office ministers, that lay beneath. Fergus and Sylvie laughed along easily, both worrying their own simpler stories were inadequate by comparison, even though Richard and Cressida listened with apparent fascination, perhaps a skill picked up during the course of their long careers.

Later in the meal, they also got to know their very different neighbours on their other side, Henry and Tabitha, who were elderly, sweet-natured and desperately missing their 'boys', who turned out to be two King Charles Spaniels left behind in kennels for the duration of their holiday. This was their first cruise too and Fergus felt sorry for them, being exposed to such a vulgar neighbour at dinner, though from a greater distance. Still, they seemed to take it in their stride.

"We were wonderwing," the elderly man said, continuing with a slight lisp: "thath's to say Tabths and I were wonderwing, whether perhapths, perhapths, you jussst might, might, jussst perhapths, be from the clergy?"

Fergus and Sylvie both smiled, stifling a not unkind laugh.

"No, I'm afraid not," Fergus answered.

"Exssthrawdinawy," said the man, "we could have thworn."

Henry and Tabitha, it emerged, were a retired vet and veterinary nurse, quietly enjoying their holiday while constantly fretting over Basil and Bugsy back home. Fergus and Sylvie found them delightful in their gentle charm. The arachnid lady, meanwhile, had focussed her attention for the first time on the unknown couple her other side and, sneaking a glance, Sylvie thought she could see despair etched across their faces as she inflicted on them another loud, soulless anecdote: they were trapped and they knew it, as if flies caught in her web, at least for the duration of the meal. Sylvie shuddered – it could so easily have been them.

The Show Troupe were back performing in the Poseidon Theatre later that evening, and a self-conscious Fergus tried harder than ever to look anywhere other than at his graceful dancer, only succumbing occasionally. Perhaps it was because he was trying to look elsewhere, that his attention was drawn to one of the female singers, who was of a similar age, but taller and with long auburn hair. Somehow she had a profound sadness in her voice, as well as the most sorrowful eyes. Then, as the song reached its climax, she lifted up her arms and Fergus was shocked to see that one of them was badly deformed. He instinctively looked away, only to find himself staring straight into the face of his dancer. A brief panic seized him as he wondered where to look next, but she quickly spun off and he could breathe once more.

Ashamed at his reaction, he gazed back at the auburn haired singer, who was now harmonising a backing vocal, and he concentrated on her voice, following it as it weaved around the main melody sung by a colleague. It struck him as intensely beautiful and, even though he wasn't with the clergy, he said a little prayer that she might be happier than her soulful eyes and singing portrayed.

"Did you enjoy that?" Sylvie asked as the curtain came down.

"Yes, I thought they were pretty good," he replied with understatement.

"Pretty good or just pretty?"

"Please give me a break Sylvie!" He pleaded, suddenly feeling very tired.

"I'm sorry, I'm just teasing. I want you to relax and enjoy yourself, but I wouldn't mind it if you found me a dashing young man to admire too!"

"The showmen do nothing for you?"

"Hmm…" she responded, unimpressed, "perhaps you can find me a mechanic from somewhere deep in the Engine Room!"

"I'll do my best."

They made their way out of the theatre, down the stairs and along their corridor. On reaching the cabin Fergus fumbled to find his key card, searching his pockets with increasing agitation. Sylvie played distractedly with the blue jewel hanging around her neck and watched affectionately, remembering he had put it in his wallet for safekeeping. Still he looked, patting his body ever more randomly for any tell-tale sign as to where it might be. Who knows why she didn't tell him, or why she didn't use her own key? Perhaps she was teaching her husband a gentle lesson – he could be so disorganised – or maybe she just wanted to stretch out a final few moments of the evening with him before they went to bed.

"Bingo!"

He held the card up to her in triumph and then inserted it in the lock, opening the cabin door to the inviting light of the desk lamp glowing softly between their crisp, freshly turned down beds, each with a small chocolate on its pillow.

"Worth the wait?" he asked confidently as he let her through, but she just smiled. Not all questions require an answer.

8

London – Late June 2006

Nicole was already finishing her breakfast when her brother, Dylan, finally made his way downstairs and into the kitchen. Summer Martins was playing on the radio:

"It's just five years ago and you think with a sigh
How she left you that morning, no final goodbye,
And life still feels so empty, 'Please why did she die?'
You ask for the ten thousandth time.
And a world rich with such beauty when she was near,
A world once filled with joy but now frozen in fear
Has lost what was precious because she's not here:
A planet that's now past its prime.
In the mountains she's absent
And she's not out at sea,
She's not lost in a forest,
Nor in the city,
And you know that you may as well roam,
'cos she's not coming home."

Of course, Hannah Webster loved both her children, but telling Dylan to do anything was trying, including getting him out of bed and to school every morning. Fortunately, Nicole was much better organised, already stacking her mug and plate in the dishwasher, singing along to the song, even emulating its steps as she danced across the kitchen floor to kiss her mother goodbye, before disappearing upstairs to see her dad. Then, she tore back down, grabbing her bag from the hallway with her good arm and slamming the front door behind her as she left the house.

Hannah turned the radio off.

"Come on Dylan, we should have left by now!" She could feel the stress building up inside her. The effort required to get her son out of the house had exhausted her almost before her day had begun; worse than that though, today she had an important presentation at nine-thirty and she was already running late. Finally, Dylan finished his cereal, gave her a weak hug and sloped off – he might still make his bus: somehow he always did.

Hannah rushed upstairs to her husband, treading the same path her daughter had taken just a few minutes earlier:

"Will you be OK?"

"Yes, yes, I'll be fine… I'll make myself some breakfast and then go for a short walk. Go, you've got to get to work!"

She hesitated – he really didn't look at all well – but her need to leave was pressing, so she turned reluctantly and headed back downstairs. A few moments later, he heard the front door close behind her too, leaving him in the now deathly quiet of their home, after its frantic start to another day.

Hannah was thirty-nine. She had met Paul when she was just twenty-one and they had married three years later. Nicole had been born on their first wedding anniversary and her brother had followed almost exactly two years after that – in terms of presents, it had become an expensive time of year, but Hannah loved the life they had built together. Although her office-based marketing job wasn't one of the exciting careers she had imagined having as a child, she felt it was secure and the money it brought in, together with Paul's Civil Service salary, meant that they were comfortable enough. As a result, they could afford the mortgage on their three bedroom terraced house without losing too much sleep, even if it was a little cramped.

Perhaps she appreciated her situation all the more because her own childhood had been very different. She had two older brothers – Sebastian (known as Bastian) and Norris (nicknamed Nu) – and they had grown up together in a house even smaller than the one she was living in now. Her father would disappear from time to time to escape the chaos but her mother repeatedly took him back, more because she desperately needed him than because she particularly loved him. When she was fourteen he had finally left for good, to Pentonville Prison, following a brawl outside a pub. She, her mother and brothers had been obliged to downsize still further, this time to a damp high-rise flat overlooking the motorway and railway lines, just west of Central London.

Hannah had always got on well with Bastian, but it was with Nu that she felt the closest bond. He was just a year older and used to tease her that she had only been born because he himself had not been the girl their parents had hoped for. They both suspected there was an element of truth to this, but in fact her conception had been down to a 'family planning malfunction'.

"It's nice to have been wanted!" she complained when, in her mid teens, she finally found this out. Despite everything though, she knew she was loved, both by her mother and by her brothers and, when first Bastian then Nu left home a few years later, she felt a surge of nostalgia for their shared childhoods: it was the end of an era.

The family came together one last time to attend Hannah's wedding in 1991. Even her father had been there, though she had only seen him a few times since, most notably at her mother's funeral in 1995, following her short battle with cancer. Hannah, Bastian and Nu had tried to support her as she declined, but it had all been very sudden and there had been little they could do. It was a consolation to her that she and her brothers had all been there at her mother's side when she had died and that those final hours had been pain-free.

Hannah kept in touch with Bastian, but she saw much more of Nu. He taught art in a school in Tooting, south London, and they spoke every week by phone, catching up in person almost as often. Sometimes he visited her, but more usually she would make the trip to his Clapham flat, either on her own or with some of her family in tow. Secretly, she preferred visiting him alone: it was like taking a step back to the best moments of their past, a brief respite before returning to the fray.

This is not to say that Hannah was unhappy, it was just that life could be very hectic. Her marriage, in fact, had been consistently good: Paul was loving and reliable, both as a husband and as a father. Recently, however, she had been worried by how tired he seemed, even culminating in him taking his first ever days off sick from work. Knowing he wouldn't, Hannah had booked him a doctor's appointment, but he needed to wait until the following week to be seen. She hoped by then he would be better anyway, but being ill was so unlike Paul and, as she rushed out of the house, a nagging fear played at the back of her mind. Perhaps this was a semi-conscious premonition of what was to come or maybe – mindful of her difficult upbringing – a foreboding that she was an imposter in her good fortune and that her luck would one day change.

With these anxious thoughts in mind, she unchained her bike from the side of the house and headed off on the five mile ride to her office near Paddington station. It had been a hot and sticky month to be commuting by bike, but the weather had finally broken a couple of days previously. This morning the sky threatened rain, but it was at least dry as she left. The traffic, however, felt worse today than it had recently and she manoeuvred her way cautiously between the frustrated drivers and their menacingly revving engines. Riding a bike in London was dangerous: a human being, protected by nothing more than a white cycle helmet, versus lorries, buses, cars and motorbikes thundering by. Two years earlier, her daughter, Nicole, had been knocked off her bike, in the relative safety of their own street, by a driver who had been distracted trying to change radio channels. She had first been flung on to the bonnet and then hurled into the road ahead as he braked, only for him then to run over her left arm as he came to a halt. Hannah was proud how her daughter had adjusted to her injuries and she thanked God because she knew it could have been horribly worse. Overall, the accident had left Hannah in no doubt as to the perils of cycling in a busy city, but it saved money, and her journey was faster than a rush hour bus and more civilised than an overcrowded tube.

Today though, the road seemed extra threatening and she was not enjoying the ride, not helped either by the pressure of running late. She hit the brakes hard, her back wheel skidding beneath her, as a white van with a ladder on its roof pulled out in front from the left, accelerating away and pouring black diesel smoke into her face. She coughed and spluttered, while on her right a large lorry drew alongside her, its engine rattling noisily and its air brakes hissing deafeningly into her ears. Emergency vehicle sirens wailed around her, adding to the noise and confusion and, as a motorcyclist shot past with an inch to spare, she felt panicky and stressed. She needed to find an escape and, on reaching the congested Marylebone Road, she succumbed and did what she had never done before, cycling a quarter of a mile westbound along its wide pavement to avoid the worst of the traffic. She then wheeled her bike across a Pelican crossing and, remounting on the other side, cycled towards the Edgware

Road and on down Sussex Gardens, finally reaching Praed Street, and a minute or two later, the safety of her office.

The last part of the route had been better, she had made up the time and had recomposed her thoughts, though she was cross with herself for having ridden that short stretch on the pavement: it had been irresponsible. In fact, in swerving to avoid a sign placed on the pavement, she had nearly ridden into a woman who had stepped out suddenly from behind a corner. She had distinctly felt her body and clothing brushing against her own and had needed to put her foot down to avoid losing her balance. She had wondered whether she should stop to apologise, but, by the time that question arose in her mind, she was already across the next street. Neither wanting to be later than she already was nor to find herself in a street row, Hannah had kept going, confident the woman wasn't hurt. But the incident had shocked her because, undeniably, it had been an extremely close call: she vowed to stick to the road in future, no matter how awful the journey.

At work, she quickly got changed and by quarter past nine was sitting in front of her computer screen. She had always been proud of her punctuality and kicked herself that today she had arrived late. Nobody had been in the office to witness her tardiness, but to her that wasn't the point. After a few minutes, her boss, Stewart, put his head around the door:

"Ready for 'Coding Tigers'?" he asked enthusiastically.

"As ready as I'll ever be!" she replied, seeking to emulate his keenness. Just before turning her mind to her imminent presentation, she made a second vow, this time swearing to herself that from now on she would get Dylan up earlier, even if she had to drag him out of bed and dress him herself. Not noticing her distraction, Stewart picked up some papers from his adjacent office and then headed down the corridor to the meeting. Hannah followed, her stressful journey finally receding from her thoughts.

The presentation went well, but by evening it was raining heavily, pouring down in a summer shower which showed no sign of easing off. Hannah, not fancying a soaking, decided to brave the Underground home rather than cycling. She ran into Paddington station, stopping to catch her breath once she was safely under its enormous canopy. There were people rushing around everywhere and barely understandable announcements boomed across the concourse. She stared up at the departure board and read where the trains were headed: Oxford, Swansea, Cheltenham Spa, Reading, Plymouth. She rarely found herself in mainline railway stations and, for a few moments, there felt something magical about a place from which trains rushed to the distant most corners of the south west and Wales, an appreciation she suspected its regular commuters might not share. She tore herself away from the spell the station had cast upon her and rode the escalator down into the heaving Underground system. Forty minutes later, having changed lines at King's Cross, she emerged gasping for air. The rain had finally stopped and the pavements shone in the early evening sunlight, as she walked the last half mile back to the house.

Already home, Nicole and (to Hannah's astonishment) Dylan were both sitting at the table doing their homework.

"Hi Mum!" they both said in unison, without looking up.

"Hi there, is your dad upstairs?"

Hannah hardly waited for the reply but made her way to the bedroom where Paul, having heard her come in, was slowly sitting up in bed.

"Oh, how are you sweetheart?" she asked anxiously, pleased to be home and putting her arm around him.

"Don't worry," he replied with a smile, "I'll live." It didn't turn out to be a good prediction.

9

Eastern Atlantic –

Friday 25th to Sunday 27th November 2016

When they woke up the next morning, they were deep out at sea once more, with no land or other ships in sight. Fergus rolled out from his duvet and caught himself singing again as he shuffled to the bathroom – he looked back anxiously at his wife but she appeared undisturbed, still at least half asleep in bed. So he was up, washed and dressed first and, while Sylvie later did the same, he went out on deck with his phone and earphones. He found a chair overlooking the sea, in a small alcove of deck between two lifeboats, and sat down with his feet up on the lowest rung of the railings. He stared out towards the horizon, uplifted by the awe of being in the Atlantic, and then began to meditate… he felt it went better today, his mind less distracted and he a little more skilled at noting and observing it when it was.

"Hey, I'm not such a bad meditator after all!" he thought to himself, before realising that that thought in itself was a distraction to set aside.

The three mornings between the Azores and Cape Verde all

began this way, with Fergus leaving Sylvie to get ready while he practised his mindfulness outside on deck. This was followed by their usual generous breakfast. The restaurant was a wonderful place to eat in the mornings: yes, it was a little frantic, with waiters rushing around carrying pots of tea and coffee and with passengers making their ways to and from the buffet, but the ocean views from the large windows were spectacular, with sea stretching out in all directions.

The only disadvantage with the free seating arrangement was that they could not always find a table for two, sometimes having to sit at a larger one, which they knew, a few minutes later, would inevitably mean them being asked:

"Do you mind if we join you?"

They didn't mind others joining them at all. What they were less keen on was the mandatory conversation which followed, often involving long tales of previous or future cruises. They both did make an effort though, Sylvie rather more successfully than Fergus, and, in fairness, most of the people who joined them were perfectly friendly and relaxed.

"You're not the most sociable animal, are you Fergus?" Sylvie said, after her husband had struggled through one such breakfast. It was more a statement than a question.

"You think?" he replied, with rare sarcasm, well aware of his social short-comings. Again it wasn't really a question. Nevertheless, more often than not they did have their own little table and, when these occasions coincided with sea days, they made for idyllic starts to the morning.

After breakfast, they would go back down to the cabin, usually meeting Rachel, their cabin maid, hovering around the nearby airing cupboard in the corridor, as she set about her preparations for making up the same fifteen cabins she had only turned down the previous evening, while their occupants had been at dinner. Yes, making up and turning down the same thirty beds every day, this reminded Sylvie of the Greek myth of Sisyphus that she had once studied at university: the man condemned to rolling his boulder repeatedly up a hill only for it always to roll back down again. The philosophical question had been whether, despite this, Sisyphus might nevertheless have been happy. Sylvie wondered the same about Rachel and hoped her cheerful singing, as she changed the sheets, was as good an answer as any, but the young maid spoke no English, so she couldn't be sure. She was pleased, though, to see the pride Rachel rightly took in her work and Sylvie made a point of looking as appreciative as she could as their two very different worlds briefly came together each morning.

Having collected their e-readers, she and Fergus would head back out on deck, usually sitting at the side of the ship, or in a sheltered spot at the stern. There they would spend the rest of the morning reading and relaxing. Time would fly and, before they knew it, they would be surprised by the noon fanfare from the public address system, heralding the daily reports from the bridge. These continued to be almost identical and to conclude with the same *"hygiene advices"* and wishing of everyone *"a very pleasant afterrrnoon."*

The reports also invariably advised passengers to hold on to handrails, on account of the swell, even on the first day out of the Azores when the sea was perfectly flat, like a shimmering plate of glass. At one stage that afternoon, a further announcement was made to the effect that the crew needed to test the engines and that passengers should not be alarmed when they switched them off for twenty minutes. For Sylvie, those were some of the best moments of the whole cruise, as the ship drifted silently, deep in the Atlantic, on a crystal ocean surface beneath a hot, semi-tropical sky. Fergus, meanwhile, was imagining the worst and had a feeling the cruise company was not always open in its communications. He feared they had fabricated the excuse of tests to disguise the fact that the ship was somehow in terrible trouble: perhaps a desperate battle against an enormous conflagration in the engine room, even as the waiters and waitresses continued to serve coffees and drinks on deck. He pictured everyone abandoning ship, floating in lifeboats in a sea of suitcases, plastic chairs, zimmer frames and other debris, waiting for rescue, even as the *Magdalena* went down in front of their very eyes.

All too soon though, to Sylvie's disappointment, the engines cranked up again and the ship continued its journey south as if nothing had happened, and of course nothing had. Fergus' initial relief quickly turned to despair at how frayed his nerves had become. He recalled how once before, a very long time ago, he had been out on the ocean aboard a vessel when the engines had been similarly shut down. That time, he had savoured the beauty and tranquillity of the experience, it had been perfect, yet today he had found the same thing frightening. He didn't need to ask himself what had changed. He mused how, with some notable exceptions, things are rarely good or bad in and of themselves, but more often only so on the basis of the labels we choose to place upon them. In this case Sylvie had, as so often, chosen more wisely and with her natural composure: a calmness to which he knew he sometimes clung as if it were indeed a lifebelt and he lost at sea.

Afternoons were spent much as mornings, though Fergus would usually also swim, more rarely getting the pool to himself in this warmer weather, and the three Caballeros invariably lounging in the nearby spa bath. On the hottest days, the stern and top decks of the *Magdalena* would be strewn with passengers sprawled out on sun beds, exposing their, by now, visibly inflating bodies to the warm temperatures and the hot sun, involuntarily conjuring up in Sylvie images of beached whales, although she sought to set them aside. Neither she nor Fergus, however, enjoyed this sort of heat and both burned easily, so they were happier in shady corners, away from the crowds.

On the second day out of the Azores they received the first of two notes in their cabin. It read:

"We are pleased to enhance your cruise by not calling at Fogo Island, the second of our three scheduled stops in Cape Verde, and instead by calling at a fourth port in the Canaries, Santa Cruz de La Palma. We will therefore arrive at the other three Canary Islands one day earlier than scheduled. As we now need to travel further between our remaining two Cape Verde ports of Mindelo and Praia, we will need to leave the former at 4pm rather than the scheduled 7pm. We hope these enhancements will enhance your holiday".

"They don't at all!" bemoaned Fergus, "we travel all the way to Cape Verde only to spend a day and a half ashore, rather than the three full days promised! And they call these enhancements!"

"They say these are enhancements that will enhance!" joked Sylvie, recalling the mindless repetition and trying to defuse the tense state into which her husband was working himself. Despite her apparent humour, she felt let down too, both for herself and for Fergus, and irritated by the way the company tried to sell this change as something good. She was also suspicious that the ship had its own agenda to get to the Canaries a day early. But with typically wise perspective she added:

"Spending a day in the Canaries rather than Cape Verde… there are people in the world with worse problems," and, of course, Fergus knew she was right.

The organised outings were expensive and so, on the whole cruise, they had only booked two: a coach tour around Madeira and a trip out from Gran Canaria on a small sailing ship, the 'Madre de la Esperanza'. The latter had particularly appealed to Fergus: spending a day sailing around the nooks and crannies of the island and then the advertised prospect of snorkelling off the boat's side. However, the next day, the second note extinguished this dream. This one was signed by Gavin, the exuberant manager of the Tours Office, who had been introduced to them at the Welcome Show a week earlier. He wrote:

"Unfortunately we are advised that the trip on the Madre de la Esperanza from Gran Canaria will be unable to operate, for operational reasons, and has therefore been cancelled. Please understand this is a decision by the operator over which we have no control. Your on board accounts will be refunded."

"'Unable to operate for operational reasons', but what does that even mean?" implored Fergus, genuinely confused.

Seeing through the flannel, Sylvie did the maths:

"With a day less in Cape Verde, we reach Gran Canaria twenty-four hours early, the sailing boat must be already booked out." And then, with a smile and noticing the childlike disappointment on her husband's face, she added:

"Come on, worse things happen at sea!" Like that child, he fought to retain his outrage, he couldn't be chirped along like this by his wife, he refused to be. Unfortunately, though, his facial muscles had other ideas and, to his irritation, he broke into a smile.

Dinner times continued to be a mixture of delight – the food and the wine – and horror – the incessant asinine conversations of the arachnid lady sitting two tables away. Throughout the meals she continued to lean one way or the other, either cupping her ear to join in her neighbours' discussions or flirting with the waiter, who by now seemed to be backing off a little himself.

"Awwww, Frederico, don't you love me anymore?"

"Of course I do madam," the waiter forced out through gritted teeth.

"Don't worry about my Charlie here, he won't hurt you. Charlie by name, Charlie by nature, that's you isn't it dear?" She cackled again, sending a shockwave through half the dining room, while her husband sat impassively, sipping at his wine.

"I don't think I can stand this much longer," said Fergus.

The next night he almost didn't have to as he was stopped at the entrance to the restaurant by the Maitre D'.

"It's semi-formal night tonight sir, you need a jacket or a tie."

"What about me?" said Sylvie, wearing a blouse and smart jeans, as she had on many previous occasions.

"You are fine madam," the Maitre D' oiled.

"I haven't got a jacket," Fergus replied.

"I can lend you a tie if you wish sir." But Fergus wasn't going to wear a tie that had been wound around a thousand sweaty male necks before his, so he trooped back down to the cabin to dig out one of his own. Finally admitted to the restaurant, he felt like the inexperienced cruising new boy as all the other men sat in open collars and shirt sleeves, with their jackets removed, once past the restaurant guard, and placed over the backs of their chairs. He thought he noticed one or two 'there's always one' type glances cast in his direction as they tucked into their second courses, before Fergus and Sylvie had even had a chance to order their first.

"I've a good mind to take my tie off and to put it on the back of my chair too!" he said with a certain logic.

Sylvie reached out and took his hands in hers: "Deep breaths!"

"Very smart!" shouted the arachnid lady in his direction, before descending into another shrieking laugh.

"You do look very smart," Tabitha on the next table said, more genuinely.

"Thank you, thank you... I'm struggling a bit with the etiquette," Fergus replied.

"I suppothse you are more uthsed to the dog collar?" Henry reflected.

"No darling, don't you remember? He said he wasn't a man of the cloth."

"Did he? How exssthrawdinawy, I could have thworn."

"I'm afraid, your wife is right," Fergus confirmed, his mood again lightening at the innocence of the elderly couple. "Cheers!" he said, smiling at them and lifting his glass.

"Cheers," joined in Sylvie.

"Cheers."

"Cheerths!"

And so cruising felt to Fergus like a mixture of heaven and hell... but the heaven easily made it worthwhile: the sea, the ship's movement, the good weather, the days of relaxation, the long, lazy hours with Sylvie. Occasionally, between the Azores and Cape Verde, he spotted his dancer, but he felt self-conscious and sought to evade her where he could. When avoidance wasn't possible or would be too obvious, he allowed himself to enjoy the easy charm she used on him and (he suspected) on half the other old male fools on board, savouring the company of someone he liked in her own right, someone who had energy, vivaciousness and her whole life ahead of her, but someone also who reminded him so strongly of the daughter he had lost. As for her taller colleague, the singer with the auburn hair, he didn't see her at all outside of the shows, until the day before they reached Cape Verde, when he spotted her on deck, staring out to sea. Uncharacteristically and spontaneously, he walked up to her:

"It's beautiful isn't it?" She turned around and he could see her staff name badge: 'Nicole Webster'.

"Yes it is," she smiled back. Without the glamour of costume and make-up he thought she was actually much prettier, even if, he concluded, she couldn't quite compete with the dancer in the pathetic beauty contest he became aware he was playing out between them in his mind. He felt ashamed: they were both around the age Justine had been when they had lost her, for heaven's sake! But Nicole was oblivious to the internal beating up Fergus was again giving himself. He allowed a moment to pass, before continuing:

"I'm sure you have people say this to you all the time, but I wanted to tell you that you sang beautifully the other night."

"Thank you… that's kind."

He wanted to hold her, not for any sexual reason at all, but because she looked sad. He longed to ask her why she looked and sang that way, but he knew that would be presumptuous.

"Well, I look forward to your next show."

"It's tonight, I'll try to spot you."

Fergus smiled.

"Anyway, I won't keep disturbing you after every show to tell you that I enjoyed your singing, so perhaps you can take that as read for the rest of the cruise?"

"Thank you, I will… but you are not disturbing me."

He was just about to leave when, without thinking, he added:

"My daughter was in shows, a dancer, you know; she worked in a holiday camp."

"Really?"

"Yes, but she died."

"Oh my gosh, I'm so sorry!" Nicole looked shocked. There was a pause and then he said:

"No, I'm sorry, I shouldn't have told you that, I don't know why I did, I guess it's just on my mind a lot."

"Of course." Another pause. "Hey, if your daughter was in show business, then a compliment from you means something extra!"

"Well, it's deserved… anyway, I'll leave you to it."

"It was nice meeting you… enjoy the rest of your cruise."

Fergus turned and left, her last words had sounded clichéd, a phrase she had probably reeled out without thinking a thousand times or more, as an American might say *'have a nice day now!'* But he felt sure there had been a moment or two before that when she had been quite moved. He also felt concern that she had something on her mind, though he supposed he'd never know whether or not he was right. Anyway, he felt pleased to have spoken to her.

That night he and Sylvie were back in the Poseidon Theatre watching the dancers, just as – a long time ago – he remembered they had watched Justine performing at a holiday camp in North Devon. How proud and amazed they had been that evening, that there on stage, dazzling the audience, had been their very own daughter! Tonight though, perhaps for the first time, Fergus was more focussed on the singing than the dancing, and more specifically on Nicole, for whom he suddenly realised he felt an unexpected paternal compassion. She looked his way mid ballad, but with the lights in her eyes, he knew she hadn't seen him.

Did they purposefully give her all the sad songs? He wondered.

10

The Chilterns – September 2004

Justine and Jones only had that one evening together in Ljubljana. The next morning he and his friends were on the plane back to the UK, whereas she still had a month's Euro railing ahead of her.

By the time she arrived in Ljubljana, Justine had already seen the Grande Place in Brussels, the twin spired cathedral in Cologne, she had taken a meandering train ride down the castle-dotted Rhine valley to Mainz and Frankfurt, wandered the ornate streets of Vienna and the old town in Bratislava. From there, she had followed the river Danube down to Budapest, Novisad and on to Belgrade where, beneath the Kalamegdan park and fortress, it joined up with its sister river, the Sava. Next stop had been Zagreb and only then, via a two hour train ride, twisting through gorges and along pretty rivers, across the border into Slovenia and on to Ljubljana. After meeting Jones there, her route was still to take her through Northern Italy, along the French Mediterranean coast, all the way to Barcelona, before returning home via Paris. Justine was not going to miss the second half of this adventure simply because she had met a young man outside a Slovenian bar, but she hoped, nevertheless, he might still be interested in her by the time she saw him again.

She knew this tour of Europe had been whistle stop, that some would be impressed by her extraordinary route, while others would seek to pour cold water over her enthusiasm by suggesting she had been everywhere but seen nothing. She wasn't moved by either perspective, for her the travelling, rather than the arriving, was most of the fun: watching her continent slip by and seeing its men, women and children going about their lives in its furthest flung corners, speaking different languages and eating their local foods. A continent of people who lived in different nations, regions and cultures, and who celebrated national traditions which had evolved over the centuries through their own unique histories, which presumably were taught in their schools, much as the Battle of Hastings and Henry VIII were taught in British ones. She was fascinated by these differences, but more so by the fact that, regarding the things that mattered most – family, friends, aspiration – people were the same everywhere.

Despite her love of trains, by the time her Eurostar arrived back in London, on a rainy Tuesday afternoon, even she had had her fill of railways, at least for a while. She crossed London and took one further, much more familiar, train back out to the Chilterns and finally arrived home, where her mother and father greeted her with a mixture of delight and relief, hoping that their daughter had exhausted her travel bug for the foreseeable future.

It felt good to be back again, in the beautiful Buckinghamshire countryside, in her family house, with those who loved her, especially after two months' travelling amongst people for whom – interesting and sometimes interested though they could be – she had been an anonymous stranger. It also felt good to be back in her own bed, the one that had served her well throughout her entire life, except for term times when she had been studying dance in Bristol.

It wasn't, however, a great time of year to be looking for dance opportunities. Her agent recommended she apply for the cruise ships and reassured her that before too long the holiday camps would start recruiting fresh talent for their next summer season; he promised also to look out for any theatre or TV work. He sounded hopeful, but warned that she may need to be patient initially. So, Justine found a job in a local bookshop while she waited, but she also wrote to a nearby dance school asking if there were classes she could teach. After an interview with a slightly timorous principal – who had seemed the rather more nervous of the two – she was assigned lessons two evenings a week for the remainder of the Christmas term, another teacher having let the school down. Justine was an optimist: as she saw it, her professional career had begun, and she steadily built up both her hours and her confidence.

Meanwhile, of course, there was Jones. She hadn't called him the day she got back from her European tour, nor even that week, rather she waited until the Sunday, five days later. She wasn't playing 'hard to get' games, she just wanted to settle in first and to re-find her home-legs, after her trip… but eventually the time came to make the call. Her name came up on his screen, so he knew who was dialling as soon as his phone rang.

"Freds… Hi there!"

"Hi there! I'm back!" She announced, half conscious that her nickname had not only stuck but been further nicked.

"Hurrah! When do you want to meet?" Justine had been encouraged by the friendly "Hi there," but the lack of any small talk surprised her and she briefly floundered at the directness of his question, so he answered it himself:

"How about I come your way on Saturday… you can show me all your haunts and tell me about your tour? How was it by the way?"

"It was great… but I'm pleased to be home. When can you get here?"

They agreed he would come down at eleven o'clock and, before she knew it, the conversation was over.

"Don't worry... men don't do phones," her father reassured her, as he entered the room to find his daughter looking a bit confused by the whirlwind nature of the call. As she collected her cat, Tiger, into her arms and headed for the couch, she suspected her father was right, but she couldn't help but be a little concerned. In fact, Jones had been every bit as pleased to hear from her as she had been to speak to him, but he had been a little scared too: he felt sure he had made a good impression in Ljubljana but, realising he now had to live up to that, he had decided to take his chances with her face to face, rather than risk fumbling around in conversation on the phone.

And so, six days later, he arrived in Justine's village for the very first time. He was half an hour early and felt illogically nervous about being spotted, either by her or by her parents, before he was supposed to have arrived – perhaps they were out and about ahead of his visit – and so he parked up in a hidden lay-by a couple of miles down the road. He got out and stretched his legs, walking up to a wooden gate in a hedge. Resting against it, he gazed out across a field which descended a quarter of a mile or so to woods below. From this vantage point, he could look clear over the trees and to the rolling hills beyond. Every now and then he heard a mewing and he wondered what it could be, then, to his right, he saw two red kites sailing high in the air, calling to each other. He watched them circling effortlessly for a few minutes, rusty red wings spread wide in the sunshine, until they were unexpectedly mobbed and chased off by a small murder of loudly cawing crows – persistent in their tormenting – leaving Jones to reflect how no life is perfect, no matter how blissful it might first appear. The calls of the birds grew ever fainter until they ceased entirely and an absolute silence was restored. Jones stayed there a while, leaning against the gate, until he gradually became aware of the distant drone of an aeroplane passing high above, as if reminding him to rejoin the world. He checked his watch – it was indeed time. Taking one last deep breath, he stood up straight again, strolled to his car, then drove the short distance back down the lane.

Turning into the driveway Jones stopped and briefly applied the handbrake, looking at the picture box house before him. He himself had grown up in a very small town, but this was in a different league: how lucky Justine had been to enjoy her childhood here, but perhaps how harsh it must have then been to venture out into life from such an idyllic setting. Still, Justine had managed it, this beautiful house releasing her, as if on a long leash, far enough for her to reach the Balkans and Spain, before gently reeling her home again. He surveyed the scene for a moment longer and then slowly continued up the gravel drive, arriving a cool, but not too cool, ten minutes late.

Meeting a girlfriend's parents, especially when you've only known her a few hours, was beginning to feel increasingly daunting: was she even his girlfriend he wondered? He told himself not to worry: he was perfectly respectable, a graduate trainee in a major retail company, he had no need to be nervous… but he was a little nevertheless and he could even feel himself sweating. The prospect of looking hot and flustered only added to a vicious cycle of apprehension.

Before he was even fully out of the car, the front door opened and Justine's father called across to him:

"Jones… hello there, welcome! Come on in." The greeting was so genuine that Jones' nerves began to ease again.

"Thank you Mr Fredricks." He closed the car door and faked a casual confidence as he took his first steps towards the house.

"Oh, Fergus, please."

"And you should call me Sylvie," said Justine's mother, appearing by her husband's side.

"Oh, Mrs Fredricks… Sylvie… hello. So nice to meet you both."

"Rubbish, I expect you're scared stiff," said Fergus, showing him inside, "but there's no need!"

Justine came down the stairs:

"Hi."

"Freddie!" He exclaimed, overcome by happiness to see her again and not noticing the confused look thrown his way by her parents. With her beaming smile and shoulder length brown hair, it seemed to Jones that she hadn't changed at all, but why should she have? It had, after all, only been a little over a month since they had seen each other, but somehow the anticipation of the moment meant it had felt much longer.

She walked up to him and gave him a kiss on the cheek.

"You found us."

"Turrahhhh!" Jones mimicked a fanfare and held his arms open as if presenting himself to an audience. He immediately wondered whether this looked humorous or alarmingly mad to his hosts, but they were already moving off deeper into the house, leaving him and Justine in the hallway.

"It's good to see you again," she said, before following her parents into the sitting room, and Jones silently reciprocated the comment with a smile. Fergus and Sylvie lingered with them twenty minutes or so: long enough to be polite and to provide a cup of tea, but hopefully not so long as to get in the way.

"But why do you call Justine 'Freddie' Jones?" asked Sylvie, looking at him quizzically.

"Yes, why do you do that?" joined in Fergus, also turning his way.

The nerves came back under this joint interrogation, he missed the intonation in Sylvie's question and was baffled as to how she and Fergus had come to the conclusion he called their daughter 'Freddie Jones'. It took a painfully long moment, under the increasingly bemused gaze of the whole Fredricks family, for the syntax finally to fall into place in his head.

"Oh, I'm sorry… well, er, how can I explain… ?" As he fumbled for his words, Justine came to the rescue:

"After we had finished eating on the evening we met, Jones said 'ready Freddie?' to me and it seems the name has stuck…" There was a brief silence… "because of our surname!" Now it was Justine's turn to feel awkward.

"Perhaps you had to be there!" Jones added, taking his turn to rescue her, "but she was sometimes called Freddie at school too…"

This was news to Fergus and he shrugged his shoulders in bewilderment:

"And you being Caspar but calling yourself Jones!"

"Casey!" Justine corrected her father, "named after a cat." Jones noticeably winced.

"Well, in any case Jones," Fergus continued, "it's lovely to meet you, and you are very welcome here." Tiger, who had crept into the room, looked less persuaded as he lurked beneath the telephone table, from where he eyed up this new male rival for Justine's affections.

"Sorry," apologised Jones to Justine a few minutes later, after her parents had slipped away, Sylvie insisting he didn't leave that evening without saying goodbye.

"What for?"

"I'm not sure I made a good impression, I was thrown by the 'Freddie Jones' question."

"Relax, they loved you!"

He seemed unconvinced and Tiger slouched out again disapprovingly, as if to confirm his doubts. Justine though was unworried. To her this had not been some major first meeting with her parents, their relationship was far too new for that. Jones was only here today because she happened to be living at home and anyway, she reassured him, it had gone well.

"How can you tell?"

"I just can… and Tiger liked you too," she lied.

"Tiger?" said Jones, the confusion descending again.

"My cat!" she explained, with just a hint of exasperation. "Come on, it's gorgeous out there, let me show you round."

11

Mindelo – Monday 28th November 2016

"Ladies and gentlemen, welcome to Mindelo, Cape Verde. The gangway can be found today on deck three, forward, port side."

Out on deck, the loud announcement jolted Fergus from his meditation.

"It's a short way into town, ladies and gentlemen, but it's a beautiful walk. For those of you who prefer taxis, these are available on the quay side. The ship leaves at four o'clock this afternoon, not the seven o'clock previously scheduled. We therefore ask you to be back on board by three thirty."

Fergus grimaced at this reminder of the enforced *'enhancement'* to their itinerary, which would curtail their visit.

"We hope you have a wonderful day here in Mindelo, ladies and gentlemen, and look forward to welcoming you back on board later this afternoon."

From his vantage point on deck, it did indeed look an attractive walk into town, though in the end (to preserve energy in the heat) they were to take the taxi option. After the Azores, Mindelo seemed very African and – amidst the heat and dust, the colourful clothes, the women carrying baskets on their heads and the lush, tall palm trees – the feeling of being somewhere truly foreign struck them as they drove out of the docks and into town. They got out of the taxi in a small harbour area where some local fishermen were cleaning their catch, ready to sell at the nearby market. Fergus and Sylvie stood on the quayside surveying the scene with a mixture of wonder and vulnerability, aware that they were now a very long way from their green Chiltern home.

The sun was hot – African hot – and this added to the disorientation they were both feeling. They realised how unprepared they were: they had brought no tourist books and the only map they carried was the very basic one provided free by the ship. In summary, they were wandering blind and Sylvie had a nagging feeling that they stood out and would make easy pickings for those looking to prey on bumbling tourists, although they were never to encounter any serious trouble. One market seller did try extremely hard to sell them tacky souvenirs and, as Fergus was drawn ever deeper into conversation with him, it became increasingly awkward not to make a purchase. Sylvie finally managed to pull her husband away and they escaped up the road until, a few moments later, the trader came running after them, presenting her with a cheap bracelet.

"A gift, to remember Mindelo," he smiled.

She dug in her pocket to find some coins, but he wouldn't take them, instead he turned and ran back to his work. Sylvie felt ashamed, would it have been such a bad thing – she wondered – had Fergus spent some insignificant sum at his stall? She looked around and surveyed the wealthy tourists haggling hard over pittances that meant nothing to them but a great deal to the traders. She had been no better, overly concerned at the prospect of being ripped off, even for an amount she wouldn't have noticed. And, in the end, it had been the trader who had given to her, teaching her a lesson into the bargain.

Their faith in people was quickly tested again when an

elderly local man came up to them in a park and cornered them in conversation, speaking remarkably beautiful English. They wondered what the scam might be and how they could get out of it, but again there proved to be none. It seemed he only wanted to practise his language skills, which he did at length and rather charmingly, while Fergus and Sylvie waited for him to pause long enough to give them an opportunity to leave without causing offence.

"Do you think we are too cautious?" Sylvie asked, after they finally broke away. "I mean, first the trader and now this man… he could have been really interesting to talk to, had we been trusting enough to do so."

"I think you do have to be a bit street-wise," Fergus replied after some consideration, "as long as you are polite and respectful, which we were."

They had been, but both were left feeling they had missed an opportunity to get to know a local man, who appeared to have an old and kindly soul.

"Still, Fergus, I hope we didn't hurt him."

They wandered around a couple of squares, one in particular was abundant with exotic greenery and surrounded by paint box bright coloured buildings of reds and blues and yellows – it was beginning to feel good to be out of the European gloom and wandering somewhere so warm and tropical. They also spent their customary few minutes in a simple church, before leisurely making their way back to the port on foot. Their map showed a beach just a little beyond and so they walked that extra half mile to see what it was like, quite an investment in energy when it was so hot, but it proved worth the effort.

The sand was white and fine, while the sea was a deep turquoise, such as you might see in an advert for a desert island holiday, or perhaps an expensive cocktail. Every now and then, a fish would jump clear out of the water, as if to see what was going on, before splashing back beneath the surface just a moment later. They both took off their shoes and socks and paddled up to their knees at the water's edge. Fleetingly Fergus felt angry at the cruise line: had they been staying all afternoon, as scheduled, he would have gone back to the cabin for his swimming things, but, alas, there was no time for that. Summoning up everything he had learned from his mindfulness training, he forced himself to observe his annoyance and then to put it aside. This worked surprisingly well and, instead of feeling cantankerous, he was able to enjoy a special moment, paddling off a tropical beach, hand in hand with his wife.

They had liked Mindelo and, despite their initial nervousness, had encountered no problems at all, but it still felt reassuring to be safely back in the familiarity of the ship later that afternoon. They sat on deck at the stern as it sailed away, passing dramatic, completely desolate islands, mountains of rock rising sheer from the mid Atlantic waters. Whoever had named Cape Verde – much like whoever had named Greenland – had not been too worried about descriptive accuracy, but nevertheless the scenery was impressive. Half way up a steep cliff on a large, barren peninsula there appeared to be a white chapel – they marvelled at how it could have been built on such a rock face, but also wondered how anybody was ever able to worship there.

After two or three hours relaxing on deck watching the rugged landscape pass and then recede into the distance, Sylvie retreated to the cabin to shower and change, with Fergus following thirty minutes later. On leaving the lift and turning the corner from the landing into the corridor he, almost but not quite literally, bumped into Mrs Huffington and her zimmer frame.

"Why Fergus, you should be more careful!" She teased him.

"I'm sorry Mrs Huffington, I hope I didn't frighten you."

"Oh, it takes much more than that to frighten me Fergus, when I was in Malaya with Lawrence we..." and she launched into a story about the years she had spent living in the Far East, but Fergus' mind was elsewhere, reminded of another collision, which had occurred at another blind corner, more than ten years previously.

"… so don't ask me Fergus if I'm frightened, the Huffingtons are made of sterner stuff than that!" She looked him keenly in the eye.

"Are you listening to me Fergus?"

"Oh yes, of course Mrs Huffington, it sounds like you had to be very courageous." Having lost track of the conversation, the first half of his answer had been a lie and the second half a guess, but he felt the former a kind one and the latter a safe one.

"Well Lawrence, you can't keep me here all evening I'm afraid, I had to eat early as they are showing 'Brief Encounter' in the Oceans Gallery and it will take me an age to get there! See you again soon."

"Goodbye Mrs Huffington, enjoy the film." She raised her hand in the simplest of waves as, with her back already to him, she began to trundle away. Fergus didn't know if it was her slow determination to get about the ship, or the fact that she had unconsciously called him by her dead husband's name, but he once again felt a surge of compassion for this old lady, her salad days far behind her, travelling the oceans, not as a single handed sailor perhaps, but somehow no less alone.

"Hi there," said a half dressed Sylvie as he entered the cabin, "Did I hear you talking to your friend out there?"

"Mrs Huffington? Yes, it was rather hard to get away."

"I could hear you, you were very sweet." She kissed him proudly on the cheek.

Fergus, despite having arrived back in the cabin long after Sylvie, was ready for dinner before her and he sat waiting patiently on the bed while she put on the small amount of make-up she ever chose to wear.

"Ready Freddie?" She asked, putting her lipstick away. She

stopped like a statue and they both stood in silence for a moment as it dawned on them what she had just said.

"I'm sorry."

"Don't be," he answered, and this time it was his turn to kiss her.

Dinner would have been eaten through gritted teeth were that physically possible, as the large arachnid lady, oiled they suspected with aperitifs, held court across their half of the dining room. Fergus actually began meditating at one stage, with his eyes closed and his hands held together on the table in front of him, between his knives and forks... Angelo arrived with his starter and stood next to him, unsure quite what to do.

"Don't worry, he's having a little Fergus time!" his wife whispered, causing her husband to open his eyes and apologise, embarrassed, to the waiter.

"Only 277 breakfasts, 277 lunches and 277 dinners to go!" he smiled, continuing the countdown to his distant leave, and Fergus and Sylvie couldn't help but smile back.

"Perhapths you could say gwace for us all Fergus?" Henry enquired tentatively from the next table.

"I'm afraid I'm really not..." but somehow Fergus didn't have the heart to argue, instead, reclasping his hands, he softly recited a little prayer.

"That was marvellouth," said Henry, "thank you." Tabitha looked across at Fergus gratefully and with a knowing little smile.

Somehow, these incidents broke the earlier tension and they were able to rise above the noise from further up the dining room, enjoying the rest of their meal and the accompanying wine. They even found themselves happily chatting again to Richard and Cressida, who were once more keen to be diverted from the drama playing out on their other side.

"I saw her still on the island at three o'clock, I was rather hoping she had forgotten the ship was leaving early!"

"Richard!" said Cressida in mock outrage.

"Can't you use your lengthy diplomatic experience and skills on her, to tame her a bit?" asked Sylvie.

"Alas, it's diplomacy, not sorcery, it can only do so much!" Richard replied. Another loud cackle came from behind them. "Believe me, wars have been declared for less!"

"Some of the bloodiest, I suspect," added Fergus and the couples felt a certain bonhomie in a trial shared.

"Would you like to go to the show tonight?" Sylvie suggested to her husband as they left the restaurant an hour or so later, but the idea did not appeal:

"It's the comedian. I bet he'll be crude and embarrassing, but we'll feel obliged to laugh… I'd much rather do something else."

And so, instead, they made their way to the mellow lighting and soothing music of the Conservatory Bar where they ordered their Pimm's, which to their initial disappointment were delivered without ice. Their waitress, however, returned just a few moments later holding a small silver bucket from which she used tongs to pluck cubes. Taking her time, she dropped them one by one into their drinks, each cracking audibly as she did, a sound Fergus had always found somehow satisfying and which tonight added to the already peaceful mood.

"Do you think many couples are as relaxed as we are in each other's company?" he asked, leaning back in his chair after the waitress had left.

"Only the lucky ones!" she observed.

Until ten and a half years ago Fergus had thought himself lucky and, for the first time since then – looking at his wife and perfectly relaxed in the easy surroundings, the ice clinking against the side of his full glass in response to the motion of the ship – he considered himself that way again. He felt a deep and quiet happiness in the moment and, for once, it was too well rooted to be chased away by the guilt of feeling good in a world where his daughter no longer existed.

12

Cornwall bound – May 1993

Fergus, like Sylvie of course, had infinite recollections of his daughter, and that memory of her dancing professionally on stage in the holiday camp was certainly a special one, but there were others that were equally treasured.

There were the big memories, the ones that came to mind frequently, kept fresh by the photos displayed around the house or in countless albums: summer holidays, family occasions, Justine's graduation from university, her first day at school. But there were also those surprisingly small, long filed away memories which bubbled up unexpectedly out of nowhere, sometimes when Fergus was relaxing quietly, other times when he was concentrating hard on something completely unrelated: Justine at a childhood party perhaps; or, when she was around eight, fascinated by an enormous house spider crawling across the living room floor; or, as little more than a toddler in his own parents' garden, laughing happily as she was chased around and around by her grandmother; or falling over while roller skating and requiring the biggest of fatherly hugs before the pain would go away; or as a young teenager teaching him to bake biscuits and excitedly showering him with praise as they emerged perfectly from the oven.

One of his favourite memories, however, lay somewhere in scale between those milestone events and those cameo moments of her short life: it was the briefest of breaks away, just the two of them, stealing a day from work and school, to enjoy a long weekend together in the most extreme south westerly corner of the country, while Sylvie was away visiting a sick friend.

Justine had been an unusual mixture: quite girlish in her love of dance, working her way effortlessly through the grades; but, in a gamine-like manner, quite boyish as well, not worrying too much about clothes and make-up, but preferring to be outdoors, enjoying nature and the fresh Chiltern air. She also loved trains, not the nostalgic love the elderly might have for steam engines, but a fascination for fast, super-sleek, modern, long distance, express trains. It wasn't that she was actually a train spotter, she wouldn't collect numbers or anything like that, but she was spellbound by the idea of trains travelling across the country to far off places at what, then at least, were considered great speeds.

Fergus lost track of the number of times he had taken her to one London terminus or another, her favourites being Euston, King's Cross and Paddington, because it was from these that trains travelled the furthest distances up and across the country. She loved the bustle, the announcements, the various sandwich and coffee outlets. It seemed to her that these big stations were almost towns in their own right. She marvelled at Euston and the prospect of trains going to Liverpool and Manchester, Glasgow even, what could be more exotic, she thought? From King's Cross trains went all the way to Edinburgh and then once, when she was about nine, they even noticed a train leaving at precisely noon and destined for Inverness.

"Where is that?" she had asked.

"It's pretty much at the very top of Scotland, I think about five hundred and fifty miles away," he had replied. To her, this was extraordinarily distant and may as well have been on the far side of the moon. Then of course there were buffet and restaurant cars: yes, people ate meals on trains! It was a world Justine longed to sample, but there was never a need for them to take a long distance train anywhere, and so she had to make the most of very occasional trips on the local commuter services from home to London and back.

When Justine was eleven, Fergus had decided to use the weekend when Sylvie was visiting her sick friend to correct this, secretly booking himself and Justine the sleeper train from Paddington to Penzance for the Friday night and the Scillonian Ferry on to the Isles of Scilly the next morning. He arranged a night there on St Mary's in a Bed and Breakfast, giving them around thirty hours on the islands in total, before taking the ship back to Penzance late on the Sunday afternoon. He thought about the night train home, but he suspected Justine would have been too tired for school the next day. Anyway, he was keen she should also experience the journey back in the daytime, with England rushing past the window, and, in particular, he wanted her to witness the dramatic and beautiful run along the South Devon coast by Dawlish. So, he booked the Sunday night in Penzance before a direct train back to London at half past ten the following morning. He wished the trip to be perfect, and, fearing disillusion at finding herself in an overcrowded standard carriage, reserved seats in first class. In so doing he also knew they would be served food on board and, in this way, he hoped the romantic imaginings of his daughter about long distance rail travel could be preserved a little longer.

This was the master plan anyway and he prayed hard that the real world wouldn't intervene, perhaps in the form of points failures, cancelled ferries, heavy rain or anything else that could foil the dream. The missed day at school on the Monday was a complication and Fergus was nervous to ask permission, in case he were turned down. Instead he decided he would simply phone from Penzance, when it was too late for the school to object, offering to come in to see the headmistress if it was a problem. As Justine was doing well and her attendance until now had been flawless, he hoped they might be tolerant about this one father and daughter adventure.

He didn't actually tell Justine about it until they were driving back from the friend's house where, in her mother's absence, she had gone after school on the Friday they were due to leave.

"You'd better pack a small bag Just, we are going on a trip!"

"Where to?" she asked. Had he said they were going around the world she could not have been more excited by what she heard and, fleetingly, his own delight at her reaction was punctured by a sadness that she would not be a young girl for much longer. Would she still be pleased to spend time with her father when she became a teenager? He needn't have worried.

So, at eleven o'clock in the evening, they arrived at Paddington station. Justine soaked up the atmosphere: all the commuters had long gone and it felt to her as if she had entered a secret world of late night activity which few were privileged to see. Their train didn't leave for fifty minutes, but it was already alongside at platform one and they looked at the sleeper carriages in wonder... by morning these would have taken them three hundred miles south west, all the way to the Atlantic Ocean. They resisted the temptation to board immediately, wandering the station a while longer, taking it all in, before finally clambering aboard and being shown to their cabin in Coach D by a particularly jovial attendant, with a strong west country accent.

Their little home from home was going to be a tight squeeze, but if there had been a world prize for cosiness it would surely have won. There were bunk beds running along the left side of the cabin, so their heads would be at the door end and their feet by the window, which was hidden by a blind. Beneath that was a table which, upon lifting its lid, revealed a basin. Between the bunk beds and the right hand wall there was insufficient space for the two of them to pass, but, as long as one of them sat out of the way, all problems were solved. A little step ladder, christened the 'stairway to heaven' by Fergus, led up to the top bunk and Justine quickly climbed it to claim her more adventurous bed.

Fergus made sure she knew how to operate the cabin door and then left her to change in private, while he did the same in one of the uncharacteristically spacious train toilets at the end of the sleeper carriage. Walking back down the corridor in his pyjamas, he knocked on the cabin door.

"Are you ready?"

"Nearly," she replied. Not for the last time in his life, Fergus found himself in a public place in his nightwear, as he muttered 'Good evening' to fellow travellers being guided towards their own berths. Eventually the cabin door opened and he could retreat inside to safety.

It was nearly time for the train to depart and Fergus had an idea. He turned the lights off and then opened the blind. Through the window they could see the empty adjacent platform and a train pulling into another beyond that. Then, on the dot of ten to midnight, and so smoothly it took them a second or two to notice, they started moving. They watched Paddington station slip away and then the city pass before their eyes – the sidings, the flyovers, the tall blocks of flats, the warehouses and factories – as the train tore contemptuously through anonymous local stations and faster and faster out into both the suburbs and the night.

"Come on," Fergus said, pulling the blind back down, "if we want to make the most of tomorrow we should try to get some sleep." She hugged him and scrambled back up the ladder.

"Dad, this is so great," he heard a voice say quietly in the darkness just a few moments later.

"Yes it is, isn't it?" he replied, "and tomorrow we'll see the sea." But he could tell that, at the end of a long day and with the rocking of the train and the rhythm of the tracks, she was already asleep. He lay awake a while longer, feeling a mixture of satisfaction at a job well done so far, anxiety as to whether he could maintain this success and happiness at the prospect of a weekend away with his daughter. Gradually these feelings blurred and merged as the clickerty clack, clickerty clack of the train overpowered him and he too was overcome by sleep.

Justine didn't wake until Truro at seven the next morning, Fergus, unfortunately, enjoyed a less good night, spending it sometimes dreaming he was on a train, sometimes conscious he really was on one, and often residing in a twilight world somewhere in between. It was fitful rest at best and he was wide awake again by Plymouth, but he still felt topped up with sufficient sleep to get through an exciting day ahead. He opened the door when the jovial attendant knocked with a breakfast tray of coffee for him, orange juice for Justine and croissants for them both:

"Good moornin', we'll be arrivin' 'n Penzaance in an 'ower."

After they had eaten, they repeated the previous night's changing arrangements, but at least this time Fergus was fully dressed as he waited patiently for his daughter to re-open the cabin door to let him back in. Their window looked out on the right hand side of the train but Fergus, who had travelled this route previously many years ago, knew that the approach into Penzance was best seen from the left. With just ten minutes to go he said:

"Come, I'd like you to see something."

They went into the corridor outside their cabin and stood watching the scenery until, between the bushes flashing by, they spied St Michael's Mount in the distance. After a few moments, the countryside fell away entirely and the bay opened out before them, shimmering in the morning light, the castle perched high on its island, which was linked to the shore by a causeway, half submerged beneath an ebbing or flowing tide.

"Wow!" said Justine, turning and looking excitedly into her father's face, and he felt he could burst at his daughter's happiness.

Five minutes later, they pulled into Penzance station, packed up their stuff, disembarked on to the platform and walked to the concourse, Justine admiring the locomotive at the front of their train which had hauled them valiantly through the night, all the way from London. Penzance in the morning had a very different feel from Paddington late in the evening: different worlds positioned at either extreme of the day and either end of a very long railway track. The laments of the seagulls added to the distinction.

"Very end of the line," remarked Fergus.

"Very," agreed Justine, seeking to take in what, for her, was the beauty of an exotic and distant railway terminus. What other station had its signs, proudly telling passengers where they had finally arrived, rising out of lush beds of greenery and palms, to the backdrop of the Atlantic Ocean? Surely they had arrived at the very end of England, perhaps even the edge of the world itself.

From the station Fergus and Justine walked, rucksacks on backs, the half mile or so to where the Scillonian ferry was docked. They breathed in deep lungfuls of fresh sea air as they marched, tasting the salt on the light ocean wind blowing against their faces, and on whose currents the gulls above wheeled, crying in joy or despair, or perhaps simply hunger. Carried on the same breeze was the unmistakable smell of old seaweed that had been abandoned by a high tide on the stony beach ahead. Meanwhile, two enormous buoys, which had once upon a time been hauled out of the ocean, lay as decorations against a cottage wall, nostalgic for the waters from which they had long ago been dragged. These were the sights, sounds, tastes and smells of the

Atlantic and they were everywhere: Fergus and Justine felt high on them.

The Scillonian sailed at nine o'clock, so the timing was perfect and soon they were on board waiting to cast off. The ship was small, with two levels of deck outside and three in, though the lowest was little more than a space for weary or nauseous passengers to crash out and sleep. The other two levels comprised lounges, a shop and a small café. Fergus and Justine found places on the starboard side of the upper outside deck, figuring that from there they would see the best views of the Cornish coastline, as they headed even further south west. Fergus had been worried that sea sickness, caused by an untimely storm, could ruin the whole trip and booking the ferry had therefore been a gamble, but by now it was clear it was one that had paid off: it was going to be a gorgeous spring day and the forecast for tomorrow was just as promising.

Slowly the ship pulled away from the quay and headed out of the harbour and into Mounts Bay, then following the rocky coast to Land's End and out into the ocean beyond. There was sufficient movement to know they were out at sea but not enough to disturb any but the most sensitive of stomachs. After they had passed Land's End, they swapped to the port side and were quickly rewarded with the sight of a school of basking sharks, enormous and clearly visible in the water, swimming mouths wide open, only it seemed a dozen or so metres off the ship.

"Not many people have seen basking sharks!" Justine thought to herself as she cherished the moment, feeling both inspired and privileged to witness their dorsal fins breaking the surface, just a few feet from where she was standing. This was a first for Fergus too and he stared at the enormous creatures with every bit as much excitement as his eleven year old daughter. Eventually, the sharks disappeared and the two of them were left staring out to sea at distant ships and lonely lighthouses, contemplating the wonder of nature and their small place in it.

Almost as soon as Cornwall disappeared in the distance behind them, so the Isles of Scilly began to emerge in front.

"We want to make the most of today," Fergus re-iterated, "so let's get a bite to eat now." They made their way to the café and ate brunch to fuel them for the day ahead, standing up every now and then to look out of the window and note their steady progress towards land. After she had eaten, Justine slipped away, returning ten minutes later with two baseball caps, one pale pink and the other a shade somewhere between blue and grey, both with *"Isles of Scilly"* written on the front, alongside an image of a seal poking her head out from the waves.

"I saw these earlier in the on board shop, we might need them, and anyway they are souvenirs."

"Good thinking Just, how much do I owe you?" her father asked, reaching for his wallet.

"Nothing," she replied firmly, "it's a present, to say thanks for a great trip." She put the pink one on her head and handed him the other.

"Wow, thank you." It seemed inadequate, but Fergus, taking the cap from her hand, somehow couldn't find better words and, before they came to him, Justine smiled and answered:

"You're welcome!" and then refocused on a last remaining piece of toast.

By the time they had eaten and returned to deck, the island of St Martin's lay immediately in front of them, with its tall cliffs and glimpses of white sandy beaches. The ship slowed right down to manoeuvre carefully around the various rocky outcrops, before steaming up the channel between the islands of Tresco and St Mary's and finally coming to its berth at Hugh Town on the latter. The trip across had taken four hours.

13

Praia – Tuesday 29th November 2016

Fergus awoke early and, wanting some fresh air, headed out on deck, where he was ambushed by the most impressive of sights. Although he and Sylvie had missed it, there had been an announcement the previous evening advising passengers that the *Magdalena* would be sailing past Fogo Island at around six thirty the following morning and that, for those willing to get up early, there would be magnificent views of its volcano, which had last erupted just two years earlier.

Only a tiny percentage of the ship's passengers had both heard the advice and mustered the will power to act upon it, but, for those who did, the reward was a classic cone shaped mountain rising nearly ten thousand feet up through the pink tinged morning cloud. Fergus felt a mixture of awe at its natural beauty and immense good fortune that, through sheer luck, he was there to see it. After a while, he rushed back to the cabin and persuaded an initially sleepy Sylvie to come out too and, for an hour, they stood together at the stern rail, without talking, marvelling at the dramatic volcanic island, as it sank ever further towards the horizon.

"I wish we could have had our scheduled day there," Sylvie mused regretfully. It was indeed a disappointment and Fergus didn't at first know how to reply, finally observing:

"Yes, but, if I hadn't woken by chance, we could easily have missed it entirely."

Sylvie smiled, this time it had taken her husband to give the perspective.

The volcano steadily receded and, eventually, they tore themselves away and headed to breakfast. By mid morning the *Magdalena* had docked:

"Ladies and gentlemen, welcome to Praia, Cape Verde. The gangway can be found today on deck three, aft, port side. Once again, ladies and gentlemen, we will be running a free shuttle bus service into town..."

The Cruise Director's smiley voice repeated the process of waiting for buses *"in the comfort of the Poseidon Theatre"* and reminded guests that the ship would sail at six o'clock that evening. Again, Fergus and Sylvie decided to avoid the rush, delaying an hour or so before going ashore. He sought to use the time to practise his mindfulness but this proved impossible as, every few minutes, a loud tannoy call invited the next set of boarding pass holders to make their way to the gangway. The announcements were loud enough to make him jump and completely unpredictable, so he found himself constantly wondering when the next might occur, rather than focussing calmly on his breathing. After a while, he realised it was hopeless:

"Still very much the beginner," he thought to himself, imagining wiser sages than he meditating undisturbed through the noise. Instead, he refound Sylvie and, once the buses were available on demand, they headed to the gangway and left for town. For a second time, they found themselves woefully ill-prepared in terms of having a map or knowing anything about the city in which they found themselves. They wandered into a central square and then up a busy street, but somehow, despite wanting to enjoy it, Praia presented itself as a hot, dusty, noisy, busy conurbation, mildly threatening to those coming from comfortable corners of Western Europe, and Fergus became nervous about getting lost or worse. They weren't even sure of the name of the street corner from where the bus would return them to the ship.

They walked back down to the square, this time along a pedestrianised avenue, parallel to the road along which they had just come. This struck them as much less intense, without either the noisy traffic or the feeling of fighting their way through overcrowded pavements. Back in the square, they sat on a bench and tried again to take in the city, but it felt somewhat edgy. Young shoeless children came up to them and, though charmed by their innocence and concerned for their welfare, Fergus and Sylvie somehow also felt a need to keep an eye on their own possessions, to which they held on tightly, whilst fighting back a guilt for feeling that way. It was a searing heat which, combined with the urban environment, left them uptight and impatient, unable to enjoy Praia and to give it the chance it deserved.

After a while, they went inside the nearby church and sat down for some quiet reflection. They both felt humbled by the local men and women who came in and genuflected before the ornate statues, spending a few moments in silent prayer, before slipping out again into the brilliant sunshine and their anonymous Cape Verdean lives. Fergus wondered what they had been praying for, what worries and needs they had privately placed before God. He felt a deep respect for them and again battled with mixed feelings: regret that they hadn't done Praia (or more importantly its people) justice, but also an urge to retreat to the safety and familiarity of the ship, where they would be able to relax again. After no more than two hours ashore, the latter feeling won and they took the bus back to the *Magdalena*.

It was by now lunchtime and they ate a crisp, refreshing salad, before settling out on deck for a relaxing afternoon with their books and a series of cool drinks. They watched in admiration as the smartly dressed waiters and waitresses tirelessly climbed up and down the stairs between decks, expertly balancing bottles, cups and glasses, and smiling naturally as if it were they who were on holiday, rather than serving drinks all afternoon, in the heat of the African sun.

In the early evening, the ship cast off on schedule and turned back out to sea, holding one of its 'sail away' parties on the rear deck as it departed. Fergus wondered what the Cape Verdeans made of the loud noise these rich westerners were making as they headed off in all their luxury. At the same time, he had to admit that the crew – for whom deep down this was just another working day – successfully created a happy, carnival atmosphere. Although he and Sylvie didn't actively take part, the mood was contagious and they felt energised as they witnessed the high-spirited celebrations from their vantage point several decks above.

Amongst those keeping the party mood going were the Show Troupe, including Fergus' dancer and Nicole, his sad voiced singer. The three Caballeros had been in their usual place, lounging in the hot tub when, all of a sudden, one made a rare venture out, running up to the dancer, lifting her into his arms and then holding her teasingly over the pool, before, to Fergus' horror, dropping her fully clothed into the water. The Caballero thought this a hilarious prank as, rather like a reptile returning to the swamp, he slunk back into the spa bath with his two friends and their cocktails. Fergus was at least relieved to note that few passengers appeared to be sharing the joke. His dancer meanwhile swam serenely to the side, climbed out and, trying not to give the impression she was as fed up as Fergus imagined she probably was, disappeared through the crowd, presumably to get showered and changed in her cabin. Fergus stared back at the Caballeros and frightened himself a little with the animosity he felt towards the one who had committed this outrage.

Meanwhile, a string quartet had boarded the ship in Praia and, before dinner, Fergus and Sylvie sat contemplatively together, this time in the Midships Lounge, listening to the smooth tones of the female violinist and the two men accompanying her, on Spanish guitar and double bass. Sylvie secretly hoped that this injection of calm would subsequently carry Fergus over dinner and, to his credit, it nearly did: just once or twice she spotted him wincing as shrieks, whines and guffaws pierced their ear drums from two tables away.

"Did you get athore?" lisped Henry.

"Yes, yes we did," replied Sylvie.

"Quite charming wasssn't it?"

"Delightful," Sylvie outwardly agreed, whilst secretly wondering quite what they must have missed that had given him this impression, but she managed to add: "especially the church."

"Oh yeth, of courssse, interesting for you in particular Ferguth."

"Yes, it was very peaceful, and quite special seeing the faith of the local people," Fergus responded, again feeling it churlish to correct him and resigning himself to (and to his surprise slightly enjoying) the clerical role in which he found himself an involuntary imposter.

"Darling, you do remember, Fergus isn't with the clergy," Tabitha gently shattered the illusion.

"Really? How exssthrawdinawy, I could have thworn..."

"I do have a faith though, we both do," Fergus quickly intervened, seeking to relieve Henry's confusion and disappointment.

"Well, that must be it then... perhapsss you could say a prayer for our boys, we're wather worried about them?"

"I'll make a point of it," Fergus replied, "Basil and Bugsy?"

"Qwite wite, well wemembered."

"You did very well," said Sylvie to her husband as they left, referring both to how he had handled 'Gentle Henry' – as they now affectionately named him – and to how he had risen above the irritation of their rather more abrasive neighbour further up the dining room. "And tomorrow is a formal night, so we can leave her to it and eat in the café."

Fergus felt relieved at the prospect, but also disappointed that they were unable to enjoy more of their dinners in the restaurant, albeit this evening he did congratulate himself: he had indeed coped better.

"Can we miss the show tonight?" he asked, a bit like a child pleading to his mother.

"Fergus! Come on… you're on holiday, you can do or not do whatever you like… it's the magician isn't it?"

"Yes, and he's bound to pick someone out of the audience for his trick, it will probably be me and, even if it isn't, I will have spent half the show worrying about it… Couldn't we relax in the Conservatory Bar instead?"

"We've unwound a lot today, why don't we liven things up a little and go to the Atlantic Lounge? There's usually a band playing late in the evenings."

This seemed a fair compromise, but Sylvie hadn't realised that, with her own suggestion, she had sentenced herself to the anxiety that, in avoiding the magician, Fergus had evaded. The ship had a number of retired men who were paid to whirl solo women around the dance floor, the cruise company called them 'dance hosts' but Sylvie playfully nicknamed them 'the Lotharios'. Between numbers they would scour the lounge like sharks hunting their next prey and Sylvie tensed up as soon as she noticed them, fearing she might be next in their sights. Fergus wished she could sometimes be a little more outgoing and, for example, enjoy this opportunity to dance with a professional. However, he quickly realised his own hypocrisy: who was he to pass judgement and when had he ever been the life and soul of the party?

"I'm just going to nip to the Gents," he teased, sensing his wife's unease.

"Oh no you are not!" Sylvie grasped him tightly.

Deep down, she knew she was being unfair and that these rather elderly men, elegant in their smart white suits, were only doing their jobs, making sure women travelling on their own would enjoy their evenings. She was even impressed by their slick, relaxed style, something she had already observed a few hours earlier as she watched them at the sail away party, dancing energetically with the Show Troupe and encouraging braver passengers to join in. Nevertheless, here Sylvie wanted to keep her head down, or at least to make it as obvious as possible that she was not alone.

They bought drinks and settled down to enjoy the band. Occasionally a lothario would sail past, apparently aiming for Sylvie but then shying off at the last moment upon noticing her husband.

"You'd be a gonner if I left you on your own!"

"Please don't," she said and Fergus was surprised by the hint of pleading in her tone.

"Come on, I'll take you for a spin myself," he suggested, reaching for her hand. Almost before she knew it, she was up and heading for the dance floor with him and, just a few moments later, they found themselves moving amongst the other couples, including the Lotharios and their latest catches. Fergus and Sylvie both realised they probably looked faintly ridiculous, but, if they did, they certainly weren't the only ones, and they stayed on the floor for the next few numbers, Sylvie slowly defrosting and Fergus' mind wandering back to discos and parties he had attended earlier in life, pre-Justine, pre-Sylvie even. By comparison, those occasions had been much harder work, trying to fit in, while fearing he never really would. It had been a less forgiving time, now was more relaxed; there how you danced mattered, here it didn't. He pictured his struggling youthful self without envy, he was happy to be when and where he was, in this time and place, dancing with his wife.

"There, I think we've done our bit!" he said, after around fifteen minutes.

"Oh and there was I hoping we'd still be up here for the slow tunes!"

"Afraid not, but…" looking across at a couple of disengaged lotharios, "I'm sure one of these gentlemen would do the honours."

She gave him a gentle punch in the ribs. They waited a moment surveying the scene, then Fergus said:

"Let's leave the youngsters to it. I'm ready for bed." Sylvie, looking at all the elderly people around them, noted the irony.

"Come on then old man," she led him towards the exit, fully intending going straight back to the cabin, but Fergus again wanted some air and so they diverted out on deck first.

"I have an idea," said Sylvie, grabbing his hand. At night, most of the ship was full of lights but, so the officers could see out from the bridge, the bow was kept in complete darkness. They couldn't get right to the very front of the ship, but Sylvie could lead him immediately beneath the bridge, from where they gazed into the blackness ahead.

"Look up," she said. Fergus craned his head and they stared together high into the night sky. Gradually, as their eyes adjusted, more and more stars appeared, until they were everywhere: shimmering reminders of both the unimaginable enormity of the universe and the inconsequence of their own place in it. They continued to gaze up as the galaxy revealed itself further, just the two of them there to witness it, holding each other and without another soul there to break the spell, though Sylvie wondered whether Justine's might somehow be nearby, observing discreetly, happy to see her parents relaxed and sharing a peaceful moment. Their lives didn't feel inconsequential at all.

"Why Sylvie, out of all the people on this ship, is it you who thinks to come up here late at night to stare at the heavens?"

"I'm sensitive don't you know?" she responded with a cheeky grin.

"Yes, I think you must be."

They stood there another ten minutes, pondering the stars, taking in the warm sea breeze and enjoying the gentle motion of the swell. Fergus remembered that two 'sea days' lay ahead and he relished that prospect and, above all, the fact he would be sharing them with his wife. He turned to look at her and thought she might do the same, but her eyes remained fixed on the night sky, her mind still contemplating its wonders. As he watched her, he once again felt that nagging fear that one day she might not be there and this sent a sudden involuntary shiver down his spine. Noticing this, she finally turned to him, enquiring how he could be cold on this warm African night, but he just told her that he was tired.

14

Lancashire – May 2013

No, Fergus wasn't a member of the clergy, but he had always believed in God… he had done so for as long as he remembered, going all the way back to compulsory church attendance with his family as a young child. Over the years, all the prayers, the rites and rituals of the services had built up layer upon layer in his soul until, now, life without God was unimaginable.

He had never, though, heard Him. Yes, he had felt God in those church rituals, also in private quiet times at home and walking through its beautiful surroundings; he had felt Him especially by the sea, gazing from some windswept headland at the untamed ocean stretching out wildly as far as the eye could see and, it seemed, infinitely beyond. And, yes, he had felt Him when holding Justine in his arms for the first time. But God's voice had always eluded him and, if he were honest, he had never felt His direction, nor ever known what He wanted him to do in life. Apart from his silent God, Fergus didn't really relate to the modern church or its people: he found services were getting bouncier and louder, more entertaining, social and celebratory, less the deep reflective, introspective rituals of his past. Yes,

Fergus was a contemplative, even if he felt his approach was increasingly considered dull, dusty and dying, steadily falling out of ecclesiastical fashion and favour.

When Sylvie went off to art school for a week in Spring 2013 (their first full week apart since their marriage some thirty-two years earlier), Fergus decided to go off on retreat: eight days of silence in a spiritual centre he had read about, a few miles inland from the coast of the Irish Sea, in rural Lancashire. The purpose of going wasn't specifically related to Justine, though the experience of her death was now an ingrained part of his spirituality and so he suspected she would be there with him, at least at times. But no, this retreat was between Fergus and God and he hoped finally to hear Him in its silence.

As he drove up the motorway he played his CD set of Bach's St Matthew Passion from start to finish… it filled up most of the journey and he hoped its weaving and soaring arias and its dramatic choruses would prepare him psychologically and spiritually for the week ahead. Shortly after the last chorale finished, towards the end of a long country lane, he arrived at the Retreat Centre's gates and, taking a deep breath, he turned in.

"You promised 'Seek and you will find'
And now I have come looking…"

Fergus closed the notebook he had brought with him to record his thoughts and prayers. His room was small and simple, with a bed, a desk, a wardrobe and some drawers, along with a window which looked out over the grounds to the world beyond and, in the distance, the Irish Sea glistening in the evening sunshine. He had been feeling anxious, turning the car into the driveway had indeed required an act of courage, as had getting out and walking inside the centre: was eight days too long? Would he climb the walls, metaphorically, literally perhaps? Would he miss Sylvie terribly?

The initial challenge had been surviving the first supper, it was the only meal of the whole retreat where talking was allowed, the silence not commencing until eight o'clock that evening. He had been worried as to what he would say as they ate, who he would meet, would they have anything in common, would he be out of his spiritual depths? In the end he barely spoke at all, beyond introducing himself to those with whom he shared a table. Everyone was relaxed and friendly, but he felt put in his religious place, firstly when two women described how they were members of religious orders and then, behind him, when someone introduced himself as a Church of England vicar. As if this wasn't daunting enough, one academic looking young man – he seemed little more than a boy to Fergus – peered dryly over his glasses and told the group he was studying a doctorate in post-enlightenment comparative monotheism. Fergus gulped and prayed hard that he wouldn't be 'found out', that nobody would ask him what he did, that he wouldn't be chased out of the centre as the fraud he felt himself to be – those prayers at least were answered. Thereafter, following a brief introductory tour of the building and a group meeting, where the rhythm of the next few days was explained, Fergus and his co-retreatants were finally released into the security of the silence.

In fact, the only daily speaking on the retreat was a thirty minute session with his guide, who would listen to how things were going and suggest Bible texts for him to ponder. Most of these passages were about seeking and getting to know God, about listening for Him in the quiet places. They were well selected and his favourite was the story of Elijah, who, from the entrance to his cave, heard God's voice not in the wind, the earthquake or the fire, but in the subsequent silence. Fergus contemplated these passages, spending several lengthy periods doing so each day in the quiet of one of the centre's several chapels.

On the fifth day, he was given a longer passage to read, John Chapter 1 verses 35 to 42:

The next day John was there again with two of his disciples. When he saw Jesus passing by, he said, "Look, the Lamb of God!"

When the two disciples heard him say this, they followed Jesus. Turning around, Jesus saw them following and asked, "What do you want?"

They said, "Rabbi" (which means "Teacher"), "where are you staying?"

"Come," he replied, "and you will see."

So they went and saw where he was staying, and they spent that day with him. It was about four in the afternoon.

Andrew, Simon Peter's brother, was one of the two who heard what John had said and who had followed Jesus. The first thing that Andrew did was to find his brother Simon and tell him, "We have found the Messiah" (that is the Christ). And he brought him to Jesus.

This was the passage that was to have the most impact, though not quite yet.

When he wasn't in meals or sitting quietly in the chapels, Fergus would walk in the garden, the labyrinth or the nearby hills. The first time he walked the labyrinth, Fergus said a vast number of prayers: for himself, for Sylvie, for Justine of course, for his deceased parents, for his few friends, for people he had wronged, people who had wronged him, as well as for those in need more generally across the world. God must have had His hands full that evening. On the advice of his retreat guide, he sought to be more contemplative the next time he walked the maze: on the way in asking himself the question Jesus had asked Andrew "What do you want?" and on the way out putting that same question back to God. After a short while waiting for God's reply, Fergus lost his nerve and started helping Him out, offering suggestions as to what He might be looking for him to do. When he reported back to his guide the next day she asked:

"Why did you feel you had to 'help God out'?"

"I was afraid I would walk out of the labyrinth without hearing anything."

"Why would such a silence have been a bad thing?"

Her question seemed both obvious and paradoxically mystical. The next time Fergus walked the labyrinth he left it to God whether He wanted to say anything. If He did, it was lost in the silence, because Fergus did not hear it, but he was less sure it mattered.

There was also a short daily mass late each afternoon where Fergus enjoyed receiving communion and where the prayers felt poetic and deep:

"Through your goodness we have this bread to set before you, which earth has given and human hands have made. It will become for us the bread of life… Through your goodness we have this wine to set before you, fruit of the vine and work of human hands. It will become for us the cup of salvation."

Supper came soon after Mass, followed an hour later by a silent communal prayer session, for which, as the light faded, the staff and retreatants gathered again in the main chapel, each praying for whatever was important on their own island. Fergus didn't struggle with any of this. He felt at home in the location and at peace in the silence. Despite his previous fears, he was never once bored, though he did miss Sylvie. In silence he found everything changed and, with nothing much to do, the world slowed down. His guide's question was challenging, but somehow for Fergus the silence wasn't enough, he still wanted to hear God, writing in his notebook:

"Your voice is too soft. I strain to hear it and
In straining I cease to relax and you disappear.
Speak more clearly, so that the first words
I hear You say will not be, when it's too late,
That I did not do Your will."

He re-read his words, they looked foreign to him on the page and he wondered if he had really written them and, if he had, whether they were inspired or crazed or (worst of all) pompous.

While he was waiting to hear God, he certainly saw signs and metaphors everywhere. Some were obvious – he got lost on a walk and didn't know the way – others were more subtle. His favourite occurred in a little chapel on a wooded hill, about a mile's walk from the main house. As he sat there on his own, it was as though he were in the middle of an endless line of thousands upon thousands of people who over the past centuries had prayed there and thousands upon thousands of others who in future centuries would do the same. He felt a connection to them across time, both into the future and back to the past, and today it was his turn. A Bible had been left open on the simple wooden altar and, waiting in the stillness, Fergus noticed the tiniest of spiders crawling across its pages. It struck him that this minute creature was quite oblivious to the fact it was in the heart of this lonely chapel, a consecrated building set in a stunningly beautiful corner of the world, walking across the pages of a holy book. How often, he wondered, was he himself walking over, on or through the sacred, but oblivious to it? He suspected much of the time.

The simple lifestyle on retreat gave other fresh perspectives, for example, mid-afternoon, small cakes were put out for the guests to eat as they served themselves a cup of coffee or tea. Fergus came to savour that little cake each day: in the outside world he would have eaten it in one bite without even noticing, here though it became one of the milestones of his new daily routine, something to be looked forward to and enjoyed.

However, the silence also did strange, less pleasant things to his mind. With nothing much else to hear, the St Matthew Passion, which he had listened to in the car on the journey up, often played inside his head, disturbing the quiet. It had been meant to prepare him for his retreat, not to be its musical backdrop, but he guessed that, had he not played this on his drive, then something else, perhaps less beautiful, would now be filling the void instead.

Also, unable to communicate with his fellow retreatants, he found himself feeling some of them didn't like him, even becoming convinced of the fact, though how they could have taken such a dislike to him on a silent retreat he wasn't sure. It came as a huge surprise when, on the last morning, after the silence finally broke, the woman he had thought most hostile asked with genuine interest, and in a super-friendly manner, how he had got on. It dawned upon him how paranoid he had become in his own mind and how much junk there was up there. He thought back to how often he had sought to read people's thoughts in the outside world: how many times had he imagined non-existent dislikes, or perhaps likes too? How much time had he spent fretting over relationships that hadn't gone wrong at all? He was resolved: mind reading was a skill best left to others.

The retreat had indeed been an adventure of the mind, it hadn't all been serene, but it had gone better than he could have hoped. Eight days had not been too long, despite his fears, and the silence had been liberating rather than restricting. He almost felt ashamed to admit to himself that, for the first time in nearly a decade, Justine had not haunted him; instead, although he had remembered her in his innumerable prayers, he had been able to focus on himself, on God and on the relationship they shared.

Before setting off for home on the final morning, he skimmed through his notebook and came to the prayer that he had written about the spider:

"In a small, lonely chapel
Isolated on a hill
Deep in countryside and weathered by wind,
A tiny spider crawled across the open pages of a Bible,
Unaware it was on a holy book and

Neither knowing the building nor the place it was in.
Help me Lord more and more to see your holiness
In my everyday life
And to walk in reverence and wonder, aware that
There is much more of your sacred presence each day
That in my ignorance I miss than in humility I see."

On re-reading his notes, they seemed rather intense and again he couldn't decide whether they were inspirational or embarrassing, he hoped the former but feared the latter, in any case they were certainly very private. He knew that the intensity would ease as he re-entered the world, he knew that there would be dark days again, but he hoped, as he had expressed in the spider prayer, he could retain at least some of the perspective and peace he had experienced, as well as the closeness to God.

Anyway, beyond all this, there had been a miracle, or at least what had felt like one, it had happened just two days earlier... a fleeting but intimate encounter with God that he would take away and ponder – he felt sure – for as long as he lived.

15

Up on deck the light was breaking through the morning cloud and Fergus was confident it was going to be another beautiful day, though he felt depressed to think they were already heading north again and (perhaps unfairly to the Canaries) he resented the fact that they were leaving Cape Verde behind. He found a quiet recess on deck, sat down with his feet on the lower rung of the rails, put in his earphones and began his meditation.

Taking in deep breaths, he settled down and, with the help of his mindfulness app, went through his routine. He closed his eyes and felt the sensation of his body weight in the chair, his feet on the rail and his hands in his lap. He listened for sounds: the deep but quiet background hum of the engines; the sea breaking remorselessly against the ship's side; and the wind blowing across deck, little more than an ocean breeze, depositing the faint and faintly familiar taste of salt on his lips. He observed his mood: definitely relaxed. He remembered his motives: he wanted his life no longer to be dominated by anxieties and sorrows, hoping that, instead, he could live more fully, for his own benefit, for

Sylvie's and for those of his remaining friends. He didn't want to lose his grief but he did want to have a healthier relationship with it. He hoped that, in getting better at sitting in silence, he would feel closer to God again and more sensitive to Him, as he had on retreat some three and a half years earlier. He scanned his body from head to toe, looking out for any tensions, pains or other feelings, pleasant or otherwise, and then finally he settled into focussing on his breath, fixing his awareness on it as he breathed in and out, in and out…

Easier said than done. Despite having been meditating like this for over a year, Fergus still found that he could only take a few breaths before his mind began to wander: some encounter he had had, some task he needed to complete, some TV programme he had seen… the potential distractions were infinite, but he had learned that they were also inevitable and so, instead of beating himself up, he had taught himself to observe these thoughts, to note them and then to return his attention back to his breathing. This would happen time and time again during each twenty minute session.

Sometimes the distractions would be in the form of short dreams and these both interested and annoyed him, a fascinating twilight world of his mind, but did they mean he was sleeping rather than meditating? Why couldn't he stay focussed on the breathing? Silent contemplation on retreat had been easier, but there the stimuli had been fewer, the whole environment had been designed for stillness and prayer. He sought to note his annoyance. The worst was – and it happened a lot – when he actually did fall asleep for a few moments or, occasionally, minutes even, because this made the whole exercise feel a waste of time. Nevertheless, he didn't get too discouraged, he understood that it was all part of the process, frustrating though it could be, and that noting the frustration was part of that process too.

Today had been no different, with its own distracting

thoughts and feelings: disappointment at the lost day in Cape Verde; worry about the accident they had seen on the drive down to Southampton; wonder at the singer and her enigmatic sadness; a memory surfacing of a train and sea trip with his daughter down to Cornwall and the Isles of Scilly, such a long time ago. He even found himself daydreaming about Katie, the detective who had become almost a friend in the years after Justine's death, seeing and hearing her in his mind as she delivered to them one of her – as they came to call them – 'No progress reports', but doing so in a way which had touched them both deeply, as she strove to be professional and sympathetic, whilst conveying an unjustified shame and awkwardness.

He was thinking about these things as his meditation came to an end. He mentally came back to his seat and sought to picture in his mind where he was, before slowly opening his eyes over an ocean that was even more perfect than he had imagined. He sat there a few minutes longer, wondering what Katie might be doing at that moment.

"Hello there early bird!" It was the dancer.

"Oh, hello there," Fergus fumbled, instantly losing his hard won calm.

"Will we see the great swimmer back in the pool again today?"

"I think there's every chance I'm afraid. Perhaps the Captain could put out a cautionary announcement: I'm a sight for sore eyes in my trunks these days."

"Oh come on…" she smiled, "trust me, on this ship you'd be quite a catch!"

Fergus almost blushed.

"Well I'm flattered, but, alas, not fooled." He felt pleased with this answer in the circumstances. "Your dancing is, erm, very good." He winced as he said it: why hadn't he quit while he was ahead?!

"Well, I'm flattered too," she smiled.

"I mean, I'm no expert, but my daughter was also a dancer."

"I know, Nicole told me, so your opinion definitely counts. Thank you." Fergus was astonished that these two young women might have been talking about him.

"She did? Tell you I mean."

The dancer smiled. Fergus tried to read her name badge, but she was slightly too far away and it felt awkward to ask.

"Well I'm sure she was very good, anyway she certainly had a caring father."

"I hope so," said Fergus. He knew from the 'had' that Nicole must also have told her his daughter had died.

"If you've ever seen the video to 'Roam' by Summer Martins, she's one of the four dancers in that, the brunette with the blue waist coat…"

"Wow, I'll check it out," she replied, sounding impressed. "Well, I'd better go tell the Captain to put out that announcement… enjoy your day and don't forget the show tonight!"

"We'll be there, enjoy your day too." Fergus answered, slightly distracted by the way she twisted her brown hair around her fingers as she spoke to him.

"I always do… this is the high life!" she called back as she walked away, leaving Fergus' head spinning. Many of his old colleagues had never really enjoyed their working days, somehow unable to motivate themselves out of ruts in which they were unhappy but secure. It felt refreshing to spend a few moments with someone young and full of life, who loved what she was doing. And she could have avoided him, but she had chosen to share a few easy moments in his company and… and, goodness, how she reminded him of Justine.

Fergus shut these ideas down the moment they had been thought and he headed back to Sylvie, humming happily to himself. His encounter had been innocent, sweetly so even, but his wife didn't need to know everything.

After breakfast, they went back to their cabin again – exchanging their usual friendly but language-hampered greetings with Rachel, who was busying herself by her airing cupboard – and they prepared for another lazy day on deck. As the sunny parts of the ship were overwhelmed with passengers basking in the tropical heat and as they themselves preferred the shady alcoves anyway, they spent the morning in the cool, towards the bow. Occasionally, one of them would go for a walk and perhaps linger for a few minutes in the sun, soaking up the rays and some vitamin D, before returning to their sheltered spot and their books. On one of these wanderings, Fergus, having climbed to a higher deck, looked down on the stern and, amongst the crowd, spied Gentle Henry and Tabitha resting on sun beds below; the former noticed him and gave a friendly wave, which he reciprocated along with a smile.

Ambling further along the top deck, he caught sight of Richard and Cressida, standing by the rail, in relaxed conversation with the Captain, who also looked completely at ease. As he passed by, Richard noticed and gesticulated for him to join them, but Fergus wasn't confident he would fit into this naturally urbane conversation, so he simply smiled and pointed downwards as if to say that he had to be somewhere, and Richard gave an understanding nod. During this brief exchange, the Captain had turned, curious as to whom Richard was waving at, and Fergus was immediately struck by his kindly face. He looked a quiet and friendly man, more at home whiling away a few minutes with individual passengers than he had been, ten days earlier, when the centre of attention at the welcome party. Fergus decided he liked him and hoped that at some stage he would at least have an opportunity to say hello. But that would have to wait, for now he had missed his chance, so he headed back down three decks to rejoin his wife.

They had both noticed how the bar and drinks staff were

divided into two very different types, with the vast majority continuing to impress them with their friendliness and immaculate presentation. Sylvie, in particular, enjoyed talking with them and hearing more about their lives, both on the ship and back home in distant, exotic countries. These bar staff always seemed willing to spend a few minutes chatting to her and, though he joined in less, Fergus would sit listening, equally touched by their gentle humility – the men as well as the women. However, there were a handful of waiters who were more wolf-like, coming around with pre-made drinks on trays and trying the hard sell, with some or other special offer.

"Drinks sir, madam?" One such waiter asked today.

"No thank you," Fergus responded.

"It's a delicious mango cocktail, and they are half price."

"No thank you."

"But why not sir? It is such a warm morning and the drinks are very refreshing."

"We will get our own drinks later, thank you."

"But I think madam wants one, sir."

"Would you like one?" Fergus said, turning to Sylvie, only half hiding the irritation in his voice.

"No."

"There you go…" Fergus said to the wolf, who slipped away to look for easier lambs, his face barely hiding his contempt.

There was, in fact, a lot of marketing and selling on board and Fergus wondered how a cruise company could make so much effort to create a relaxing atmosphere only then to sabotage it with incessant attempts to separate passengers from their cash. It began to grate. Strategically placed staff with cameras, for example, sought to charge for photos in front of various themed backgrounds, the latest being a snowy Christmas scene, besides which one of the Show Troupe (not experiencing the highlight of his Show Business career) had been co-opted to play a reluctant Santa. Meanwhile, it seemed wine-waiters had been instructed to encourage those asking for glasses to buy bottles instead.

"No, just two glasses please," Fergus had pleaded one evening.

"A bottle is much better value, sir."

"No, tonight we only want a glass each, thank you."

"We can keep the rest for tomorrow…"

"But we don't know what we are eating tomorrow."

"Are you sure then?"

"Quite."

"Is that 'quite' as in 'reasonably' or as in 'completely'?"

"Very definitely 'completely', thank you."

"Well, if you are certain?" the wine-waiter half asked, conveying surprise anyone could make such a choice.

"We are."

Even at Reception, where a display of decorative Christmas cakes had been set up, staff worked hard to persuade passengers to part with a few extra pounds and take one home. At one stage, there was also a 'fashion show' in the nearby lobby, which the ship had somehow hyped into a must-see event. Staff took their turns to stride the cat-walk, posing around in expensive garments, to the eulogy of a host with an over-loud microphone who, if you were to believe him, had never before seen such bargains. Amazingly, a number of passengers appeared taken in, gawping, applauding, gasping even, and Fergus was reminded of the crowd admiring the emperor in his new clothes. Sylvie was particularly unimpressed, seeing all these hard sells, along with the disingenuous communications they had received, as glimpses behind the cruise company's mask – beneath all the smiles, it was very definitely a business.

Back on deck, both jumped as the fanfare heralded the Captain's latest update, which proceeded to be broadcast to a captive but increasingly uninterested audience – dozing on sun loungers or legs splayed from white plastic chairs. Only Fergus, on this occasion, listened a little more attentively, suspecting it wasn't the Captain's favourite moment of the day either.

After it had finished, they continued to sit there for a further hour before making their way up to deck ten, where they had discovered the waiters opened up the external doors to the restaurant, enabling passengers to have lunch outside. They kept to a simple salad and bread roll, accompanied by iced water, exchanging few words as they gazed out at the tropical sea and watched the swells passing by on their long migrations to break on distant shores. It was a lazy, idyllic way to spend lunch and a world away from the rushed sandwiches, eaten over a computer keyboard, which for Fergus (and millions of others) had long been the routine.

Looking down on the stern again, they noticed the Caballeros in the Jacuzzi.

"Rub-a-dub-dub, three men in a tub!" Sylvie joked, inspiring in her husband a chuckle even as he sought to identify which of the villains had thrown the dancer into the pool. Just then she appeared, smiling and laughing with the sunbathers, working her way across the lower deck. Fergus leaned forward, watching nervously as she neared the spa bath and the lurking Caballeros. Suddenly, one wolf-whistled piercingly in her direction, the sound carrying clearly to Fergus and Sylvie observing from high above, but she did not react. The Caballero sank back into the bath, laughing boorishly with his two friends and hiding any disappointment at her lack of response. The dancer herself continued unperturbed through the crowd, eventually disappearing from Fergus' protective sight.

As he sat back in his chair, Fergus felt a surge of animosity towards the Caballeros. He could not help but worry how many times Justine may have been confronted by their type – it was almost unbearable to consider. Such thoughts did not cross Sylvie's mind and, even had they done so, she would have been more confident her daughter could have handled such situations.

She was able to see, though, that her husband was brooding over the incident – this was so typical of him and she sometimes wished he would lighten up, but she said nothing, certain he could not remain affronted long in these perfect surroundings.

Sure enough, Fergus' indignation imperceptibly melted away in the sunshine and, sensing it was time to move on, Sylvie took his hand and slowly they ambled back to their immaculately made-up cabin, where they rested, both wondering how doing so little could prove so incredibly tiring.

16

London and the Chilterns – early April 2010

Katie got into one of the pool of unmarked police cars at Paddington Green and headed to the A40. Subsequent to her visit to the Fredricks' a few days after Justine's funeral, she had returned to see them on half a dozen further occasions, though none had been as difficult as that initial time, when deep down she had known that all the best leads had already been explored. And all in vain.

She remembered, on first arriving in the area and driving those last few miles to their house, how beautiful she had found the countryside and how terrible she had thought it for someone who had grown up there to have died so impersonally on a cold London street. These feelings had been further confirmed when she reached the house itself, with its well kept lawns and the encircling woodland beyond. The building exuded a quiet serenity and it had struck Katie as being both perfectly where it belonged – deep in the Chiltern countryside – yet somehow not belonging at all to the wider world and all its troubles. But now troubles had even reached here:

"It looks like it's going to be difficult," she had confessed on that first visit, after they had ushered her in and exchanged pleasantries.

A ginger cat with black markings had wandered into the room and jumped on to her lap, just after she had started to speak. Mrs Fredricks had been about to get up to dislodge him, but Katie had signalled she didn't mind: in fact she loved animals, though it was strange to be having this sort of conversation with one on her knees. She had briefly wondered if the cat realised Justine was gone, whether he missed her, or if the entire tragedy was passing over his head, he being the only one who would not have been amazed had Justine walked through the door at that very moment. Katie gave him a stroke, which had reassured her more than him, then she continued:

"We have interviewed the witnesses but, beyond the cyclist being a woman, they have given us very little to go on. We have placed signage up at the accident site, asking people to come forward if they saw anything. We have done as much work on the CCTV as we can, following the cyclist both as far back and as far forward along her route as possible. We have also interviewed women cyclists using those roads. I have not given up, really I haven't, but I want to be honest with you too that, in my experience, it's not looking very hopeful."

Katie now shuddered a little as, turning on to the A40, she remembered her own words from four years earlier. At the time she had worried that she had been too blunt, but she hadn't wanted to pretend, to give false hope simply because it made a difficult conversation easier for her. Above all, she had felt ashamed… ashamed because she knew she was failing them and because, somehow, that must have shown as – though at that stage they barely knew each other – Mrs Fredricks had come and sat next to her, while her husband had sought to sound reassuring:

"We are sure you are doing your best. We both understand it is difficult, but we also know that, whether or not you find her,

Justine is gone. Finding the cyclist does matter, but it wouldn't change anything."

"They're lovely aren't they?" Wendy had said as Katie walked back with her to the car.

"Very, the cat too... but I am not going to be able to give them what they want and, I don't know, I feel so unprofessional... no result and then them comforting me!"

"You are doing fine, Katie... how would anyone else do any better? Just be as good as your word, don't give up on them. Not yet anyway."

As Wendy's words came back to her years after Wendy herself had moved on to other tragedies, Katie wondered how long 'not yet' should last? She had never given up but, to be frank, until a fortnight ago, she had run out of lines to follow and her subsequent visits to the Fredricks' had been little more than social calls to a couple of whom she had grown quietly fond. They had always greeted her warmly, asked how she was, made her tea and provided biscuits, and they had never quizzed her in too much depth about the case, knowing it only embarrassed her to reveal how little progress she had been able to make. Where others would have been less understanding and bullied her to do more to find their daughter's killer, the Fredricks had listened attentively to anything she had told them, but had also understood she was doing all she could. Then, two years ago, Mr Fredricks had said:

"Katie, thank you so much for all you have done, for caring and for trying your best, but, Sylvie and I, we both know there's nothing more you can do. Torturing yourself won't help either us or our daughter."

He was right, she knew that... in fact he would have been right had he said the same thing eighteen months earlier.

"You have to know when to let a case go," her inspector had said only a few months after the accident, but he had said it out of concern for her rather than for wasted police time.

Of course other crimes increasingly consumed her attention, but every now and then, she would still make the effort to try something new: fresh posters on each anniversary and, on days off when she was at a loose end, occasionally going to one of the sites along the cyclist's route and watching for women riding recklessly. Even as she did these things she knew they were completely hopeless, that these excursions were merely temporary insanities on her part and that, short of a miracle, the case would never be solved.

She was relieved Mr Fredricks had said what he had said, it needed saying and she was not sure when she would have had the courage. It wasn't fair on them to keep pretending there might be a positive outcome. So, they had both hugged her, and then she had left for what she imagined would be the last time.

Two years later and it felt good to be driving out to see them again. She had phoned them first, making it very clear that there had not been a breakthrough, but explaining that there was, nevertheless, something she wished to discuss with them.

Katie switched on the radio and a loud trailer screamed out at her for a football match to be broadcast that evening, a man excitedly commentating on a goal from an earlier game. The noise went straight through her and she desperately and randomly punched at other buttons to quell it and find another channel. In this way, she stumbled upon a music station and soon found herself singing along to Summer Martins' 'Roam':

"It's now ten years ago yet you're sensing her still
And it makes you so sad but it gives you a thrill,
You hope you might glimpse her but you never will,
She's gone and she's gone for good.
And all of those memories you hold deep inside
Are more precious than gold and you're so full of pride
That she was once yours and oh how you tried

To protect her, you thought that you could.
In the mountains she's absent
And she's not out at sea,
She's not lost in a forest,
Nor in the city,
And you know that you may as well roam,
'cos she's not coming home."

The song for some reason suddenly felt a little too close for comfort, maybe in view of where she was headed, and so she switched it off, driving on in silence.

Perhaps it was that silence, perhaps in combination with the optimism of the early spring weather, but, as she headed deeper into Buckinghamshire along the M40 and spotted the first tell-tale red kites circling high overhead, her heart began to lift – the area was gorgeous, even from a motorway along which most people tore at seventy miles an hour. Yes, Justine had died far too early and on a cold London pavement, but millions lived in London, some never seeing anything beyond its streets, how lucky Justine had been to grow up here! Off the motorway, Katie navigated the familiar leafy lanes that led to the Fredricks' home, remembering how in summertime these little roads were like tunnels, with lush green branches reaching across from both sides and overlapping in the middle overhead. She pulled into the driveway and surveyed the house and garden, wondering what that childhood must have been like, had it been as idyllic as she imagined or was the reality rather more humdrum? Knowing the Fredricks as she did and with a well developed picture of their daughter in her mind, Katie felt that, even if her upbringing hadn't been perfect, it surely hadn't fallen far short.

"Katie! How lovely to see you again!" Sylvie called across, already out of the house and in the driveway, before her guest had even stepped out of the car.

"Hi… and you…" They embraced and Sylvie led her into the house where another familiar face appeared.

"Katie!" Fergus said, surprising himself by how pleased he felt at her return, maybe because this was someone who had tried her best for them and who had felt pain when that best had not been good enough.

For twenty minutes or so easy small talk followed, washed down with the same familiar cups of tea that they had used to drink when Katie previously visited. She asked after Tiger:

"Oh, I'm afraid he passed away last year," Fergus said.

"I'm so sorry, he was lovely…"

"Yes, he was rather… and somehow a link back to Justine too. Still, he was getting on, and they are together now… we buried him at the end of the garden, by the path into the woods." He briefly worried that this intimated Justine was buried there too, but Katie had known what he meant. She also knew that, no matter how good it felt to see them, she was here professionally rather than as a friend and so, when the moment felt right, she turned the conversation to the matter in hand.

It had started a fortnight ago when the BBC had approached the Metropolitan Police about a TV programme they were making on the tensions between drivers and cyclists in London. In turn, Katie had been asked to be involved. Initially her eyes had rolled, she had no desire to be on TV and the debate itself anyway was an old one, and one which always missed the point. She predicted the show would include cyclists complaining how they had been knocked off their bikes by motorists (and Katie had seen plenty of that in her job) and motorists criticising cyclists for weaving dangerously in the traffic and jumping red lights (she had seen a lot of that too, including a spate of pedestrians knocked over while crossing the road under a green man). Katie found the 'us and them' nature of the debate tiresome and knew that it wasn't really about drivers and cyclists at all, it was about considerate and inconsiderate people: someone who ignored a red light on a bike would jump a queue in a car, someone who tailgated in a car would ride a bike on the pavement.

She had been about to decline when they mentioned the broadcast date, the four year anniversary of Justine's accident. Perhaps it could serve a purpose. She agreed to speak with the producer, who seemed delighted to hear that the programme would tie in so well with the anniversary, and he agreed to highlight the case. It was just now a question of seeking the Fredricks' permission and even asking if they would like to appear.

Katie explained all this to Fergus and Sylvie and they were immediately excited about the prospect, though both wanted to have a think about actually appearing themselves. Justine's life didn't need marking, but it felt good that it would be and that her death might just prevent someone else's. None of them liked to think too much about the other possibility: perhaps someone would be watching who would know what had happened, perhaps even the cyclist herself and, perhaps perhaps, they or even she would come forward.

After about ninety minutes, Katie said her goodbyes, knowing this time she would be back in touch with them again soon. As her car crunched its way down the gravel of the Fredricks' drive and back out on to the open road, the adrenaline pumped through her body and she consciously sought to contain her excitement. She knew that, although she had hidden it beneath a friendly professionalism, she felt exhilarated: it had been good to see Fergus and Sylvie again, they had picked up easily and naturally, and it had felt invigorating to be out in their quiet, beautiful corner of the world once more, even to revisit their house. This powerful combination had refuelled her optimism and she felt as if the TV programme – though not without risk of painfully dashed hopes if not managed carefully – meant Justine would still be remembered more widely, even if only through references to her death.

Above all, Katie felt that there was a chance, no more than that, that she might yet deliver for Justine and her parents after all.

17

After their rest, Fergus went for a swim in the pool at the ship's stern, while Sylvie found a quiet spot nearby with her book. The water was lovely, heated from the sea and almost bath like. What's more, he got lucky, nobody else was in it and the three Caballeros had even absented themselves from the adjacent spa bath. He savoured floating effortlessly on his back in the salty water, without the need to move a muscle, riding the swells either with his eyes closed (he felt he could easily fall asleep) or staring up at the blue sky as the occasional cumulus cloud floated by. Eventually, the perfection was broken by a man plunging in, creating waves which flooded over Fergus' face, causing him to wake coughing and spluttering from his reverie. The man began ploughing athletically up and down the short pool and Fergus decided to leave him to it, climbing out and gathering up his things.

Getting changed was always awkward here as there were no facilities, but he had found there was a changing room on deck ten, at the very top of the ship, by the smaller pool there. Fergus climbed up the three levels, leaving a trail of water behind him, and he wandered along the deck until he reached the door.

"*Closed for cleaning.*"

Fergus couldn't help but think that, of all times, mid to late afternoon would be when the changing room was most likely to be required. What were his options now? The easiest, despite being in his swimming shorts and just having a towel draped around his shoulders, would be to take the lift inside the entrance to the nearby Conservatory Bar, which would drop him within a few metres of their cabin six decks below. So this is what he did, trying not to feel too ill at ease as he waited, dripping, for the lift to arrive. When it finally did, Gentle Henry stepped out:

"Goodneth! Baptithing by emersion?" he asked with a slight tilt of his head.

"No, no…" Fergus replied, "Just been for a swim, but the changing room is closed so I need to get back to the cabin."

"Yeth, yeth of courth, I musssn't keep you… but wouldn't it be a marveloussss setting? Perhapsss an idea for the future? Now, where I wonder is Tabths?"

"Yes, but…" however, before he could remind Gentle Henry that he wasn't qualified to perform such rites, the lift doors closed between them and Fergus began the descent back to his cabin, feeling increasingly self-conscious and cold each time the lift stopped to allow others in or out along the way.

Finally it reached deck four and the doors opened.

"Why, hello there Fergus! It looks like you have been the sporty one today!"

"Oh, hello Mrs Huffington… yes, yes, I've been in the pool."

"Well I didn't think you had been horse riding Fergus!" Mrs Huffington replied. "Oh, my Lawrence and I, we used to love our horse riding mind you…"

"Did you Mrs Huffington?" said Fergus beginning to shiver and feeling conspicuous and exposed as he stood in the lobby in his swimming shorts, his small rucksack hanging from his right hand, while his left held on to the towel around his neck.

"Why yes Fergus, he and I were quite sporty ourselves, don't you know? We used to ride for hours in the New Forest, it didn't matter what season. We used to love it. Do you ride Fergus?"

"No, I can't say that I do Mrs Huffington. I'm rather chilly, I think I'd better…"

"Oh, you'd love riding. If you like nature that is, and I'm sure you do. You look the sensitive type. My Lawrence was too, but don't get me wrong, he was also a man of the world. He made his fortune before he was forty… unfortunately, he didn't live long enough to enjoy it. You must look after yourself, you see, Fergus, and I'm glad to hear you go swimming, but you should try the riding when you get home, you really should."

"Thank you for the tip Mrs Huffington, I'll…"

"But you must ride somewhere nice Fergus, otherwise it is wasted. Do you live somewhere nice Fergus?"

"The Chilterns, Mrs Huffington…"

"Oh how lovely! Lawrence and I had friends there… oh yes, we used to visit them often Fergus, and they us… how lucky you are to live in such a beautiful area, and perfect for riding too. I'm surprised you don't, what a terrible waste!"

"Well, perhaps I'll give it a try, it's just that…"

"Why Fergus, you are going blue, what are you doing standing here in the lobby in those wet things? I can't let you keep me anyway, I'm late for my bingo. I won a £10 voucher to spend on board yesterday Fergus…"

"Gosh, congratulations Mrs Huffington!"

"Yes, valid on any products priced £50 or over, so I'll be looking at the jewellery later, I have my eye on something quite special." And with that, almost magically, the lift doors re-opened and she and her zimmer frame shuffled inside, while Fergus made a dash for the cabin, wondering whether he had avoided catching his death. A hot shower warmed him up and thirty minutes later he rejoined Sylvie on deck. Soon they were sipping their lattés and diving deep into their e-readers.

"Dolphins!" The shout went up from somewhere on deck and everyone who was able rushed to the rail. Sure enough, there they were, some twenty of them leaping out of the water on the port side, just behind the ship. Fergus and Sylvie had caught sight of the occasional one before, but it had always vanished again the very moment that they had spotted it. This time they were impossible to miss, their silver skin reflecting the bright sunlight as they fleetingly cleared the water to the "oooohs" and "ahhhhhs" of their admiring spectators. Just a couple of minutes later and the show was already over. A few of the passengers waited there a short while, scouring the sea in the hope of an encore, but gradually each gave up, one by one retreating back to their sun loungers, until it was only Fergus and Sylvie left at the rail.

"What is it about whales and dolphins, in fact what is it about seeing any animal in the wild, that feels so magical?" mused Sylvie.

"I suppose, we all live such busy, modern lives that seeing an animal in the wild reminds us of the natural world... it's good for the soul," Fergus answered. "We feel it when we see the red kites circling high above us at home..." For a moment they both pictured the birds wheeling effortlessly in the Chiltern skies, a wing flap being no more necessary to them than a swimming stroke had been to Fergus in the salty pool.

"... and the badgers, foxes and deer," added Sylvie. They loved, especially on summer evenings, going out into the countryside near their home and spotting all these creatures. It always felt like a Buckinghamshire safari and Justine had often been their guide... when they continued these walks after her death, they both frequently felt that if they turned round they would still see her, perhaps as a teenager, a short way behind them, sometimes lost in her own world but often alert and eyes peeled for any sign of wildlife.

"It's all about patience and keeping quiet," she would say as she sat down somewhere and waited for the wildlife to come to her. Fergus and Sylvie would wait patiently too, occasionally with incredible luck: once a badger walked past Sylvie's legs, almost brushing her; another evening, a barn owl surprised them, flying silently between the trees and landing on a branch right above their heads, looking down inquisitively with its beautiful moon face at the open mouthed band of three below. Sometimes, though, they would wait with no luck at all, until eventually either their legs would ache from standing or their backsides from sitting, and Fergus or Sylvie would suggest it was time to head home.

"Just one more minute…" Justine would plead, before reluctantly conceding, and the three of them would slowly troop back through the late evening, often with the bats swooping above their heads catching insects in the late evening sky, while Tiger waited impatiently for their return.

Fergus and Sylvie were woken from these daydreams by the sight of an enormous whale, just some forty metres off the ship, breaking the surface and then vanishing again beneath the swell. It did this three times before disappearing for good. They looked at each other as if they could hardly believe what they had just seen… and they had been the only ones to see it, even though they had heard it clearly, breathing out through its blow hole. How had everyone else missed it? It was one of those rare moments in life: another jewel to recall when the going got tough, or perhaps even an omen signalling the end of the hardest times and the breakthrough to happier days ahead.

"Justine would have gone crazy to see that!" said Fergus as the surprise faded.

"It was a gift," replied Sylvie.

As it was a formal night in the restaurant, they again ate early in the café, before retreating to the calm of the Conservatory Bar for their Pimm's. They didn't talk much, not because they had nothing to say, but because neither felt the need to say anything and, anyway, the string trio were playing. It was hard to imagine a more relaxing ambience and so they just sat quietly, enjoying their drinks, each other's company and the music floating around their ears. An elegantly dressed Richard and Cressida crossed over to them on their way from their pre-dinner drink to the restaurant.

"Good luck!" cried Sylvie.

"Thank you… as it's formal night we're gambling she'll be on her best behaviour!" Cressida replied, crossing her fingers.

The couples smiled at each other and, just for a moment, as the diplomat and his wife disappeared through the doorway, Fergus again regretted he wasn't more naturally sociable himself, envying the couple's easy ability to talk to anyone. He knew the diplomatic service wouldn't have been for him – the prospect of those embassy parties appalled him – but he wished he could nevertheless mix more readily. As Fergus brooded on this, they continued to sit quietly together, both feeling they could happily remain there the rest of the evening, but Fergus also felt an illogical loyalty to the dancer and, a little later, he suggested they should go to the show and Sylvie agreed.

So, once again, they found themselves in the comfort of the Poseidon Theatre with the lights dimming at the start of another performance. If he were honest, it was quite amateurish, something halfway between a very good school show and a rather average West End one. However, he understood how important singing and dancing would be to this troupe of young men and women, whose faces were now so familiar to him but whose characters he could only construct in his mind, and he clapped encouragingly at every opportunity, whilst wondering whether any other audience member had invested quite so much of themselves into their performance. He didn't mean to be critical of any of them – least of all his nameless dancer and Nicole, his wistful singer – but, once more, he supposed there was only so much anyone could do song-and-dance-wise on a small stage rolling around on the Atlantic swell.

"Enjoyed?" he said to Sylvie.

"Yes, a great deal," his wife responded with an enthusiasm that again surprised him but which, without him knowing, had been partly for his benefit. She knew that he enjoyed the shows and, while she did too, her pleasure was more in her husband's enjoyment. Occasionally, she would turn and look at him, rather than at the singers and the dancers, and she felt happiness at his absorption in the performance, with his mind temporarily free of the sorrows and sadnesses which had become so much a part of their lives. So perhaps her "yes, a great deal" was because she had been watching another show entirely, the one that had played out on her husband's face.

Again, they stood at the bow of the ship star gazing, this time alone save for one deck walker putting in some late evening laps, coming round predictably every five minutes as he clocked them up. They relaxed there in silence enjoying the moment, each other's company and the warm wind blowing agreeably against their faces, but – for Fergus at least – there was also the creeping awareness at the back of his mind that this perfection couldn't last and that another day had quietly slipped by.

18

London – Wednesday 23ʳᵈ June 2010

Hannah kicked off her shoes and crashed on the couch with her Chinese take-away, it had felt a long day and she was pleased to be home. Nicole, who had just finished her A-levels, was out with friends and Dylan was upstairs in his room doing homework. As the aches lifted from her tired feet, she could finally relax.

Life had been tough these last few years but, though she missed Paul terribly, she felt it was settling down again and that, actually, she had made a good job of raising her family through the year of her husband's illness, the trauma of his death and the grief and emptiness beyond. She was fairly sure that Nicole had done well at her exams and, if a good thing can come out of losing your father so young, Dylan had grown up a lot – she hoped not too much – and was so much easier than he had been a few years earlier.

Stewart, her boss, had been very sympathetic while the family went through the nightmare from which they were finally emerging, although she felt she would grieve for her husband for as long as she lived. But life was at least stable again. And she was repaying the company for their support by being in the most productive phase of her career: a rich vein of success with a string of new, high value clients. So, although her crash on to the couch was a tired one, it was also a satisfied one, the only frustration being the song she could not get out of her head.

The previous week, a pop star, with a string of hits over the preceding years, had died of a brain haemorrhage which had come out of the blue, and her songs were being played everywhere, with broadcasters competing to pay their respects. The chorus of her most famous song 'Roam' had been spinning in Hannah's head all day and still tormented her now:

> *"In the mountains she's absent*
> *And she's not out at sea,*
> *She's not lost in a forest,*
> *Nor in the city,*
> *And you know that you may as well roam,*
> *'cos she's not coming home."*

Hannah was shocked to hear the young singer had died but, although she liked the song, it wasn't exactly poetry and she had been amazed over recent days at the crowds weeping out from her TV set, as various tribute programmes had been squeezed into the schedule. Thank goodness, no sign of any tonight as Hannah zapped between the channels looking for something to watch. Finally, she settled on a documentary about the dangers of cycling in London, which she knew to be a hazardous pursuit from her own days riding to work, something she had abandoned upon realising her children were going to lose their father: they didn't need their mother taking undue risks too.

She sat there, internally nodding at the tales of how cyclists were obliged to take their lives in their hands and how London's politicians needed to do much more to make the capital a bike-friendly city. Towards the end of the programme, however, there was a twist, as the focus turned to the duty cyclists also had to ride their bikes responsibly:

"On this very day, four years ago, at half past eight in the morning, twenty-four year old pedestrian Justine Fredricks was hit here, as she turned a corner into the Marylebone Road, by a cyclist riding fast along the pavement. The cyclist – also a woman – didn't stop and was never caught to take responsibility for the death of this young woman and for the shattered lives of those left behind."

The picture switched, initially to the same female police officer who, earlier in the programme, had highlighted some of the poor driving she had witnessed in her career. She was now standing on the corner between Great Central Street and the Marylebone Road, explaining how cyclists too could cause mayhem and tragedy on the streets by ignoring the rules. Then the image switched again, this time to the young woman's parents, sitting in a beautiful garden somewhere outside London, speaking with love and pride about their only child. Hannah could clearly hear song birds excitedly chirping in the background and, every now and then, one would swoop into shot collecting seed from a feeder placed on a lawn, which stretched away to a purple blooming rhododendron bush in the distance, just visible at the top of the screen, apparently at the start of a wood. She briefly wondered where this demi-paradise might be, but the scene changed again, this time back to one of bikes weaving precariously through city traffic, as the narrator wound up the programme with a summary of the issues affecting cyclists in London, finishing with a sentence inspired by a conversation with Katie:

"Ultimately, what drivers and cyclists have in common, far more than anything that separates them, is that they are people. Of course most are considerate, but every day we see how others cause havoc on our roads, however they are travelling, and it's usually innocent people, in the wrong place at the wrong time,

that pay the price. Perhaps road users of all descriptions should be arguing less between themselves and instead fighting together for the Mayor to do much more to ensure our streets are safer for all, including those who, like Justine Fredricks, are neither on two nor four wheels, but on foot."

Something made Hannah rewind:

"On this very day, four years ago, at half past eight in the morning, twenty-four year old pedestrian Justine Fredricks was hit here, as she turned a corner into the Marylebone Road, by a cyclist riding fast along the pavement. The cyclist – also a woman – didn't stop and was never caught..."

Distant memories of just avoiding a woman at that very junction slowly began to surface. No, surely it couldn't have been her? She racked her brains, eventually remembering that her near-miss had been on the date of her presentation to 'Coding Tigers', a software company in need of marketing. Theirs had been an important account and it had been crucial to win it, in fact they had turned out to be her first big client. She had been running late that morning, she remembered it clearly now, and she had cycled on the pavement, just along the Marylebone Road and only that once, though she felt certain that she had not been riding fast. Despite her caution, however, she did recall that she had undoubtedly brushed against a woman pedestrian emerging from that corner: it had given her a real shock. She hadn't, though, believed that she had actually hurt her... although it's true she hadn't stopped to check for sure. She should have done so, in hindsight she realised that, only it had all happened so quickly. But what date had it been?

Hannah put her tray down and walked to her desk the far side of the room. She knew all her old diaries were there and it did not take her long to find the one for 2006. She quickly flicked through to June 23rd and there in her own big, black letters was written *"9.30 Coding Tigers Presentation."* She didn't move as her brain made the creeping but inevitable connections between what she had seen on the television, what she had read in her diary and the logical conclusion:

"I killed someone!"

She couldn't believe it. She had thought she was a morally good person, a woman who had come through a difficult start in life to raise a decent family and to hold down a respectable job. She was someone who cared, not someone who killed! She had nursed her husband through illness and been resilient after his death, for the sake of her children. She had survived all that, finally everything was going well and now this! All the while the police had been searching for her – a fugitive, a wanted person who hadn't even known she was on the run – and a family had been grieving for a daughter whose life she unknowingly had taken.

She felt sick. She didn't know what to do. Should she call the police immediately? Should she keep it to herself? Should she talk to Nu? She didn't know whether to sit down, stand up, walk around, stay in, go out. Her head was spinning and she couldn't think as the panic set in. Eventually, she rushed upstairs, grateful that Nicole was out and that Dylan's music was playing too loudly for him to be aware of anything beyond his closed bedroom door. She shut herself in her own room, falling onto the bed she had once shared with her husband, and uncontrollably sobbed.

She emerged ninety minutes later, having composed herself and ensured there were no visible signs of her breakdown. She was now resolved what to do, she just didn't know when she was going to do it. She tidied up her dinner things, throwing away the congealed remains of her half eaten meal and washing up her plate and cutlery, before bracing herself to say goodnight to Dylan. When, a little later, she heard Nicole come in, she resisted the urge to go back downstairs and give her the hug she desperately needed – it might reveal something was wrong – instead, she called down to her, asking if she had had a good evening, and then explaining that she was having an early night.

Shortly afterwards, though, she crept halfway back down the stairs, peering through the banisters and into the living room at her daughter sitting on the sofa, on the phone to the same friend she had only minutes before left, entirely unaware that her life had just changed.

Hannah watched sadly for a few moments and then tiptoed back up to bed. Amazingly perhaps, she slept.

The next morning she woke up and for a few seconds everything was normal, but then the awful truth seeped back into her consciousness and again she wept. Pulling herself together once more, she put on a brave face for Nicole and Dylan and then found an excuse to leave early for work… except she wasn't going to the office at all, but to the person she trusted most in the whole world, and for that she needed to take the Northern Line down to Clapham.

Hannah was relieved to find Nu in. He opened the door and she instantly threw herself into his arms.

"Oh Nu, something terrible has happened!"

"Come in, come in," he said, ushering her into his living room and beginning an alarmed guessing game, "Is it Nicole? Dylan?"

"No, no, they're fine," she replied, "but, oh Nu, I think I've killed someone!" Nu was a poet, a nature lover, one of the world's carers, but he had the capacity for a very level head too. He sat down next to her on the sofa, took her hands in his, waited a moment for her to compose herself and then asked her to start from the beginning. It all came pouring out, unstoppable as the sobbing returned, but this time with the comfort of knowing someone who loved her unconditionally was there with her. After she finished, he put his arms around her and gave her the hug she had been unable to ask from Nicole the previous night. Neither spoke for a couple of minutes and then Nu became businesslike.

"You have definitely done the right thing coming to see me," he said, both strongly and reassuringly, "we can talk it through, take our time and be sure you are happy with whatever decisions you are going to make next."

"I know what I'm going to do," she answered, "I'm handing myself in, I've got to, I just don't know when. They'll send me to prison, maybe for a very long time, but for the moment Dylan needs me. Nicole is leaving for university in a few weeks, but I'm still her mother, she depends on me as well..." Hannah started crying again. "Perhaps I could wait until she's graduated, or even until Dylan has too... but that could be seven years from now, more maybe... even then, he may not be able to afford somewhere to live on his own... how am I going to..."

"Slow down, slow down," Nu said, breaking his sister's stream of panic, "first of all, we don't know for sure that it was you, going to the police now might clear this all up..."

"But it's the right day, the right time and the right place that I remember hitting a woman, and we know the pedestrian was a woman and that the person who hit her was too." Nu had to agree that it was pretty damning. His sister continued "... how can I leave those poor parents without at least the small satisfaction of knowing who was responsible?"

This was a problem that needed some thought and they agreed that, with Nicole able to babysit for her younger brother, Hannah would stay the night with Nu, giving them the rest of the day and then the whole evening to talk it through calmly together, coming up for air from time to time. In this secure environment, a way forward was found and the next morning, while her brother went to buy some envelopes and paper, Hannah wrote a letter on his computer:

"Dear Detective Sergeant Brady,

I saw you on television on Wednesday night when you marked the exact 4th anniversary of the death of a young woman who was knocked over by a female cyclist near Marylebone Station. Until seeing the programme, I had no idea I had hurt anyone, but I now feel sure that I am the cyclist you described. I remember being late for a meeting and riding on the pavement along the Marylebone Road on the 23rd June 2006. I distinctly recall brushing against a woman who suddenly appeared in front of me from Great Central Street. I was not, however, riding fast (as claimed in the programme) and I didn't think she had fallen over, though I admit I did see her spin round and I should have stopped to check she was unhurt. I know it was the 23rd June because I still have my 2006 diary and my meeting is shown on that day.

I want to do what is right, but I am a single parent and I have my children also to consider. I promise to hand myself in as soon as they no longer need me. I would like to tell you more, but I can't for fear I will give you clues which will help you find me. I know this letter is a clue in itself and if it helps you identify me so be it, but I needed to tell you that I will come forward, that I hadn't realised what I had done and that I am terribly, terribly sorry.

Please will you pass this message to the parents of the poor girl I killed. I can't begin to imagine what they have gone through and I feel totally deserving to find myself in this nightmare. It will be a relief to come forward: I will do so in a few years, when I will accept full responsibility."

Wearing rubber gloves, Nu printed the letter on to a sheet of paper from the ream he had just bought. He folded it into an envelope he had unwrapped from the cellophane of a new pack and on to which he had printed the police station address. They did not know if these forensic precautions were necessary, but felt sure the paper and envelope would be scoured for any possible clues. Neither's DNA or fingerprints were on file, but they wanted to avoid any possible future link. They were even wary of CCTV tracing them to a post box, and so Nu alone took the letter to the busiest one he could find in central London. Hoping if any cameras did trace this moment they would discount him as being a man, he discreetly emptied the letter from a plastic bag into the box and then slipped away back into the crowds.

"All done," Nu said to his sister back in Clapham. "Still OK with it?" It was a little late had she wanted to change her mind, but the one small mercy was that Hannah felt sure now that this was exactly the right way to deal with this nightmare situation, she just did not know how she was going to get through the next few years and the prison sentence which she assumed awaited her beyond that.

"Remember," said Nu, "it was an accident."

Hannah stepped out into the late Clapham afternoon. It was time to go home.

19

The swell got up substantially on the second full day between Cape Verde and the Canaries and Fergus and Sylvie were both delighted – secretly they had been disappointed that there had been very little movement on board, today though promised to feel more stormy and, even as they made their way to breakfast, they could see fellow passengers stumbling around as if half drunk.

Afterwards they headed to the laundry. You need to pack an awful lot of clothes to last three weeks and they had decided not to try, but instead to do some simple washing of socks, underwear and T-shirts about half way through the cruise. That day had come. First stop was Reception to buy a token and then they took the lift down to the only publicly accessible part of deck two, where the launderette and the medical centre were hidden away. Down here the passageways were uncarpeted, bare pipes ran up, down and along the walls, flashing lights with accompanying bells and sirens leaked through the half open door of a dingy games arcade and a slightly dank smell filled the air. Most corridors were cordoned off with a chain and presumably led to the mysterious parts of the ship which only the crew ever saw – an oily-overalled mechanic emerged from one as if to prove the point, stepping over the low-hanging barrier and smiling at a disoriented Fergus and Sylvie as he passed, before disappearing again behind an intimidating heavy metal door.

As soon as they entered, the laundry room felt hellish, with around a dozen washing machines churning noisily and half as many tumble dryers also whirring away infernally. The sound wasn't deafening but it was intense, and the heat coming from the machines, together with the lack of any windows, added to the feeling that the devil himself might enter the room at any moment, carrying his own laundry basket, along with a pitch fork with which further to torment his guests.

They could see that one machine would finish its cycle in fifteen minutes and so they hung around ready to pounce on it as soon as it did, fretting whether the person using it would return to remove their items or whether anyone else might walk in at just the wrong moment, grabbing the empty washer before they had a chance to claim it. These tensions added to that infernal feeling, but fortunately the user was indeed there and she removed her damp clothes promptly when the cycle finished, while Sylvie stood her ground nearby, ready to throw her clothes in at the first opportunity. The triumph of getting the machine was short lived – how the hell (and the phrase felt appropriate) did the wretched thing work? They closed the door and inserted the token: nothing. They pushed every button they could find: nothing. They tried to open the door: it was locked, with their underwear and T-shirts stuck inside.

The heat, the noise, the claustrophobic feel of this room deep in the bowels of the ship, together with the aggravation of not being able to work the machines, all added up to the antithesis of their experience watching whales and dolphins from the stern the previous evening. Both felt the frustration, but Sylvie was better at taking deep breaths and not letting it get to her, while her husband ever more frantically turned dials, randomly pushed buttons and pulled harder and harder at the locked washing machine door. After a while he gave up. Moments later, there was an audible click, Sylvie tried the latch and the door opened.

"Well, at least we've got our clothes back!" she sighed. A nearby woman, who looked completely at home in the laundry and as if she would happily spend the entire cruise there, came up to her:

"Did you close the door and then put the token in? Because you need to put the token in first and then close the door." She pointed to some faded, peeling instructions pinned inconspicuously to the far wall.

"Oh, thank you," said Sylvie, again repressing her frustration, "Fergus, we are going to need another token." He stomped off to Reception to obtain one, ready for a fight should anyone seek to charge him for it, but instead the young Thai lady behind the counter smiled sympathetically and said:

"Oh, I'm so sorry sir," and, handing him another one, added "don't forget to put the token in first and then to close the door."

"Thank you, thank you... I won't... forget I mean."

Fergus retreated back down to deck two, hurrying past the flickering lights and nightmarish noises emanating from the arcade, finally returning to the laundry room to find his wife valiantly fighting off a man who wanted to use their machine. They inserted the token, closed the door, watched the washer spring into life, then made their escapes.

"Good afterrrnoon, ladies and gentlemen. An update from the brrridge..." The Captain began his daily report of temperatures, wind speeds, position and estimated arrival times, but Fergus and Sylvie barely listened to these pearls of wisdom as they sat, out on deck again, deep in their e-readers.

"Since therrre is some significant swell, please do hold on

to the hand rrrails as you move about the ship, in orrrder to avoid acc-Sea-dents." For the first time this advice was sound and both Fergus and Sylvie were relishing the pitching and rolling motion as the *Magdalena* ploughed on through the waves. Every now and then, someone would walk by and be sent stumbling off sideways as the ship passed over another roller, but in most instances this experience was greeted with laughter and good cheer, like children on an exhilarating fairground ride.

"A few hygiene advices, please wash yourrr hands fre-Quent-ly throughout the day for 20 seconds using hot soapy water as this is the best method to prrrevent infection..."

"Yes, yes, yes, we've got the message!" Sylvie said out loud, remembering how she seemed to spend much of the day washing her hands or using the various hand sanitisers dotted around the ship and at the entrances to its restaurants. The Captain finished his message and peace returned.

Sylvie stayed put much of the time, relaxing in her chair, though she did go for occasional walks. Fergus, however, continued to enjoy wandering about a bit more. He would roam the ship, mainly outside but also in, exploring and savouring being on board, wanting to squeeze as much out of the experience as he could. In doing this, he found various nooks and crannies with new views over the Atlantic and he would stand gazing out towards the horizon, loving the fact that land wasn't to be seen in any direction. The swell today only added to his sense of euphoria.

As he heaved open a door and ventured inside the ship, he passed the entrance to the Poseidon Theatre and could hear the criminologist giving a lecture about 'Jack the Ripper'. Peeping in, he noticed how the audience appeared captivated by the little man as, whisky glass in hand, he paced the stage, excitedly expounding theories on these gruesome Victorian murders. Fergus again could not help but wonder why anyone would wish to sit indoors through this grisly detail when it was such a magnificent day outside, with the thrill of the Atlantic Ocean, but clearly many did.

He continued through to the Reception area where there were also a handful of small boutiques:

"Excuse me sir. Can I interest you in a video of the cruise?"

"No thank you."

"But sir, they are tremendous value and beautifully shot, let me show you…"

"No thank you," Fergus barked, shaking the steward off and heading towards the Salt of the Earth pub.

"And which European Airport has the code FCO?"

Fergus noticed Jennifer (the bespectacled librarian, crafts teacher and unlikely chatterbox introduced to them on the first evening) sitting on a bar stool with a microphone, hosting the twice daily quiz. He resisted the urge to shout out 'Rome' to her as he made his way through the pub and into the sleepy atmosphere of the bingo being played in the lounge beyond, in the corner of which he saw Mrs Huffington marking off her numbers with an oversized pen.

Finally, Fergus headed back out on deck, relieved to hit the fresh air again. As he walked, he noticed the Captain heading towards him. This was his chance:

"Good afternoon!"

"Good afterrrnoon," the Captain replied with a warm smile, though without stopping. It had hardly been the leisurely conversation Richard and Cressida had enjoyed the previous day, but the only words he and the Captain would ever exchange still felt like a small victory to Fergus and he rejoined Sylvie feeling buoyed by the brief encounter. He sat a while with his wife, but, checking their watches simultaneously, both knew the respite would be short lived…

"I think our washing may be ready soon," he half-heartedly suggested.

"Once more unto the breach?" Sylvie ventured.

"I fear so." They headed down to the laundry and their machine showed just five minutes to run. The next challenge would be finding a spare tumble dryer. Several were already in action, but those that were not were still filled with clothes awaiting the return of their owners.

"Do you think we can just empty one?" asked Fergus. Sylvie looked unsure and, for some reason, this insignificant question felt like a matter of war and peace as they pictured someone furiously demanding to know who had dared to handle their knickers. However, their indecisiveness was resolved by a man:

"Mine will be finishing in a moment, you can have that. It's a bit of a hell hole down here isn't it?" They both felt relieved, mainly at the availability of the dryer, but also at evidence of another civilised presence with them there, an ally with whom to battle the machines, the heat and the noise. They restricted their answer to a unison:

"Yes it is. Thank you."

So, with near perfect co-ordination, as their washing machine stopped so did the man's tumble dryer, and they were able to transfer their clothes across, switch the machine on and escape for a further sixty minutes. During this interlude, they ate their usual light lunch on deck ten, outside the restaurant, smiling across at Gentle Henry and Tabitha who were sitting quietly, enjoying theirs in the sunshine, a few tables away.

"We seem to be yoyo-ing between heaven on deck ten and hell on deck two," Sylvie observed to her husband, who was sitting eyes closed and face tilted up towards the sun.

"One more trip to hell!" Fergus responded, reluctantly, and without initially moving position, but then slowly coming back to life. Bracing themselves a final time, they collected their laundry, gave their T-shirts the most cursory of irons and, having gathered up all the socks and pants they could find, retreated back to their cabin to put it all away.

"Finally, job done!" Sylvie smiled.

They ventured out again, walking a couple of laps around the deck, before settling back down to their books and, in Fergus' case, also to his meditation.

"Paradise regained!" He said, before putting his ear plugs in and starting his deep breathing. His wife took hold of his knee and gave it a shake.

"Paradise regained," she agreed.

The line between paradise and hell is, however, thin and not always delineated so clearly as it was at that moment between the top and bottom decks of the ship. A few hours later, listening to the string trio playing in the Midships Lounge, Fergus bristled at a man holding a loud conversation with someone back home on his mobile phone:

"Surely they will sell for 54k? OK try offering them 58, but make it clear that we won't go a penny higher... yes, the Melta Media presentation needs to be on the 6th January... no, it has to be the 6th... get Brett to start working on the slides..."

They had both thought that, while on board a ship, they would be free from what, to them, was a modern plague, but this naivety had been shattered as early as day two or three, when they had been awoken from an afternoon snooze out on deck by a female voice proclaiming loudly, to someone nearly a thousand miles away, that she was in the middle of the Atlantic, on her way to the Azores.

They had rolled their eyes at each other as the woman reported back every detail of the cruise to date and had then gone on to ask about *"Archie and the girls,"* before expressing shock at hearing that *"Chardonnay has been suspended from school... again!"*

Every few days a peaceful moment would be blighted in this way by someone oblivious to, or uncaring about, the volume of their voice. Some spoke so loudly that Fergus wondered whether they really needed a phone at all. This man particularly irritated him: talking while a string trio played was, Fergus preached to Sylvie (though quietly enough for the man not to hear), "disrespectful to the musicians and inconsiderate to everyone else."

"Come on," she replied, "while you are on your high horse, we may as well trot along to dinner." Sylvie cut through his indignation, a skill she had refined over the course of their long marriage.

"Yes, the Farthly deal takes precedence over all the other accounts, it's too important… can't you tell Jacoby to…"

"Giddy-up now!" Sylvie joked as they got up and headed to the restaurant, without waiting to hear what Jacoby should be advised to do.

They enjoyed dinner. Yes, the Maitre D' as usual stood at the restaurant entrance squeezing hand sanitiser into their palms without ever looking up at their faces, but at least the arachnid lady had toned down her volume switch for the evening. The food was excellent and washed down with another rich and smooth Merlot. Meanwhile Angelo, their waiter, hurried around chaotically with plates and trays, somehow never quite dropping anything, joking with them as he rushed by that he had to get back to his chickens, which were busy laying eggs in the galley. Had the Maitre D' loitered long enough after asking *"is everything alright?"*, the answer from both Fergus and Sylvie would have been a firm *"yes"*, but typically he was gone before they had time to respond. Instead, they just laughed and enjoyed the madness of the moment, along with the last sips of their wine.

Easily resisting the lure of the comedian performing again that night in the Poseidon Theatre, Fergus and Sylvie settled down in the card room and played Scrabble, before venturing out one more time to try to catch the stars, but there must have been cloud cover, because the sky above was a murky black.

"Canaries tomorrow," said Sylvie.

"Hmmm!" replied Fergus, as the frustration of a lost day in Cape Verde resurfaced, but this time he caught himself in his grumpiness without the need for his wife to intervene.

"How do you put up with me? Why do you put up with me?" He asked.

"It's a good question. I think it must be something about love." She gave him a kiss and, as she did so, the moon emerged brightly from the clouds.

"How did you do that?"

"Spooky isn't it?" She teased… "but I'm out of tricks for one day. And I'm dropping. Let's go to bed."

20

The Chilterns and beyond –

September 2004 to June 2006

Following that slightly awkward first meeting with her parents, Jones set off on his walk with Justine hoping that the Ljubljanan magic they had shared together had made it safely back to Britain with her. It quickly became apparent that it had.

She didn't appear to share any of these anxieties, leading him eagerly through countryside she knew like the back of her hand, but which was for him all new. He liked it, but more than that he liked the enthusiasm with which she showed it to him, as they wandered up and down hills, through woodland and emerged into open valleys. They stopped to rest by a stream, where they witnessed streaks of blue shooting through the air as a pair of kingfishers dived for their tea. Justine was clearly proud of where she came from, Jones thought to himself, and rightly so.

"How was that for starters?" she asked as they completed the circle.

"Excellent," he replied, admiring more red kites circling overhead.

"You've seen nothing yet, my biggest surprise is reserved for later, at least I'm hoping…"

They went into the house and Justine started to prepare some pasta while Jones sat watching on a kitchen stool.

"It's good to see you again Freddie," he said, as he mused to himself what the surprise might be.

"You too," she responded, looking up briefly.

They ate their food, talking easily and also easily not talking. By the time they had finished it was early evening.

"Come on Jones, rest period over, it's back out into the wilds… not far this time, but you'll need to be quiet, and patient." He put his boots back on and followed her down the garden and, ever so quietly, to the edge of the wood, where she sat down on a fallen tree, patting it for him to do the same. Then they waited. Occasionally Jones went to say something but she put her finger to her lips and whispered for him to be patient. He had never been on a date like this before, he was in new territory literally and metaphorically, but he felt strangely peaceful in the tranquil surroundings with nothing expected of him but to sit quietly in the warm late-summer evening.

After about thirty minutes, there was a distinct rustling sound, followed a moment later by a snuffling and a sniffing. Jones heard it clearly.

"Don't move!" Justine whispered, as a black and white snout emerged from the bushes, hesitated and was then followed out by a large grey body. Jones' first badger! Five others emerged behind, also snuffling at the ground with their snouts, two looking distinctly younger and more playful than the others. Jones was mesmerised and Justine clutched his hand tightly with excitement that her surprise had come off, just as she had hoped, and that he had been patient enough to wait. One of the younger badgers came within five feet of

Jones and he was scared it would spot him and run away in fear, but it never did.

"Badgers have terrible eyesight and, as long as you don't move, you keep quiet and you stay down wind, then they can come quite close... but I admit that was pretty good today!" Justine explained, as they retreated back to the house. The badgers, after fifteen minutes or so, had shuffled off into the woods and she had signalled to Jones that they should back away quietly. Even then the action had not been completely over, as a fox ambled slowly across the lawn in front of them and sat down, like a sentinel, by the front door, washing itself calmly.

"Look, brother fox!" whispered Justine. They stopped for a moment and then crept forward stealthily, until finally they got too close and it trotted away, disappearing into the trees the far side of the house.

"It was a date to remember!" Jones concluded.

"For good reasons, or because it was crazy or boring?"

"It was a little crazy, but it was never boring," Jones replied.

"But was it good?"

Jones felt touched by her first sign of insecurity. She clearly loved this place and he felt privileged to have been shown into her magical world.

"It was the best, Freddie," and he took her in his arms and kissed her, just as he had done in Ljubljana.

"It's funny isn't it," she said dreamily and looking up into his eyes, "how neither of us calls each other by our real names!"

"Do you mind?"

"No, but I've not been called Freddie since school and, as for you, well I like the name Casey."

"Freddie suits you Freddie... and Jones suits me and, anyway I told you, I'm named after a cat, so I prefer not to be reminded."

"My parents will get terribly confused."

"Sounds like fun!" he joked, then suddenly fearing she was serious, "but Justine is great too, so if you prefer..."

"No, I think I'm getting used to Freddie," she interrupted decisively, kissing him again and leading him back into the house.

The next year and three quarters was Jones' and Justine's time. There was to be no wedding, no children, no growing old together, no happy ever after. This was the deepest personal relationship that Justine would ever know and, although it wasn't going to prove quite that for Jones, it would still be a chapter of life that he would remember and treasure, even as an old man. Neither knew it at the time, but this fleeting period was all that they would share. For Fergus and Sylvie these were the months when they saw their daughter become (perhaps a little late) a grown woman, something which – on balance – they greeted with joy.

Jones had always wanted to be an airline pilot, but somehow the training opportunities were not there. His disappointment gnawed at him, even though he knew that, in being taken on as a management trainee at a major high street retailer in Cambridge, his safety net had been other graduates' unattainable dream. Meanwhile, Justine had a number of interviews for dance roles, including on cruise ships. In the end, like buses, three offers came at once: two at sea and one a six month contract from March working at a North Devon Holiday Camp. She opted to be closer to home and chose the latter.

She was thrilled about this, her first proper contract, and the experience exceeded her already high expectations, as she settled into life with her small group of fellow singers and dancers. She enjoyed rehearsing, performing, being with children and working amongst people who were on holiday, having well-deserved fun and building their own special memories with their families. The whole place felt happy and she knew she played a small but important role in creating that atmosphere. What's more, in this tiny corner of Devon, she was (as her boss put it) a 'star in a jar' and she enjoyed the attentions that this brought, with children (and occasionally even adults) excitedly rushing up to her – the girl from the cabaret – as they saw her wandering the park.

Jones visited her twice a month over the next spring and summer while she was working there. He couldn't believe how good a dancer she was the first time he watched her on stage, and he felt proud that this beautiful, skilful young woman – who he imagined entranced half the men in the audience – was his girlfriend. When she had time off, they would head to the sea, or sometimes to Exmoor, and they would hike along trails, not always with a golden sun on their backs, enjoying being on the beach or deep out in the countryside, even when it was pouring with rain. Chances for Justine to come home during this period were rare and she spent most of those occasions at her parents' house, sometimes just with them, sometimes with Jones as well. By now, Fergus and Sylvie were growing to love Jones, all the more because he was sensitive enough to give them some time alone with their daughter. They visited her once in Devon too, also coming to see one of her shows, and Justine had been touched by how captivated they had looked as she fleetingly glimpsed them from the stage.

Devon ended in September and Justine again found herself at a loose end. She was not worried: her agent had found her a four month contract from January, dancing at a major holiday resort in Florida. She was excited by that prospect and, back home in the meantime, she had more opportunity to see Jones and even to enjoy a holiday in the Lake District with her parents.

A bonus came when, unexpectedly, her agent found her work appearing in a music video, the whole shoot taking the best part of a fortnight, though most of that involving a lot of hanging around. She danced with three other women and with the singer, Summer Martins, who was already famous for her fun, upbeat style, though this particular song was more melancholic. Juxtaposed to the lyrics about grief and loss, the tune, however, somehow retained Summer's happy personality, and this combination of 'sadness with a smile on its face' seemed to create something fresh and poignant. Justine realised that there was a good chance the song would be a hit and that her dancing would be seen on TV and across the internet. She found learning the steps easy and, though she didn't say it to anyone, when she saw snippets of the video she thought she danced very well, perhaps slightly better even than the others. It was another boost to her confidence and she looked forward to the song being released.

That Christmas was the only one she and Jones ever shared. He came down late on Christmas Eve and, along with her parents, they went to midnight mass together. For Justine, this was always the best part of the whole festive period: a snug Christmas Eve full of anticipation, then venturing out into the night to their candle-lit church for carols and an hour spent remembering the very first Christmas and its message, before emerging at half past midnight into the magic of Christmas Day itself. The evening was rich with atmosphere, as well as the promise of more earthly pleasures when they woke up the next morning. They spent Christmas Day enjoying the usual big dinner, exchanging gifts, pulling crackers and wearing ridiculous hats. These were finally removed only when all four headed out in the afternoon for some much needed oxygen on a short walk.

Jones had first visited in late summer, but at this time of year the Chilterns looked very different: then it had been green and dry, but now the trees were bare and the ground caked in wet mud, in places almost impassable where it had been churned up by horses. The party slipped along these footpaths, wrapped up against the frosty wind, to the sound of crows cawing from their nests, swaying in the exposed branches high above. There was no snow, but nevertheless the scene to Jones seemed very bleak, though it was bleakness with a beauty and it felt exhilarating to live in a country where the seasons changed the landscape so completely four times a year. After a while, the house came back into view, a streak of grey curling up from its chimney and into a sky that was, even at four o'clock, already fast losing its daylight. Yes, smoke from a crackling fire that promised the walkers warmth and the prospect of a long, cosy evening ahead, pecking at snacks, soaking in mindless TV and playing old, worn out games.

All too quickly, New Year came and went and, a week later, Justine found herself on a plane bound for America. Her four month contract there was in hindsight a mixed blessing: she gained more experience dancing professionally, saw more of the wider world and made new friends; but she was a little homesick throughout for – in no particular order – Jones, her parents, her friends and her familiar corner of England. Had she known she only had weeks to live, she would certainly have chosen to spend them in the place and with the people she most loved. What her parents most wished after her death was either that she had never gone in the first place or, better still, that she had stayed out there longer, thereby avoiding her fate – unfortunately she chose the middle way and destiny wasn't to be cheated.

On the bright side, Justine enjoyed the dancing in Florida and grew further in confidence whilst there. But it was a world away from Devon and the resort lacked the down-to-earth, family charm of the holiday camp where she had danced the previous summer. It also felt very temporary: many of the resort's usual dancers were taking a break between the Christmas and summer peak seasons. It turned out that Justine was providing cover in some of the backing roles during a quieter time of year. There were a handful of others in the same position, including Tanya, a young dancer from Koblenz in Germany, with whom she quickly became firm friends. They spent half their free time happily exploring this sunny, new environment together and half pining for their homes. Tanya was touched that, out of all Justine's two months of inter-railing, it had been her train journey between Cologne and Mainz, snaking down the Rhine valley and through her own home town, that she had found the prettiest. Neither girl was miserable, but Justine did observe that they had both chosen careers which all too often might take them away from homes they loved.

Come late April, it was with a mixture of emotions that both headed back to their respective countries, a close, but ultimately short, friendship having been established. For a month, Justine did not have a great deal to do, but May in the Chilterns is a wonderful time and place to be at a loose end, with spring blossoms bursting from the trees and swathes of woodland bluebells carpeting otherwise freshly green woods. After having ventured away so far, Justine enjoyed relaxing in this, the place where she felt she most belonged, staying out all day and wrapping the gentle scenery around her like a comforting blanket.

"I can't believe it!" She bemoaned to Jones one day with mock despondency, "I've discovered I'm a home bird!"

"Surely not!?" he replied sarcastically. In fact her love of home was one of the many things he adored about her, sometimes he felt it little short of a miracle that she had ever gone inter-railing and met him in the first place, but he also knew her well enough to know that she had a strong independent streak too, perhaps that had pushed her to explore.

Justine's agent had booked her an audition, just after May bank holiday, a week following her return from the States. It was for a London show which, if she were offered the part, would run from the autumn. The audition had gone well and she secretly felt confident, but without daring to hope too much. Just a week afterwards an envelope arrived asking her to go back for a further two days of try-outs and, at the end of the second morning, she was offered a role in the dance chorus. It felt like her biggest break to date, plus it was near home. Initial rehearsals began in London a fortnight later.

And so, on 12th June, Justine bought herself a Season Ticket, presciently only for a month (ironically she felt that buying anything longer was tempting fate), and she arrived for her first day at the East London dance studio with a mixture of excitement and terror. She surprised herself that these emotions quickly dissipated into a feeling of confidence, with the experience she had gained in Devon and Florida (and of course the dance video she had done with Summer Martins in between) reaping its rewards. She felt at home in the world of dance and fell in easily with her colleagues, also spending extra time watching the principals rehearse, seeking to learn from them and dreaming that one day this might be her. Her parents took great pleasure in witnessing their daughter's success and Jones was telling anyone who would listen that his girlfriend was going to be in a West End show... in reality it wasn't quite going to be in the West End, but it wasn't so far off.

"I am so proud of you Freddie!" He said to her the last time they were together, some sixty hours before her accident, as he dropped her off at home after a final shared weekend. "And desperate to see the show!"

"You'll just have to be patient!" She had teased, stepping out of the car and pulling her bag from its back seat, "all things come to those who wait!"

Alas, that is not always true and for Jones the wait was to prove eternal. He could picture her turning back one last time as she walked to her front door, he knew she waved at him and that he had flashed his lights in reply. But he didn't remember having told her he loved her, not that night when it mattered most: he racked his brains as if doing so hard enough might mean he could conjure up the memory, but it was no good, you can't recall something that didn't happen.

So, life was going well for Justine as she sat on the train, heading for her eighth day of rehearsals, feeling content. More than content, she was happy. She was dancing for a career, rehearsing for a London show, and she felt she had held her own amongst the other dancers in the first seven days. More importantly, she had Jones.

Three days after her death, a small square package arrived for him through the post: he immediately recognised the writing. Shaking, he opened it. It was a CD, the soundtrack of the show in which Justine was to perform. There was no note, but on the CD cover she had scrawled:

"Jones, all things come to those who wait, but here's a little taster for those who can't! Love you, Freddie."

21

The Canaries –
Friday 2ⁿᵈ to Sunday 4ᵗʰ December 2016

The Canaries –
Friday 2nd to Sunday 4th December 2016

So far, because a stop in Cape Verde had been dropped, the cruise had comprised four days in port and eight days at sea; now, because a day in the Canaries had been added, they had five days at four different ports ahead, the first three being Las Palmas de Gran Canaria, Santa Cruz de Tenerife and Santa Cruz de La Palma.

On the first of these days, over breakfast, a smiley announcement rang out from the Cruise Director:

"Ladies and gentlemen, welcome to Las Palmas de Gran Canaria. The gangway can be found today on deck three, forward, port side..."

"Where else?!" Sylvie heard a waiter say sarcastically under his breath, as he rushed across the room with a plate of food.

"... and it is just a short walk into town, but, ladies and gentlemen, it's another beautiful one. Please remember the ship departs at nine o'clock this evening, so do be back on board by eight thirty. We hope you have a wonderful day here in Las Palmas."

Almost identical, overly cheerful, announcements followed

the next two days and Sylvie understood why, having heard hundreds upon hundreds of them, they may have grown a little stale on the derisive waiter.

After the Azores and Cape Verde, the Canaries felt a bit more on the tourist trail and, although the temperature was a little cooler, walking in the crowds became tiring, leaving them to wonder whether they were really enjoying it or just going through the motions because they felt they should. In both Gran Canaria and Tenerife, where the crowds were by far the worst, they opted for sightseeing buses to show them around and, once on board, they settled down and enjoyed the open top rides. Fergus, in his sunglasses and faithful baseball cap, didn't worry about the commentary (available through earphones), instead he just relaxed in the warm breeze as the towns and their surroundings rolled by, occasionally lifting his arms into the air so his hands ran through the low-hanging leaves of the trees lining much of their route.

Each of the two locations had its highlights: for Las Palmas de Gran Canaria it was a late afternoon walk along the promenade of the Playa de las Canteras, watching the locals and the tourists relaxing as they strolled beside the beach, with the Atlantic waves breaking in the distance; for Santa Cruz de Tenerife it was the lush Parque Garcia Sanabria, with its sub-tropical green plants (from which they could all but feel the oxygen oozing) and its tall, exotic palms, some leaning slightly, reaching high up towards the sun and the azure sky above.

Santa Cruz de La Palma, on the third day, had a much quieter feel to it, and their walk up the cobbled pedestrian street towards the town was more peaceful. Two thirds of the way along, there was a church to which they retreated, escaping the heat of the sun and hoping to enjoy some reflective silence. These plans however were thwarted by three women, minding the building, who shouted out to each other across the nave and the pews, as they dusted and carelessly clattered around, performing various bits of minor maintenance. There is nothing more wonderful than sitting in a tranquil church, but little more frustrating than being there when that peace is lost amidst the intruding din of others. Eventually, Fergus and Sylvie gave up and, worn down by three days in a row ashore in similar places, they made their way early back to the ship.

Fergus took advantage and decided to meditate again, but it was to prove a patience testing day. He was just getting into his deep breathing when he was tapped tentatively on the shoulder:

"Excuse me sir, we need to do painting here."

The maintenance man said it with utter politeness, as well as a smile, and Fergus was proud of how he rose above the irritation, quietly finding another location. He got a bit further through his session this time before a drilling started up behind him. He sought to put it out of his mind, even seeking to see it as a wonderful opportunity to practise detachment… but who was he kidding? The drilling stopped. Would it restart… ? Perhaps not? Then, just as his hopes were raised, the noise began again, stopping and starting every few minutes thereafter, the gaps often filled with two voices shouting loudly at each other in Mandarin. Fergus opened his eyes, feeling more uptight than he had felt before he had even begun.

Both he and Sylvie had previously found the amount of maintenance going on throughout the ship, especially outside, to be quite irritating. With their heads they understood it was necessary: the ship was kept in excellent condition, but one cruise began the same day the previous cruise ended, so most maintenance and repairs had to be done when passengers were on board. This logic did not, though, prevent it from becoming frustrating, especially because it always seemed to be taking place wherever they were… even once, when Fergus had been meditating outside at six thirty in the morning, his peacefulness had been interrupted by the ever approaching noise of water being used to hose down the deck, until he felt the inevitable tap on his shoulder and the courteous request to move on.

Finally giving up on the drilling and the loud Chinese chatter, Fergus got up and, seeking to maintain a calm which he wasn't really feeling, he once again found another corner: third time lucky perhaps?

"Ladies and gentlemen, the crew will shortly be embarking on an emergency exercise. This is purely a drill and we apologise for any inconvenience."

The tannoy jolted Fergus out of the trance into which he had just settled... he tried to relax again, but a series of announcements followed, each preceded by a loud fanfare:

"Code Gamma – Fire in the Engine Room... Fire crews to muster deck 2 aft!"

"Crew to emergency stations... seal all Fire Doors!"

"Close all water tight doors, close all water tight doors!"

"Lifeboat crews to lifeboat stations, lifeboat crews to lifeboat stations!"

"Code Yankee, Code Yankee, launch lifeboats, launch lifeboats!"

By now Fergus had given up on mindfulness for the day and, instead of battling on with his meditation, he wandered across to the side of the ship. Once there, he found his frustration was quickly diluted by fascination, as he watched the starboard side lifeboats being lowered into the harbour. He had to admit, although the timing of the drill had been annoying, the professionalism with which it was carried out was impressive, and he felt reassured should disaster strike the ship between here and Southampton, though he remained not at all certain how some of the more fragile passengers would fare. He hoped he wouldn't have to find out.

About forty minutes after the drill had begun, there was a final fanfare:

"The Exercise is over, the exercise is over. Re-open Fire and Watertight doors. Crew Code Zulu. Officers to the bridge for

debrief. Ladies and gentlemen, thank you for your patience. This concludes today's test."

Lifeboats were re-raised and peace quickly restored to the ship, although Sylvie found herself briefly trapped on the stairs, trying to come up, as hordes of staff swarmed down, back to their duties from their muster points. Amongst them, she spotted Rachel who smiled and shrugged her shoulders as she passed, as if to say *"sorry, but what can I do?"* Sylvie, pressed against the wall, smiled back, pleased to see their cabin maid was in the company of a barman and two waitresses, all of whom were laughing happily together: it felt good to know Rachel had friends on board.

In truth, for Fergus and Sylvie, the calm they had built up from so much time at sea had been eroded by these days in the Canaries and, for him, there was a steadily increasing sense of tension. This wasn't helped at all in the evenings, as they sat through three more dinners with the arachnid lady loudly talking inanities just two tables away, screeching with laughter, waving her arms about and flirting with her waiter:

"How's your love life Frederico?"

Poor Richard and Cressida, next to her, got enmeshed in this drama every night and one sensed that their diplomatic skills, honed in the most desperate corners of the world, might fail them at any moment. While Fergus and Sylvie witnessed this from a slightly safer distance, it still left them feeling that evening meals were rather like endurance tests, and ones which both feared, beneath their English repression, they were failing. And didn't the woman look more arachnid-like every day, with her spindly limbs, the lower ones sometimes wrapped around the table legs, holding them in a vice-like grip, while her upper ones shovelled food relentlessly into her mouth. In Fergus' eyes, it was as if she were slowly but remorselessly turning into a monster.

For Sylvie, the food was also beginning to grate. She didn't eat meat, but the vegetarian main courses were proving to be the poor relation on an otherwise excellent menu and she was growing tired of feeling a second class diner. As at so many restaurants ashore, she only ever had one vegetarian choice, which in her view was no real choice at all. On one night, pepper and courgette soufflé with a creamy sauce and fresh minted peas had appeared on the menu and her hopes had been raised that she would finally fare better. Alas, too many others before her had been tempted by it, away from their normal roasts, and the restaurant had run out by the time she sought to place her order:

"We can do an omelette madam…" Angelo said, without any obvious shame.

Seeing the usually carnivorous arachnid lady getting stuck into the last of the soufflés did nothing for the way Sylvie felt about her and, for once, it was Fergus who tried to take the placating tone:

"Try to enjoy your meal, I'm sure they can put cheese in the omelette…" It wasn't obvious whether he was being serious or ironic, but the look he received in response communicated clearly to him that this was a line of conversation best not pursued further. The next night there were no such shortages, with the vegetarian option back to its normal tick-box status, and 'mushroom risotto' turned out to be an upturned cup of rice with a few mushrooms tactically placed around its sides. Sylvie resigned herself quietly to this, betraying her disappointment only with a half suppressed groan.

Although the Maitre D' still appeared somewhat remote, they had grown fond of Angelo: there was a naivety in his manner and they felt empathy for him as he continued his countdown of seemingly innumerable meals to serve before he could see his family again. In all though, dinner times were not the most relaxed part of the day, especially on the night Fergus – not having noticed it was another semi-formal evening – was again dispatched back to his cabin to fetch a tie, while all the other men sat open collared in the restaurant, with their jackets slung over the backs of their chairs. In fairness, most of the food was of a remarkable quality, bearing in mind the number of passengers and the fact that they were at sea after all. Nevertheless, rather than truly enjoying meals, Fergus and Sylvie usually left the dining room with a sense of relief, counting on an evening walk around the deck to restore their mental calm.

After they had taken that stroll, their evenings varied. On the first Canary Island night they had a drink in the Conservatory Bar, before heading downstairs to hear the band in the Atlantic Lounge, with Sylvie again trying her level best to look attached to her husband while the Lotharios circled around, looking for potential partners. Fergus was unable to resist another:

"I'm just going to nip to the Gents…" tease, which received the same "Oh no you are not!" response from Sylvie that it had generated four nights earlier.

The next evening, they wound the night down playing cards, appropriately enough, in the Card Room. It was completely empty, with their fellow passengers either filling the various bars or attending the show in the Poseidon Theatre, this time featuring an old crooner from the 1970s. Fergus and Sylvie savoured the peace, disturbed only when a woman came into the room in order to escape the noisier areas and make a phone call: apparently there was a crisis at the pony club. The conversation only lasted ten minutes, though it would have taken Einstein himself to explain to the two card players why it had felt infinitely longer.

"Hmmm," said Fergus as the woman shouted down her phone, "didn't we say that the Card Room would make an excellent place to find a body?"

"Don't think I'm not tempted too!" Sylvie retorted. But at that very moment the woman finished her conversation with:

"Kisses kisses darling," leaving the room without realising her murder had by that stage reached the point of mid-planning.

As she left, so a man entered, settling down quietly the other end of the room, with a laptop computer open in front of him and a large reference book to one side. They could hear him tapping on the keys, but softly, so it was background noise and not disturbing. Every now and then there would be a pause and these became increasingly frequent, until eventually the typing stopped altogether, replaced only by the sound of occasional heavy sighing.

After they had finished their game, Fergus and Sylvie stood up to leave and, heading to the door, she caught the man's eye and enquired:

"Not working surely?"

"Writing a book actually, or at least trying."

"How interesting!" Sylvie exclaimed with genuine surprise.

"Oh, I don't know," the low key response came with a hint of despondency and was followed by another sigh, "I'm not sure it's going to be much of a success."

"That all depends how you measure success," interjected Fergus thoughtfully, "maybe books are like people: a few become famous, the vast majority don't, some might just be known by a handful of friends, some only by their creator even, but they all have value, at least if they have soul."

There was a silence while the author digested this uninvited wisdom and Fergus momentarily worried that he had made a fool of himself, but then the man replied:

"That's rather insightful. You do put a lot of yourself into writing a book, that's for sure."

"How is yours coming along?" Sylvie probed gently, wary that he appeared to be struggling.

"I'm a little stuck I suppose. It's a story set in the late nineteenth century and I'm finding it difficult to capture the period... it's not easy to put yourself in a different time and place," he thumbed through the thick reference book, as if to illustrate the weight of his task, discharging motes of dust into the light of the lamp he had angled over his keyboard.

Not wanting to disturb him further, they left him there with the Card Room to himself, she wishing him good luck and happy to hear the sound of the tap tapping restarting as its door slowly closed behind them: perhaps he was making progress again. Fergus, however, said and heard nothing, something about the encounter had left him contemplative, as if somehow lost in a memory. As she led him back to the cabin, Sylvie noticed this but sensed it was not a moment to intrude.

The third evening was very different again, this time involving the latest show, which had an "*Around the world in eighty days*" theme. The lead male performer played Phileas Fogg, encountering his colleagues dancing in traditional costumes from various nations, while the band played songs from around the world, or at least songs with names of countries in their titles. The show culminated in a raucous gypsy number from Spain and the girls twirling around in fabulously colourful flamenco dresses, into which somehow they had 'quick changed' between numbers. The songs didn't exactly trace the route taken by the original Phileas, but the combination of exotic costumes together with diverse tunes and dances created an atmosphere in which Fergus and Sylvie were able happily to lose themselves, though he again worried a little as to how Nicole was able to convey so much sadness in her vocals.

"Didn't you think the leading lady singer was good, the auburn haired girl?" He ventured to ask his wife afterwards.

"Do you mean the one with the deformed arm?" Sylvie queried rather bluntly, trying to distinguish between the singers, but immediately regretting her choice of words.

"Oh come on, she's so much more than that!" Fergus almost

barked back, feeling defensive of Nicole and in a rare moment of disappointment in his wife.

"I know, that was insensitive. Sorry."

Relief swept over him that his wife had recognised her tactlessness, as well as some embarrassment that – without thinking – he had reacted so strongly. They headed out of the theatre and back on deck, star gazing once more from beneath the bridge.

"Speaking of the singer... have you gone and got yourself another little crush?" Sylvie asked delicately. There was a pause, which surprised her, then:

"There is something about her... something sad," he answered. Sylvie recognised the sadness too, in hindsight she could see it, but she said nothing. "I don't know," he went on, "I'm a bit fascinated with them I suppose, the singer and the dancer I mean... but more than that, I'm a bit concerned for them..." Sylvie looked dubious, but she could see he meant it. "Maybe it's the singer's arm, maybe it's the dancer's friendliness... maybe it's what might have been... perhaps I feel protective towards them."

Sylvie was sufficiently attuned to her husband to hear the unspoken "because I failed to protect Justine." She gave him a hug, before audibly whispering:

"And maybe it's because they are a little bit pretty too?"

"Hmmm... yes, there might be a bit of that in the pot as well!" Fergus admitted sheepishly, "but you know..." She put her fingers on his lips before he could finish:

"Shhh, quiet Romeo, you are over-thinking and over-worrying... take me to bed."

22

The Isles of Scilly – May 1993

Fergus knew his daughter liked extremes and so they took a launch for the twenty minute trip to St Agnes, the smallest, most westerly of the inhabited islands. Once there, they walked down a narrow lane, past pretty cottages and then along a footpath, until they were out on moorland overlooking the Atlantic and towards America, more than three thousand miles beyond. Justine, the peak of her pale pink baseball cap protecting her eyes from the sun, stared out to sea, as if it were possible, if you strained hard enough, to look all the way across.

They collapsed on the grass, ate chocolate and enjoyed being at this extremity, breathing in the fresh air and feeling satisfied to be at the very end of their nonstop journey of fifteen hours from Paddington, and a couple of hours longer than that since they had left home. They rested there a while, before leisurely completing their circle, finding themselves once more at the small quayside where they had first arrived. A few minutes later, the same launch collected them and took them back across the sea to Hugh Town, dropping other passengers off in time to catch the return ferry to Penzance. Fergus and Justine, meanwhile, made their way towards the small, but inviting, hotel they had booked for the night in the town centre.

They settled into their twin room and each had an urge to go to sleep there and then, but Fergus rallied both himself and his daughter and they found a nearby pub in which they ate fish and chips, recounting to each other their favourite moments of the preceding twenty-four hours.

"Mum, guess where we are?" Justine said down the phone once they were back in their room, "the Isles of Scilly!" she continued before her mother could answer. Sylvie listened to her daughter tell her all about the sleeper train, the ferry, the basking sharks, the launch across to St Agnes and back again. Visiting her sick friend had been something she had wanted to do, but it was also rather depressing, and she felt her spirits revive as she listened to the joy and excitement in her daughter's voice. Eventually, Fergus was handed the phone:

"So it's going well?" Sylvie asked.

"So far, perfectly," he replied. Sylvie felt a moment of regret that she wasn't there with them; but then she recalled how she and Justine had often shared time together and, reassuring herself that there would be plenty more of that to come, her sorrow was replaced by a deep contentment that Justine was enjoying such a great trip with her father.

"I'm pleased... and proud, but I'm missing you both..."

"And we you, but we'll see you the day after tomorrow... are you OK?"

Sylvie insisted she was fine, even though secretly she felt a little lonely away from home without them, the trials of her own day catching up with her.

"You're not a bad father, Fergus." She gave this verdict tiredly, pulled between the draw of her awaiting bed and a reluctance to say goodbye to her only family, who suddenly felt very far away.

"And husband?" He asked cautiously.

"Not bad, not bad at all."

They said goodnight, Justine shouting a "sleep well Mum" from across the room, and they returned to their separate corners of the country. Justine got changed in the bathroom and by the time her father had done the same she was already sound asleep. He switched off the light, stifled a cry as he stubbed his toe fumbling for his bed in the dark, and then quickly fell into a deep sleep to rival that of his daughter.

After breakfast the next morning, they packed up their rucksacks, put on their new baseball caps and headed back to the harbour, the idea being to take a boat trip out to the Western Rocks, where Fergus knew they were almost bound to see seals, though he hadn't told this to Justine. Then the plan took them on to the Bishop Rock Lighthouse, after which, were they to keep going, it would be 'next stop America!' And so they found themselves back on a launch, with a dozen or so other nature lovers, skirting around St Agnes and then the Annet island bird sanctuary, where, to their astonishment, they saw puffins in significant numbers on the cliffs and bobbing around in the water. Through her father's binoculars, their clown like faces stared back adorably at Justine as the boat gently sailed by. Meanwhile, Fergus was quietly thanking God for another piece – this one unexpected – of a jigsaw which was coming together to create a perfect weekend away with his young daughter.

When they reached the Western Rocks there were seals everywhere, some gently dozing upon them, some swimming in the sea and others simply bottling, that is to say floating in the water with just their noses breaking the surface, so they could breathe. Justine, chalking up yet another spectacular member of British wildlife, was again ecstatic, romantically envying their lives lazing around in the Atlantic. Had they been able to speak, the seals may have invited her to come back in the winter and see if she still envied them then, but perhaps they wouldn't have sought to argue that overall it was such a bad life. After half an hour or so, the boat's motor cranked up and, despite Justine willing it not to, the launch headed deeper out into the Atlantic, leaving the seals behind. She didn't know it at the time, but she was to see seals several times again in her short life, including four years later when she was swimming off a Cornish beach and, for a few fleeting but magical seconds, came face to face (or perhaps face to snout) with one, so close that she swore she could smell the fish on his breath. That, however, was for the future…

The launch approached the Bishop Rock Lighthouse, a tall tower rising some fifty metres into the air and standing on a rock so small they couldn't actually see it until they were extremely close. They circled the lighthouse a few times and both Fergus and Justine found themselves wondering what it would have been like to be a lighthouse keeper in such a location:

"And in the winter you'd be stuck there for weeks!" Fergus exclaimed, unsure whether the prospect appalled or appealed, though suspecting the latter. Justine was in no doubt:

"How fantastic!"

The launch then did something unexpected but wonderful, throttling up its engines and heading a mile or so deeper out to sea, before powering them right down again, until they were off completely. There, in what felt like the middle of the loneliest part of the Atlantic, they spent ten minutes floating in a silence broken only by waves washing against the boat, the gentle sea breeze and the occasional cry of a distant gull. It felt as though everyone in the boat understood the magic as barely a word was spoken. Eventually, and perceptively, Justine whispered to her father:

"We must remember this is here, when we are having bad days at school or at work."

"Yes we must," her father replied succinctly. He took off his cap a moment, ruffling his hair in the sea breeze and then, with his mind, took pictures in all directions: of the horizon deeper out in the Atlantic and of the lighthouse and the Isles of Scilly in the distance back the way they had come.

A painful moment lasts an age and a perfect age lasts but a moment. All too soon the engines came back to life and the launch swept them home to St Mary's and the quayside at Hugh Town, arriving at noon, just over two hours after they had left. But Fergus' plans were not yet finished...

They wandered into the town and had a drink and a bite to eat, before returning to the quay just in time to see the Scillonian docking. It would sail for Penzance in a little over four hours, with them on board. Fergus had researched that there would, in the meantime, be a little ferry to the neighbouring island of Tresco, for any day trippers from the mainland who wished to see its famous Abbey Gardens. The same boat would, of course, bring them back to St Mary's again before the Scillonian sailed. And so, having been on the Isles of Scilly for just twenty-four hours, they clambered aboard a launch to their third island, this time little more than ten minutes away across the sound.

The Abbey Gardens were a short hike up from the quayside and Fergus and Justine soon found themselves wandering amongst lush green plants and trees, the like of which he would not see again for another twenty-three years. It was hot too, for spring at least, and there was definitely a sub-tropical feel in the air as they wandered the paths, stopping occasionally to enjoy the views and the exotic flora, resting at one stage in a beautifully coloured shelter made from a mosaic of sea shells. Fergus had wondered whether, after the wildlife, plants would be a little dull for his daughter but, whilst it was true they were not as exciting, he could see she was entranced as she walked around this Eden: a paradise which surely must have been cut loose from somewhere far more distant, drifting on the Atlantic currents, winds and waves until it finally ran aground here, just off the south-western-most tip of England, no more than four hundred miles from their own home.

"I know it was a long trip to get here," she said, "but it's still incredible that all this is so close." Fergus agreed and wondered why they hadn't paid a visit before. He was, however, also just a little nervous about missing the launch back to St Mary's, so, after two and a half hours wandering the gardens and taking a drink in the café, they headed back down to the little harbour and sat on a wall waiting for their ride, which duly arrived fifteen minutes later, eventually chugging them back across the water to where the Scillonian was patiently idling. On deck, Fergus asked:

"So, the Isles of Scilly, hit or miss?"

"Bullseye!!!" Justine replied with a beaming smile.

The ship left the islands by a different route, turning left out of the harbour and squeezing between St Mary's and St Agnes, before setting its sights on Land's End some twenty-eight miles away. They savoured every moment of the return trip but Fergus was adamant that they should eat on board, as it would be past eight by the time they reached Penzance. The food in the little café was basic, but it more than did the trick and both ate hungrily after their eventful day. When they finished, they could see through the window that they were alongside the Cornish coast and they returned up on deck to watch it go by, better wrapped up now against the evening chill. Finally, they sailed past the village of Mousehole and turned into Mounts Bay, with the lights of Penzance glimmering in the distance and the dark tower of its church outlined against the evening sky.

They quickly found their nearby hotel, but decided they should take their one opportunity to investigate Penzance itself, before collapsing into bed. Again, they felt it had a mysterious, end of the line feel, with a long promenade from which streets turned off to the right, up towards the centre of town, while to the left the high tide lapped hungrily at the steps leading from the beach. They looked in on a park, shrouded by trees, and in the dusk could just make out a traditional bandstand on a lawn. Between the paths, colourful flowers flourished amongst abundant greenery in immaculately kept beds, such that, had they not already seen Tresco Abbey Gardens, they would have been cursing their lack of time to explore.

Back on the promenade, they watched the lights of a fishing boat returning slowly across the bay, eventually entering the safety of Newlyn Harbour, just a mile up the coast. Penzance seemed honest and hard working: there were none of the usual tourist trappings, no pretence or desire to be a resort, no noisy nightlife spilling out on to the streets. Here the Atlantic was not an extraordinary wonder but an unpredictable neighbour – sometimes kind, sometimes furious – with whom the town had long learned to live and work. It may not have made many of the history books, but both Fergus and Justine had the impression that it, nevertheless, had many centuries of stories to tell.

"I don't think we did Penzance justice," Fergus concluded.

"There's only one solution… we'll have to come back… next weekend!"

"Hmmm, that is an option it's true," Fergus reflected, putting his arm around Justine and turning back towards the hotel, "or we could save it up for the future?" Justine looked up at him with a smile.

"Promise?"

"Promise," he replied, giving her shoulder a squeeze. But he wasn't quite the perfect father after all, because this was a promise that was to be forgotten by both. In fact, neither was ever to see Penzance again: Justine because she died young and Fergus because, thereafter, a visit would have been far too painful.

There just remained an awkward phone call and then the journey home. After breakfast the next morning, Fergus rang Justine's school and spoke to the headmistress, explaining, as the fait accompli it was, that they were in Penzance, having had an unexpected (he winced as he said it, knowing it was a half truth,

189

in other words, true for Justine but not for him) trip to the Isles of Scilly and that his daughter would not be in school that day.

"That sounds wonderful, Mr Fredricks," the headmistress replied… "and is it likely to happen again?"

"It was perfect, so I don't think I would risk spoiling the memory."

"I'm glad you had a good time." She knew that, prior to this, Justine's attendance had been flawless, she also felt that a child spending such a weekend with her father sounded – at her stage of schooling at least – rather more valuable and educational than a few hours of missed classes. However, she decided she should still go through the motions: "but your daughter's schooling is very important, please try to avoid term times in the future, or at least to ask permission before you go."

"Yes, yes, I will, I will," Fergus fumbled before thanking her and saying goodbye. "Phew!" He said to Justine, "that was scary!"

"Oh, she's not so bad…" Justine replied, and Fergus had the impression she was right.

Rucksacks back on, they hiked to the station and, walking all the way along the platform to the very first carriage, they boarded the train and found their seats, sitting opposite each other. And so, from her first class luxury, Justine watched Penzance and Mounts Bay slip away. She continued to look out of the window, like watching a film, as Cornish scenery and villages passed by. Fergus, meanwhile, just watched his daughter and felt satisfied at a plan well executed. After a couple of hours of gentle progress up through Cornwall, the train turned a sharp curve to the right and headed over the Tamar Bridge and into Devon and the city of Plymouth.

It was the ride after this that Fergus had been keen for his daughter to witness in the daylight, and it was the reason he had opted for seats on the right hand side of the train. They wended through the Devonshire countryside just south of

Dartmoor before rejoining the coast and, with the sea lapping just a few feet beneath them, the train hugged the water's edge, passing through tunnels in the red cliffs and finally emerging into Dawlish, with the town itself on the left and its promenade on the other side of the tracks to the right. They could see people strolling along enjoying their day by the sea and Justine thought how pretty it looked, even though it couldn't compare to the natural wilds of the extreme west from which they had just travelled.

The train eventually turned inland and picked up pace until, after Exeter, it was whistling through the English countryside at a speed which Justine felt sure was as fast as ever she had travelled. She also fulfilled another ambition by having lunch on a train: it was served at their seats, but with table cloth, napkins and crystal glasses. Again, time worked its tricks and the journey, which for some on board felt interminable, for Justine flashed by. She kept checking her watch, not out of boredom but for how long remained – time was passing far too quickly. All too soon, the grey outer suburbs of London began to emerge, gradually replacing the rural green and, fifteen minutes later, the train pulled into Paddington.

It was three twenty and Fergus was pleased they had been punctual, he didn't want Justine being brought back down to earth by witnessing London's miserable rush hour. She took in the station one final time as they walked to the taxi rank, and half an hour later they were on another train heading back out of London and into the Chilterns. Fergus was amazed to see his daughter still glued to the window as the more familiar hills and fields came into view.

"Can you ever have enough of trains?" he asked her. She thought for a while before answering:

"Is that possible?" He smiled and again thanked God, this time that the trains had all been on time, that there had been no signals stuck on red, no breakdowns, no overcrowding, no drunken yobs… none of the things that could blight modern rail journeys, leaving them dreadful affairs, something he feared she would inevitably find out for herself one day, but he was grateful it had not been on this trip. Fergus' car was waiting for him where he had left it at the station less than seventy-two hours earlier and they drove the short distance home, initially in silence, then a simple:

"Thank you Dad, it was wonderful!" as they turned off the lane and into the drive.

Justine jumped out, grabbed her rucksack and ran up to her mother who had seen them arrive and was waiting by the open front door, having only got home herself that lunchtime. Fergus gave his wife a wave but then sat a moment longer in the car by himself: satisfied, content. He – like Sylvie of course – had infinite memories of Justine, but this action-packed, lightning, father and daughter visit to the Isles of Scilly was the most perfect.

23

Madeira – Monday 5th to Tuesday 6th December 2016

The ship had sailed from Santa Cruz de La Palma late the previous afternoon, but it wasn't until lunchtime that they came alongside in Madeira. It was Fergus' sixty-third birthday and, after so many shore days in a row, they had enjoyed a slow start and the lazy morning at sea. Out on deck Sylvie presented Fergus with his gift, an early edition of his favourite book 'The Wind in the Willows'.

"Wow!" he said, on unwrapping it and carefully opening the front cover.

"Is that wow at the present or wow at what it must have cost?" Sylvie asked apprehensively.

"Definitely at the present... what I don't know about won't hurt me! Thank you." Sylvie was pleased that the book had been so well received and she watched him contentedly as he leafed through its pages, until he was distracted by a fanfare introducing the Captain's first report in four days:

"Good afterrrnoon, ladies and gentlemen. An update from the brrridge..."

Meanwhile Madeira drew closer and closer until, eventually,

the *Magdalena* squeezed into the harbour and came alongside the quay, behind a larger ship. Small ropes were thrown by the crew and collected by men in bright orange jackets on the wharf below, these were then used by them to pull up the hawsers, which in turn were deployed to secure the vessel, fore and aft. Finally, the gangway was lowered and another smiley announcement from the Cruise Director welcomed them to Funchal.

Unusually, Fergus and Sylvie were booked on an organised trip and this was scheduled to leave at half past two. It was a three and a half hour tour of the island, culminating in tea at the famous Reid's Hotel. This was the one time the ship was berthed for the night, and their plan was to see a little of the island that afternoon (including some of the dizzying view points) and then to have a leisurely wander around the town the next morning, before the ship departed sometime after lunch.

Quite quickly after boarding the bus, they felt pleased they had not been on any other tours. It did feel a little like an organised day out from the old folks' home and only Richard and Cressida, whom they spotted towards the back, looked similarly out of place. Nevertheless, as the bus climbed up out of Funchal, both decided to make the best of it, savouring the view of the city from Pico dos Barcelos, their first stop. Then it was ever higher and higher, round bendy roads with sheer drops, and they began to feel this was much more fun than they had originally feared. They developed a certain admiration for their older travelling companions, all of whom (perhaps emboldened by the fact that they had already lived long and well) gasped and cheered, deriving a certain metaphorical high out of the sheer drops, from which they were separated by little more than a rusty old barrier and their driver's skill.

The coach took them all the way up to Eira do Sorrado where, having climbed to a height of some 3,500 feet, they had giddying vistas over the valley below, after which it twisted them down the same roads back towards Funchal. At Reid's Hotel they drank English tea poured from beautiful porcelain teapots into delicate bone china cups, accompanied by cakes and scones served from ornately tiered stands, with the option of plenty of jam and fresh cream from little silver pots dotted around the table. This was not Fergus' natural environment, but you would never have guessed this as he and Sylvie chatted easily to Richard and Cressida, for whom, after so many Embassy parties and diplomatic receptions, this was very much home from home.

"Gosh, you can be quite sociable, when you make the effort," Sylvie joked as she and her husband headed down some stairs and out into the expansive hotel grounds. For some reason, none of their travel companions discovered these gardens, so Fergus and Sylvie had them all to themselves, taking their time as they strolled at leisure amongst the sub-tropical plants which, for Fergus, brought back memories of a distant, happy day with his daughter. They also had wonderful views over the sea, and of the *Magdalena* patiently waiting for them in the harbour below.

All too soon, it was time to rejoin the others on the bus and for the party to make the short drive back to the port.

"That was surprisingly nice!" Sylvie said as they re-entered their cabin.

"I agree, well worth doing." And both felt satisfied that, with their sailing trip from Gran Canaria cancelled, the one tour they had ended up taking had been money well spent. They thought about going back into town to eat, even felt they should, but somehow it was a 'should' feeling, rather than a 'want to', and they both resisted it. Instead, they dined on board, to the usual background banter of the arachnid lady, whose eyes seemed to have developed a strange red tint and who took badly to being served by a new waiter:

"Where's my Frederico?" she demanded, leaning out in the

direction of the Maitre D', as if suspended by a thread, as he passed.

"He has been deployed to help in another restaurant madam," came his pre-prepared reply, and he disappeared into the kitchen without stopping to discuss the matter further.

"Lucky Frederico!" whispered Sylvie, though she suspected the redeployment may not have been down to chance at all.

They both managed to rise above the noise, perhaps because they had enjoyed a good day out, or maybe because they were now celebrating Fergus' birthday over a bottle of Shiraz. Towards the end of the meal, the waiters gathered around their table, complete with guitar and tambourine, and performed a cha-cha-cha styled 'Happy Birthday to you!' Although he had seen this happen to others, somehow it had not occurred to him that they would know it was his birthday; Sylvie, however, had half-expected it and was a little nervous as to how her husband would react. She anxiously scrutinised his face for clues, thinking she discerned embarrassment and pleasure in equal measure, and was relieved, when the restaurant broke into a round of applause at the end of the song, to see him smiling broadly as he thanked the waiters.

They sat for a few minutes, letting their meals settle and finishing the last of their wine. Then, feeling relaxed and at ease, they stood up to leave, Fergus even managing to squeeze out a "Good evening" to the arachnid lady and her silent husband as they passed. The woman lifted her head in response and a wave of motion went all the way down her spine, her red eyes seemingly glaring back at him as she shouted out loudly enough for the whole dining room to hear:

"We know where you two are going! Hahahah!"

For a moment, Fergus imagined he saw extra limbs bent unnaturally beneath the tablecloth, but – feeling the centre of the restaurant's attention and his face as crimson as the monster's eyes – he couldn't look long enough to be sure, as he hurried to the door, dragging Sylvie as he went.

"I can't abide her!" he pronounced to his wife in the lift going down to their cabin, the happy birthday bubble quite burst.

"Try not to let her get to you, we're home in five days and then you'll never see her again." She felt shocked at the strength of her husband's feelings and she was a little worried for him. "You were enjoying your evening, please make the most of the rest of your holiday, you so deserve it. We both do. And tomorrow we can eat in the café – it's a special Chinese buffet. It might be nice."

Fergus was also a little shocked, he could see she was not far from tears and he cursed himself that, despite all his meditations, he still took the bait when something irritated him. He waited until they were back in the cabin and then said:

"I'm sorry. Your husband's an idiot… and yes, the Chinese buffet sounds a great idea." He held her for a few seconds.

"My husband's not an idiot, he is just being severely tested by his spiritual guide!"

"Yes, as far as spiritual guides go, I must say she really is quite tough!"

"She would infuriate the Buddha himself!" Sylvie said, disappearing into the bathroom. They decided on an early night, just going out once more to walk along the deck, admiring the lights of Funchal glowing from behind the harbour and the Madeiran hills rising in the distance beyond.

The next morning, Fergus wasn't so keen to go ashore again, he was feeling a little tense, but he sought to hide it from Sylvie, knowing she wanted to see more of the island. They took a shuttle bus into the heart of Funchal and then their third open-topped sightseeing bus in five days, choosing a route which took them around the city and its surroundings. They liked Funchal, by day or by night it was pretty, and the banana plantations were thick and tropical, despite them now being over a thousand miles north of Praia, which had been their most southerly calling point. It was certainly cooler than Cape Verde, but still much warmer than England would be when they arrived home in a few days' time. As the bus took them higher, they basked in sun and temperatures which would equate to a very reasonable British summer's day, whilst also enjoying the cooling breeze blowing in from the sea. Fergus began to relax. Suddenly, as the bus turned a corner and entered a particularly exposed stretch of road, a strong gust of wind caught under the peak of his blue-grey baseball cap, lifting it off his head, high into the air and then dropping it somewhere in the gorge far below.

"My cap!" he cried out, putting his hands to his bare head and just catching a glimpse of his souvenir from the Isles of Scilly hanging in the bright sky, before it disappeared out of sight.

"My cap!" he repeated, this time with resignation and barely aware of the uproarious laughter from his fellow sightseers in the rows behind.

Sylvie didn't know what to say, it was irretrievable, irreplaceable.

"Oh Fergus, I'm so sorry."

"Justine…"

"I know, I know, Fergus," she interrupted gently, taking his hand, the sadness in his face breaking her heart. She wrapped her arm around his, laying her head on his shoulder as they continued the circuit in silence, leaving the baseball cap somewhere further and further behind, while the same wind that had stolen it in a moment of spite, blew tenderly against their faces, as if seeking still to be friends.

Once the tour was over, Fergus, slowly coming to terms with his loss, said that he had had enough of sightseeing, and Sylvie was graceful enough not to try to persuade him otherwise. They ambled back contemplatively from the town centre to the ship, which around three hours later slipped its moorings for the final time.

When they next walked on solid ground it would be back in England. Neither was quite sure how they felt about that prospect: they loved being out at sea, but they were also a little jaded from so many ports of call in quick succession. Anyway, three weeks was a very good length for a break and they were increasingly feeling the call and the pull of their idyllic home. To quote Justine, deep down they were both 'home birds' after all.

They watched from deck as the ship moved sideways away from the quay and then slowly forward, before turning a sharp right to exit the harbour, lose its pilot and head north east along the coast, eventually leaving Madeira behind and ploughing on in the direction of Southampton. The holiday, though, was not yet over, there still being three full sea days to go and, whilst they knew the weather would only be going in one direction too, they both looked forward to them, as well as to seeing their house again thereafter. Sylvie slipped away while Fergus sat on deck, dozing and lazily watching the sea and the island of Porto Santo come and go in the distance.

After a while, he too headed back to the cabin but, predictably, encountered Mrs Huffington in the corridor. He really didn't feel like talking, but it was too late, she had seen him.

"Why Fergus, you appear very distracted."

"I'm sorry Mrs Huffington," then, thinking of his lost baseball cap, "I suppose I have something on my mind."

"Madeira can do that to you Fergus," she stared at him intently as if expecting him to ask why, but he didn't, risking another question instead:

"Do you still miss your Lawrence, Mrs Huffington?" There were a few moments of quiet while the old lady considered her response to this unexpected query.

"I carry him with me Fergus." It was a good answer and Fergus was about to say something to that effect, but she hadn't finished:

"Anyway, we'll be together again soon enough, I'm sure. You see death isn't what most people think Fergus. There's a curtain yes, but I believe there has to be, that what comes after is so wonderful that if we could see it we would all immediately jump through. But we have to live here a bit first, some of us longer than others. Just as we grow physically in the womb, so here we grow spiritually, it's like the gestation for the more important life that follows."

Fergus was momentarily stunned, he hadn't expected such a thoughtful reply from the old lady and he couldn't match it.

"I hope you are right Mrs Huffington."

"I am right Fergus…" again she eyed him as if daring him to disagree, one hand on the zimmer, the other playing with the silver chain and medal she had bought herself at a discount with her bingo winnings.

"I very much like your pendant Mrs Huffington."

"Thank you. It's a St Jude, he's the patron saint of lost causes, because everyone always confuses him with Judas Iscariot."

"But you're not a lost cause Mrs Huffington."

The old lady again stood there silently for a few moments and then slowly put her hands around her neck, unfastening the chain's catch.

"I hope you aren't either Fergus." She held out the pendant: "I hear it was your birthday yesterday, so please…" the silver glistened in her palm as she held it out towards him.

"I couldn't possibly."

"But you must Fergus, you must, otherwise I shall simply drop it here."

He tentatively took it from her hand and stared at it, losing himself in thought. By the time he looked up again she had already turned and was shuffling away from him.

"Thank you Mrs Huffington, I shall treasure it," he called out, but she just lifted her hand in a wave and continued down the corridor.

Fergus rejoined his wife in the cabin and showed her his gift.

"The patron saint of lost causes," he explained, perversely proudly. They both reflected again on this old lady roaming the seas, dispensing unique wisdom and poignant presents, in Fergus' case a well-timed substitute (inadequate, but still a consolation) for the priceless gift he had just lost.

They washed and changed and then slowly made their way to the Chinese buffet, he wearing his new St Jude pendant, Sylvie her lapis lazuli necklace.

The café was heaving with people who had plainly had the same idea, but Fergus and Sylvie managed to find a table to themselves and they delved into the buffet which, for vegetarian and non-vegetarian alike, was delicious; so much so that they both subsequently realised they had eaten far too much. They went outside to walk it off on deck, feeling a little better with each lap.

"I think we overdid it," remarked Sylvie.

"Yes, I rather fear we did," Fergus agreed.

They drew two chairs up next to each other in one of their favourite spots, a sheltered area at the stern where they had spent many hours reading and drinking lattés.

"I have something for you too," she said, holding out a small package. "I bought it… in the boutique… as a holiday present, to say I'm sorry about your cap, thank you and that I love you." This time it was Fergus' eyes that widened with surprise.

"But you already say you love me in so many ways."

"I want to say I love you in every way," and they both smiled as they realised that, consciously or sub-consciously, they had repeated a conversation of a fortnight earlier. Fergus slowly opened the package and found a silver watch with a deep blue background.

"It's beautiful," he wondered.

"I know," she answered cheekily, "and it's deep blue like the sea."

"Deep blue like the sea," he echoed. "You couldn't have chosen better!"

She put her arm around his and once again leant her head

on his shoulder. A few minutes later he realised she was asleep. He sat there like that for an hour or more, reviewing the holiday, reviewing also their lives with Justine and in the long years since she had died. That precious cap, he should have kept it safely at home, what had he been thinking? He pictured it lying, even at that very moment, amongst the thorns of the Madeiran scrubland.

"I'm sorry Just," he apologised softly and the wind caught his words, stealing them too, both out to sea and into the blackness of the night. After a while, he tried to practise his mindfulness: what more perfect setting than a warm evening, far out at sea, with nobody around except his wife, whose head rested comfortably against his upper arm? However, he quickly realised his own eyes were rapidly growing heavy: it was indeed a lost cause and any attempt at meditating was only going to end one way.

He gently roused Sylvie and led her sleepily to bed.

24

Ljubljana – December 2013

His sixty-third birthday was spent in Madeira, but three years earlier, for his sixtieth, Sylvie had treated Fergus to a week in Slovenia. In fact, without intending it, they had followed much of the initial route around the small country that Jones and his friends had taken some ten years earlier, although at slower pace. Jones had seen it in summer, lush and green with warm mountain airs; the Slovenia they saw was transformed by an early cold spell, which had laid blankets of snow and ice across its higher ground.

Their itinerary began by hiring a car at Ljubljana airport and heading north towards Bled. On the way, they diverted to see the Vintgar gorge, where they strolled the boardwalks fastened to the sides of the canyon, while an icy cold river gushed dramatically beneath them. There, suspended as they were between the two cliff sides and with trees towering overhead, the rays of the winter sun could not reach them and the already low temperatures dropped further, a cold they could feel sharply against their faces, even though their bodies were warm in the winter coats they had bought a few days earlier. As they exhaled, their breath visibly froze in the air before them, as if they were old steam locomotives and the boardwalk their tracks. They had grown up in an age before mass, budget travel and there still felt something miraculous to them that they could board a plane in a grey corner of England and disembark just two hours later in Scandinavia, Spain or in this case Slovenia, a country which immediately felt so different and whose beauty (as well as whose cold) could take their breath away.

Ultimately their new jackets were no match for the extreme temperature and, after ninety minutes, both were pleased to return to the car. Fergus cranked the heater up to full and, as they set off again, they waited impatiently for the engine to start pumping warm air into the cabin. Sylvie kicked off her shoes, ready to thaw her toes in the heat:

"You'll never get them back on again!" Fergus warned, but at that moment, as she massaged her feet to restore the blood flow, she didn't particularly care.

It was already early evening by the time they arrived in Bled and they quickly installed themselves in the modest but comfortable hotel which would be home for the next two nights. This was the first time they had properly stopped since leaving their house that morning and a wave of tiredness overcame them both, so they allowed themselves an hour to recover, before going down to the restaurant for a birthday-eve meal.

Replenished by this supper and warmed by a large, open fire, they emerged outside again for a brief wander around the town and down to the lake itself, which they were surprised to discover was completely frozen. It was too dark to see much, except for a few lights dotted around the shoreline and, there in the centre of the lake, the tower and steeple of the famous island church, illuminated softly and pointing up into the clear night sky, as if a chimney for the petitions of those who prayed there.

In daylight, the following morning, they could better see the field of shimmering pure white ice which surrounded the church. Fergus briefly wondered whether they could have safely skated across, but – having neither the daring nor the skates – they contented themselves with two circuits of the lake on foot, one either side of lunch. As dusk fell, they returned tired and red cheeked to their hotel, where the fire seemed to be waiting impatiently for them in its hearth, crackling and spitting its contempt. Every now and then, a waiter served it logs from a pile stacked by its side, and the flames consumed these ravenously. As they warmed themselves nearby, Fergus and Sylvie were far better humoured, but no less hungry.

"You're really going to get chilblains!" Fergus cautioned his wife once more as she rubbed her toes in the heat, but again she didn't care, focussed only on restoring her circulation after so long out in the cold.

The next day, after a final walk around the town, they drove the more mountainous of the two possible routes to Bohinj, where a cloud hung low in the valley just above its larger, half thawed lake. On all sides there were pine trees, weighed down by snow: dark forests which climbed up the slopes from the water, mirrored with crystal clarity in the pools where the ice had melted. The bridges along its perimeter and across its tributaries were also reflected on the surface, their arches forming perfect ovals as they reached down to meet their counterparts in the water below. Mountains rose all around, bleak and beautiful in the winter sky. The lakeside path was rough and slippery, while to its sides, in the places without tree cover, snow lay thickly on the ground, as it did on the roofs of the few buildings along the shore, including the churches, though it had slid off their steep Balkan spires.

After an excursion to the water's edge, Fergus and Sylvie checked into their hotel and planned a lap of the lake for the following day, though opting to do it by car. And so they set off the next morning, driving its length, but pulling over frequently in order fully to enjoy the scenery, the snow crunching satisfyingly underfoot as they explored. When they eventually reached the far end it was lunchtime, so they found an inn where, asking a waitress to recommend something traditional, they ate a warming bean and sauerkraut hotpot, followed by a pastry filled with cottage cheese and walnuts for dessert.

They emerged back outdoors, lethargic after their meal, but the fresh air quickly reinvigorated them. Finding no road to drive back down the opposite shore, they walked contemplatively along it instead, engrossed in a silence broken only by the burbling and splashing of the occasional mountain stream cascading down to the lake.

"How are the toes now?" Fergus enquired, after twenty minutes.

"Still toasty," Sylvie replied cheerfully, "the hotpot's working wonders!"

A little later however, when they turned round to head back, the chill was once more beginning to bite and Sylvie was relieved finally to arrive at the car, where again she quickly removed her footwear. This time, though, the relief was short lived because the drive to the hotel was too brief to enable her feet to thaw properly and, as they approached its entrance, she could not put her shoes back on.

"What did I tell you?" said Fergus, with an irritating hint of triumph.

"Oh, just drop me by the front door, I'll make a dash for it…"

And so Sylvie found herself hobbling up the cold hotel steps in her socks, feigning composure as she collected their key from the disapproving receptionist, before stumbling on up the stairs to their room. By the time Fergus joined her there, she was already soaking in a deep, warm bath.

Later that evening, in the hotel's restaurant, they were again confronted by a menu of incomprehensible dishes, leaving neither of them under any illusion that they were becoming experts in Slovenian cuisine. Fergus found himself tucking into a grilled meat dish, without being entirely sure what it was, while Sylvie, as a vegetarian option, was pointed to the unpronounceable široki rezanci z jurčki, which turned out to be a wide ribboned pasta with local mushrooms.

The following day was a Sunday, which made for a leisurely drive back to Ljubljana, where they returned the hire car and checked into their hotel for two nights. They were to spend the next day and a half ambling through the streets and parks of this small capital city, which to them, apart from the graffiti here and there on its walls, seemed a world away from the stress and grime of its larger European cousins. They wandered through Tivoli, across the Three Bridges, around the Farmers' Market and into the old town. They visited churches, museums and, snubbing the newly installed funicular railway, hiked to the castle, climbing the spiral stairs up its turret. There, Sylvie's head span as, protected from a sheer drop by just a waist high wall, they gazed out across spectacular vistas of a Slovenia which was slipping ever deeper into winter.

Early their final evening, outside a bar on the banks of the Ljubljanica river, not far from where Jones and Justine had first met, Fergus and Sylvie waited for their meal in the warmth of a patio heater, sipping at wine and watching life go by. An old man with a walking stick unhurriedly made his way step by step across the cobbles, as if engaged in a quietly determined act of rebellion against the pace of modern life. A woman with long brown hair walked past more briskly in the opposite direction, a coat of the same colour buttoned up and stretching down to her knees, as she pushed her two year old daughter home in a buggy, talking softly, perhaps about what exciting things they might do the next day. A street sweeper assiduously brushed dirt into a pan and tipped it into his bin, before taking a brief respite from his toils to lean against his broom and look back at his work, proud to be keeping his Capital clean.

On the far bank, they could see the stall holders from the

Christmas market packing up their wares for the night, looking forward to warm evenings at home with their families, after a long day out in the cold selling festive trinkets and steaming hot mulled wine. They banged around, taking down trestle tables and shutting up their little wooden huts: noises which carried across the river, along later with the sound of their vans starting up and driving away. Fergus and Sylvie only became aware that Christmas music had been playing gently in the background when it suddenly stopped mid-carol, leaving a strange silence hanging in the air, a vacuum which the city quickly filled with the clattering of cutlery on plates, a nearby child crying at a perceived injustice and, in the distance, a siren wailing, as if to prove that emergencies could even happen here.

They went for one last walk later that evening around Prešeren Square, with its festive lights, pink cathedral and enormous Christmas tree; the river glistening with reflections as it flowed nearby. The scene felt enchanting and they didn't want to leave. Instead, they loitered briefly around the Three Bridges, gazing up at the castle, illuminated high above them on the hill behind the old town, with the city's fairy tale 'castle and dragon' flag billowing out in the mountain wind from the turret where, just a few hours earlier, they had giddily stood.

"I can see why she liked it," said Sylvie. "I mean, I know she was here in summer rather than winter, but you can still tell."

Of course there was no need to say who 'she' was. They hadn't come to Ljubljana just because of its poignancy to Justine... but somehow the city had drawn them and, in truth, this had felt something of a pilgrimage.

"Yes, it's been a good trip," Fergus replied succinctly, with his right arm around his wife's waist, and they slowly turned and made their way back to the hotel.

A freezing fog hung over the city as they climbed into a taxi the next morning for the drive to the airport. They arrived early and there was little for them to see from the departure lounge, until the gloom was finally pierced by the bright lights of their plane feeling its way towards them across the apron. Boarding began just ten minutes after the last inbound passenger had disembarked and Fergus and Sylvie were pleased to find they had a row to themselves, three from the back.

"Good morning, ladies and gentlemen, I'm First Officer Casey Williams and it is my pleasure to fly you to London Stansted this morning..."

As the announcement continued, Fergus and Sylvie looked at each other:

"Did you hear that?" he said.

"Yes, it's Jones flying the plane!"

For two years after the accident, they had kept in close contact with him, but his life had then moved on, while theirs had stood still. He had continued to write to them every Christmas and around Justine's birthdays, but he hadn't ever mentioned flight training. They didn't begrudge him any of this though and, as their plane trundled its way back across the airfield, they felt excited that they might now have a chance to see him again and thrilled that he had achieved his ambition.

For Jones, this success had not come without cost, having indebted himself to levels which, if bordering on the excessive, at least demonstrated his commitment. This had all been rewarded when, just twelve months ago, he had obtained his Commercial Pilot's Licence and, soon afterwards, a junior First Officer position. It had been in early 2012, during this flight training, that he had met Samantha, his girlfriend, who was now similarly qualified, though flying with a different airline. It seemed that both their professional dreams had come true and Jones now had no further career ambitions, happy to be a First Officer flying short and medium hauls across Europe.

At the end of the runway, Jones completed the final checks with his Captain and then spooled up the engines so that the plane pulled hard against its brakes, until finally they were released and the throttles pushed to takeoff power. Fergus and Sylvie were pressed back into their seats as the jet accelerated and took off into the Slovenian sky. The freezing fog, which had lain thick on the ground, was not particularly deep and, as the plane climbed and turned, they soon emerged through it into bright sunshine and clear air. It seemed, through the window, as though they were rising over a mystical sea, the hilltops like islands poking through the dense mists, captivating Fergus and Sylvie with wonder, while Slovenia sank ever further below.

Just two hours later, juddering through some light turbulence, the plane wheeled high above the Essex countryside and began its final approach towards Stansted. "50, 40..." the autopilot counted down the last feet to the ground, "30, 20..." Jones moved the throttles back to idle and, a couple of seconds later, they landed. There was a brief roar as he used reverse thrust to help slow them down, then stillness as the plane turned off the runway and taxied to the Terminal. Jones reached up to switch off the seat-belt sign and, moments later, Fergus heard another favourite sound, that of a hundred buckles undoing at the same time, signalling the safe end to another flight.

They were at the rear of the plane anyway, but he and Sylvie purposefully made sure they were the last to walk down the aisle and, on reaching the front, they asked a stewardess if it would be possible for them to speak to the First Officer. She disappeared into the flight deck, briefly revealing a dazzling array of cockpit lights. Fergus and Sylvie waited nervously until a few moments later he emerged.

"Jones! You made it! You're a pilot!"

"Yes I am... oh my gosh, Sylvie!" he stumbled in astonishment, his mind grappling for a few seconds, both with this wholly unexpected reunion and with the sudden coming together of his personal and professional worlds. Regaining some of his composure, he gave her a hug.

"And Fergus!" he turned to Justine's father and another embrace followed.

"It's great to see you both, I had no idea you were on board…" he hesitated, not quite sure what to say. Having had a couple of hours to prepare for this moment, Sylvie jumped in:

"Well, we heard your announcement, but we thought we shouldn't say anything until after we had arrived. It's great to see you as well, it's been too long…" She hadn't intended it harshly but Jones looked awkward.

"I know, I know… I'm sorry, it's just that…"

"I didn't mean it as a criticism Jones, it's just such a nice surprise."

The truth was that for two years after Justine's death he had struggled to get on with his own life, all his thoughts had been fixed on her. After a while, he had concluded that the close touch he kept with her parents wasn't helping and so he had cut back contact dramatically, until he was only sending them cards at special occasions.

"No, I should have stayed in touch… I was just finding it so difficult…" he faltered and, realising he was struggling, Fergus intervened:

"We know. We are just pleased to see you again. Come on, you'd better compose yourself, you'll be making your next set of passengers nervous!"

Jones gave a short laugh. "Yes, I really should be getting ready, we are off again in thirty minutes. Amsterdam."

"It's all glamour!" Fergus joked.

"Ljubljana is my favourite route though… I always remember…" again his powers of speech waivered as the memories rushed back.

"We know you do Jones," this time it was Sylvie who provided the reassurance, "come and see us sometime won't you?"

"I will, I will, I promise. I'd like that."

"Well, we'll leave you to get on with… whatever it is you do next," Fergus said, shrugging his shoulders in ignorance as to what that might be, "but we will see you again soon, yes?"

"Yes, definitely."

They turned and left the plane, disappearing gingerly down its steps.

Meanwhile, the Captain was busying himself with paperwork in the flight deck, enabling Jones to slip back into his seat, grateful for a few moments to reflect on the encounter. Through the windscreen, he studied Fergus and Sylvie traipsing slowly across the tarmac and it struck him how vulnerable and alone they appeared. For a moment, he felt unbearably sad but then, just before reaching the terminal, Fergus turned round and waved towards the plane. Without thinking, Jones raised his hand in response. Neither could have known whether the other saw, nevertheless Jones was cheered by the exchange, though it felt very private, and so he was pleased too that, head still deep in his documents, the Captain had not noticed.

25

North East Atlantic – Wednesday 7th December 2016

Fergus woke at a quarter to three in the morning and, while Sylvie slept soundly the other side of the cabin, he grew ever more restless and ever wider awake, fretting about his lost cap, the Caballeros and his humiliation by the arachnid lady. After half an hour, and with sleep still eluding him, he opted to get up and go for a walk rather than lie there restlessly any longer, hoping by the time he returned to bed he would have broken the grip of this insomnia.

He put some trousers over his pyjama bottoms and a jumper over his top. He slipped on some socks and shoes and crept out into the corridor, which stretched a short distance forward and seemingly endlessly aft towards the stern. He walked to the stairs and climbed two floors to the main reception area. The only soul in sight was a woman, some distance off, lurching drunkenly from side to side, as she stumbled away from him through the deserted ship. Fergus watched her a moment before quickly climbing another level, for fear she would turn around and spot him. From here he was able to get outside, walking a lap of the deck, now completely alone. Despite the hour and Fergus' lack of a coat, it was not cold and he found the combination of sea air and solitude a heady mix, it felt almost magical to be out here by himself while the *Magdalena* slept.

He put his hands on the rail and looked out into the darkness of the night-time Atlantic and at the swirling waters below. A familiar feeling stole up on him: with just a few seconds of madness, of loss of control, he realised he could easily climb over the rail and throw himself overboard. Nobody would witness it, he would certainly die, never to be found, leaving everyone wondering what on earth had happened. He'd had similar feelings ever since, as a very young child at the local train station, he had felt a tangible force pulling him towards the platform edge and on to the tracks. He had needed to hold tightly onto his mother to resist it. Now, nearly six decades later, his mother was not there to grasp and the magic he had felt just a few minutes earlier had suddenly changed into an unanticipated feeling of fear.

Not trusting himself, Fergus went back inside and walked around the empty lounges and bars, places which during the days and evenings were crowded with a captive clientele, but which now were empty, save for the ghosts of the passengers who had cruised on the ship in years gone by... it seemed to him that they melted away as he turned a corner, resuming their hauntings only once he had disappeared around the next, the eerie night-time creaks and groans, unheard during the day, the only clues to their vaporous presence.

Eventually, he climbed down the stairs back to deck four and reached his cabin. For some reason, before opening the door, he looked back down the endless corridor towards the stern. In the distance he thought he could see shapes moving... he decided to take a closer look, but perhaps had only got a tenth of the way there when he stopped dead: he was almost certain it was a group of monks in hoods and orange robes padding aftward, away from him. Instinctively, Fergus put his back to the wall, making himself less visible, lest one should turn around and spot him. He watched as they walked ever further down the corridor before, finally, turning left through an inner door and disappearing into the bowels of the ship.

Fergus waited a few minutes and then nervously crept all the way to the mysterious door, which was shut tight and bore a sign reading 'Strictly No Admittance'. Fergus shivered and hurriedly made his way back up the corridor, occasionally looking behind anxiously, but there was nobody in sight. A sense of relief swept over him as he closed the cabin door behind him. Sylvie was still sound asleep and oblivious to his nocturnal wanderings. He got back into bed, but the whole point of the exercise had been lost and he was wide awake again, with his mind racing: who had the hooded and orange robed monks been? And why had they been wandering the ship in the depths of the night? Fergus sat up in bed as his mind conjured up ever more sinister explanations... Finally, after half an hour or so, he realised that he had briefly dropped off to sleep and, taking this as a good sign, he lay back down hoping that before long the rest, which had been so elusive for much of the night, would finally come. In the dark, with the hum of the engines and the gentle rocking of the ship, sleep did indeed sneak up on him, much like a gently flowing tide flooding unnoticed over his anxious thoughts, bringing him peace, at least until the morning.

For once, Sylvie was awake and up before her husband.

"Hello sleepy head!" she said, ruffling his hair. It took Fergus a few moments to come to and, during these, the memories of his strange night-time encounter came back to him. He considered telling Sylvie but held back. Instead, he lay in bed, preoccupied with his recollections, for another ten minutes or so, while Sylvie washed. He then did the same. Once they were both dressed, they headed to breakfast and the previous night quickly receded in his thoughts as they slipped into their familiar sea day routine.

The Captain gave his usual monologue. It felt as though he should be saying words of wisdom, or at least warmth, and every noon time they hoped he just might, but he always disappointed them.

"... *and finally a few hygiene advices, please wash yourrr hands frrre-Quent-ly for 20 seconds using hot soapy water, as well as using the hand sanitisers you see about the ship and at the entrrrance to the rrrrestaurants. Have a very pleasant afterrrnoon.*"

Suspecting that fine weather might now be at a premium, they ate a final time on deck ten, outside the restaurant, again surveying the Atlantic around them. Fergus pondered a final swim, eyeing the pool far below, adjacent to which, in the spa bath, the three Caballeros laughed and joked between sips of their lurid coloured cocktails. Fergus stared with venom as they lounged cockily amongst the bubbles, shouting raucous words that could be heard but not quite understood at this distance. By the time he actually got to the pool an hour later, they were still in place, but their cocktails must have taken effect because they lolled their heads against the sides of the bath, one of them occasionally raising just enough energy to press the button to restart the bubbles. Fergus looked up at the sun and half hoped it remained strong enough for them to wake up burnt, but he caught himself in these feelings and settled for being grateful that they were at least now quiet. One last time, he lowered himself into the empty swimming pool, turned onto his back and floated effortlessly as he watched the clouds drifting by high above.

Suddenly, he felt a gentle splash on his face and he immediately lifted his head and started treading water. Getting his bearings, he noticed his dancer crouching by the poolside and smiling at him:

"Couldn't resist, sorry!" Seeing her there only added to Fergus' surprise and, for a moment, he coughed and spluttered so much that she wondered whether her tease had been misjudged.

"I'd pull you in if I could reach!" he joked, immediately regretting his words as he remembered her experience at the hand of the Caballero.

"I'm keeping my distance!" she laughed back. "Anyway, I'm impressed, you are still up to your old mermaid tricks even after nearly three weeks."

Looking up at her, he was angled so he could finally see her name badge: it read 'Holly Parkin'.

"I think this might be the final time, I doubt we'll have this weather tomorrow."

"Nevertheless, on this ship you are quite the athlete: I think you were first in the pool at the start of the cruise and it seems that you are going to be the last out," she surveyed the sleeping pensioners all around, none looking likely swimmers. Fergus felt a certain pride that this little achievement had been noticed, he had never received a compliment for his sportiness before, and certainly not from a young woman.

"By the way," she continued, "I watched the video... of your daughter... she was great, really. Nicole thought so too."

"You did? You thought so? She did too?"

"Yes, yes and yes," Holly replied cheerfully, once again twisting a lock of hair around her finger. "She was pretty as well, you should be very proud."

"I am, extremely."

"Will you come and see our last show tonight?"

"Of course!" he answered, still feeling flattered that she should have been interested enough to look up the video and now, doubly so, that she should care in the least whether or not he came to her show. "But it's the last one already?"

"Tomorrow night is the farewell cabaret, we just do one number, and then the final evening is the crew show... so yes, tonight's our last one. Catch us while you can!" she smiled.

"I'll be there." He watched as she stood up, gave a little wave and walked off. He lay on his back again but, with the adrenaline pumping, he was no longer relaxed and he soon climbed out of the pool. He noticed that the three dozing Caballeros seemed to be glistening in the sun, as if they were gently roasting. A cocktail glass had fallen on its side beside the Jacuzzi and was rolling back and forth in a semi circle to the motion of the ship. Fergus picked it up and placed it on a table.

"Be careful of the sun, boys," he warned, but they did not stir. He tried again: nothing. He hesitated, wondering what he should do, but, despite the sunshine, the sea wind whipped across his wet body and he was starting to shiver, so, his conscience half clear, he leapt three levels up the stairs to the changing room on deck ten:

"*Closed for cleaning.*"

Fergus couldn't believe it. Trembling violently now on the more exposed top deck, he eventually made his way its length to the lifts in the entrance of the Conservatory Bar. The journey down seemed to take an eternity, stopping at every floor and, more often than not, just as the doors began to close, someone would rush up and stick a foot between them, or press the button, and they would re-open. Sometimes the process would then repeat... when, with two floors still to go, an old lady started manoeuvring in on her mobility scooter, Fergus had had enough, but hid it by playing the gentleman:

"Here, let me allow you more space," he said as he squeezed out.

"Thank you, that's terribly kind... oh, you're dripping wet!" But Fergus was already rushing down the stairs, desperately hoping he would not bump into Mrs Huffington.

"Oh my goodneth!" said a startled Gentle Henry, making his way up with Tabitha, as a half naked Fergus charged down in the opposite direction towards him.

"I can't stop I'm afraid... I'll see you both at dinner?"

"Yeth, yeth, of courssse... the Lord doesss indeed work in mysterwious wayths..."

Finally, back in the cabin, Fergus climbed out of his trunks and stepped into the shower, letting the hot water cascade over him, rubbing his face as shampoo washed down from his hair. Swimming on the *Magdalena* was idyllic, floating effortlessly beneath a warm sun, rising and falling as the water sloshed around him, but (as so often in life) there was a price to pay afterwards and he couldn't help but feel relieved that this had been the last time.

An hour later, he was back on deck with Sylvie and their e-readers, lattés on order. As she started reading, Fergus was horrified to hear himself start singing one of the songs from the cabaret, he stopped himself, but too late.

"So you bumped into your singer or dancer again?" Curses! How was she so perceptive?

"The dancer yes, her name is Holly… You miss nothing!"

"You don't make it hard for me… most men keep their fancies quiet, you sing whenever you see yours!"

"She's not my fancy…"

"I know, I know," said Sylvie, fearing from his tone that she had pushed the tease a bit far and wary that her husband's mild obsession may be more fatherly than anything else, the ghost of another dancer never far from his thoughts… or hers for that matter. She held his hand reassuringly.

Only one coffee arrived.

"Oh, I'm sorry madam, I thought sir did not want one… I will get one straight away."

"No, no, it's OK," Fergus replied, "I'll just take a sip or two from my wife's." The waiter made certain they were sure and then disappeared. Sylvie stood up and took the coffee to the rail, where a few seconds later Fergus joined her. She offered the glass out to him and they held it between them, each releasing it occasionally to enable the other to take a sip. Had Justine's ghost been there, the scene of her parents tenderly sharing the one coffee in this way may have reminded her of something she had once witnessed from a railway carriage window. But that was a long time ago.

"Come on, back to our books!" Sylvie said decisively, emptying the last dregs of coffee from the glass.

And so they continued reading out on deck, at first only peripherally aware of the breeze blowing balmily against their faces. Occasionally, they would lift their heads from their e-readers and gaze across the ocean, tracking a sun which was imperceptibly arcing down towards the horizon, until eventually it disappeared into a low lying haze. The wind no longer felt so companionable in the faded light, blustering around them more wildly, billowing out their clothes. Realising they were cold, they finally retreated indoors.

After resting briefly in their cabin, they changed and headed to the Midships Lounge for an aperitif. This time there were no mobile phone conversations to intrude upon the string trio, whose delicate music combined with the soothing motion of the ship (and perhaps the drinks) to lull Fergus and Sylvie into a blissful calm.

Alas, it was such that comes before a storm.

On their arrival in the restaurant, the arachnid lady and her silent husband were already seated, waiting to be served. Fergus nodded to them as he passed but had the impression that she just gave a malevolent shudder in response. And then, was it his imagination, or were her eyes redder than ever, as if to get to her evening meal she had had to exit through the fiery gates of hell itself?

"Awwww, where's our starters?!" The shrill, loud voice grated on Fergus and he prayed hard that Richard and Cressida would arrive quickly, creating a barrier between him and his nemesis... as if by miraculous response, he noticed them approaching down the restaurant.

"Awwww, Fergus, had a bad day have we? You look a real grumpy chops... give us a smile my darling? Awww, you can do it if you try…" Why were their dining neighbours walking so slowly? Fergus forced a smile…

"Awwww, isn't he sweet. We love you Fergus, you know we do… Where's our starters?!"

Mercifully, Richard and Cressida finally took their places, exchanging sympathetic glances with Fergus and Sylvie as a piercing rendition of 'Why are we waiting?' rose from the table beyond, until at last a waiter brought a prawn cocktail, which temporarily silenced her.

As Fergus watched her eat, he could hear her long tongue slurping up the poor prawns – what a way to end up, he thought sympathetically towards the mercifully already dead creatures! The arachnid lady wiped her mouth with her sleeve and leaned over, cupping her ear, to hear what her neighbours were saying…

"Awww, Bar-Bay-Dos… you'll luv it! We went there last year, the men are goooooogerous, even more gorgeous than Joseph here!" She feigned to give the unfortunate waiter a slap on the backside.

"Hey!" he said, startled at the prospect and regretting he had ever been persuaded to swap restaurants with Frederico.

"Awwwww Joseph, it's only me-ee!" Joseph retreated behind the doors to the kitchen and, by this stage, the Maitre D' himself was looking on as if he were about to intervene, but somehow never quite reaching that stage.

In this way, the meal continued until, at its end, the woman's table was a catastrophe of spilled food and drink and she gave the most enormous belch.

"It's a compliment!" she roared, outraged that anyone could think differently.

To Fergus, the transmogrification was now complete. Her squat body sat splayed on the chair, her lower limbs curled around its legs. Her abdomen was distended with the excesses of her meal, yet her spiderish arms still darted across the tablecloth, gathering up the last pieces of half finished baguette and transferring them machine-like into her mouth. Her jaws smacked noisily until, with an almighty swallow, the bread was gone and she was left there, sitting behind the detritus of her meal, looking around defiantly with her red eyes, as if for further prey, and sinisterly running a finger around her gums to dislodge any final remnants of dough.

Fergus couldn't stand it a moment longer and, getting up suddenly, he fumbled his way to the exit, crashing into the dessert trolley as he departed and with an astonished Sylvie left trailing in his wake.

"I could kill her!" he exclaimed to his shocked wife as she finally caught up with him outside the restaurant.

"She's awful... but you must calm down!" She said it firmly, standing directly in front of him, holding his upper arms in her hands, as if both to steady him and to hold him in place until, as quickly as it had been lost, his composure was restored. "Come on, let's get some fresh air outside, before the show," she suggested, finally relaxing her grip. Picking up jumpers on the way, they headed out on deck, where the wind resumed its indifferent blustering against them, uninterested in their petty dramas and placing them in perspective against the vastness of the ocean.

A little later, in the Poseidon Theatre, for the first and only time, they had seats in the front row. This felt a little perilous lest part of the act involved grabbing an unsuspecting audience member and dragging them up on stage. However, it also gave a spectacular view, not just of legs and feet flying around, but also of the dancers' faces and expressions. Those in the first row, from the light-dazzled stage, were the only passengers the performers could really see and Holly spotted Fergus early on, definitely now giving him a smile. He didn't quite know where to look and, by the time his brain had told him to smile back, it was too late, she had turned away. The singers, meanwhile, joined in with some of the simpler dance moves, but otherwise concentrated on their songs, often performing them solo from one position.

Towards the end of the show and by chance, Nicole moved to the part of the stage immediately in front of them and, standing there in a soft spotlight, she began singing "Roam". Fergus fell into a trance, perfectly focussed on nothing but her face and the familiar words of a song that had been his companion for eleven years, since his daughter had danced to its video; its words like a prophecy he was fated to live out after her death a few months later.

> *"You're lying awake, can't go to sleep,*
> *The grief too profound, the pain far too deep,*
> *The tears that you cry the sole crop that you reap,*
> *You were happy, but now you just weep.*
> *Her bright light is gone and your heart starts to crack,*
> *But your mind still returns to the love that you lack,*
> *And all that's around in this world spun off-track*
> *Is just darkness and blindness and black.*
> *In the mountains she's absent*
> *And she's not out at sea,*
> *She's not lost in a forest,*
> *Nor in the city,*
> *And you know that you may as well roam,*
> *'cos she's not coming home."*

As he looked up at her, Fergus again felt an overwhelming intensity: he was suffocating, but strained to remember how to draw in oxygen; he felt a surge of panic, he needed to breathe, he needed to breathe! He was hot, his body taut; air, air, he had to get air! He knew that he would surely die if she were to look down at him now, surely die if... and then she did. He was paralysed, hypnotised, mesmerised, as she smiled at him through the sad lyrics and as his asphyxia tightened its grip, until finally... finally... after an eternity and just before he was sure he would pass out, she looked away again, and then (and only then) with an enormous in-take of breath, he automatically filled his lungs and the hot, sticky oxygen of the theatre cleared his head enough for him to regain some control and his body at long last began to relax.

But why, oh why, did they give her the sad songs and why, oh why, did she sing the saddest of them all to him?

26

Lancashire – May 2013 and Galilee – AD31

On retreat in Lancashire, a fifty-eight year old man was sitting in a chapel, meditatively, in silence. If he had been listening, he would have heard the birds singing as they flew to and from their nests in the eaves of the building, and as their young called out for more food. If he had been looking, he would have seen the sun streaming through the chapel window, illuminating the stained glass images as if, at any moment, they could spring to life. If he had been breathing deeply, he might have smelled the salt in the air, perhaps even tasted it on his tongue, as it blew in under the chapel door and through the cracks and crannies of the old building. But Fergus noticed none of these things as he travelled through space and time to be with John the Baptist, on the banks of the river Jordan, along with Andrew and another of John's disciples.

They were resting there, that's all. Yes, there were people around, but not that many, and John wasn't baptising, just relaxing in the sunshine. He had told them that, only the previous day, he had seen the Messiah, knowing it was Him because the Holy Spirit had descended upon Him as he walked. It was Him whom Fergus had come to Galilee to see... but he was getting hot and so he hoped there was time for a swim first.

The stones crunched as he made his way to the water's edge and then, as he stepped in, he felt the coolness, first under his foot and then rising above it. He waded in deeper, gingerly, both because it was cold and for fear his bare feet might hit a stone. Once the water had reached his chest he started to swim and, finding his courage, he ducked his hot, dusty head under the water. He refreshed himself in the river for a few minutes before finding a submerged rock, about a third of the way across, and, heaving himself up, he sat on it, facing upstream, with the Jordan's waters flowing coolly around his waist.

After a while, he swam back to the side and, without towelling himself, put on his robe, tying it with a cord and knowing the sun would quickly dry him off. He walked back up to his three companions, sand and dust immediately sticking to his damp feet and ankles as he went. Shortly afterwards, John pointed up the shoreline to his left:

"Behold the Lamb of God whom I saw yesterday!" The man was walking down the side of the river and at one stage took His sandals off to step in, also to cool His feet.

Yes, Fergus had transported himself to Galilee, and back nearly two thousand years, all at the suggestion of his guide on the sixth day of his retreat. Until then he had, each day, been given short Bible passages to mull over; however, she had that morning suggested a new meditative technique, taking a whole Bible story and imaginatively placing himself squarely in it. It turned out that this was something Fergus could do and, while his physical body was indeed sitting quietly in one of the chapels of the retreat centre, his consciousness was very much watching the 'Lamb of God' step back out of the water and continue His way down the riverbank past them, as described in the text from St John's Gospel given to Fergus by his retreat guide.

Andrew, the other disciple and Fergus followed Him and suddenly He turned around:

"What do you want?" He asked. Taken aback, Andrew fumbled for his words:

"Rabbi, where are you staying?" To which the man replied:

"Come and see." And they followed Him. As they walked, Andrew or the other disciple asked:

"Are you the son of God?" To which the man responded:

"There will not always be time, but for now there is – I am Jesus of Nazareth."

They arrived at Jesus' little encampment, a short way back from the river, in a sheltered spot beneath a palm tree. Here it was cooler and Jesus prepared a fire, lighting it with ease and the wood cracking as it burned fiercely. He put a stone over the flames and heated some breads. There were some containers nearby from which they drank, while, later, Jesus made them a hot drink that tasted a little like tea.

Afterwards, Andrew went off to find his brother, Simon. The other disciple also stepped away and Fergus found himself alone with Jesus. Fergus was aware that once Simon arrived he would dominate, so this was his own opportunity to speak with Jesus. He took it:

"Lord, I am at an advantage. I know who you are. I am praying to you from a long way away and a long time away. Help me to know you here." And Jesus immediately replied:

"I am in all times and in all places."

For a fleeting moment, it felt to Fergus as though he knew that, although not with him physically, Jesus was every bit as much present as when, all those years ago, he had been with his disciples in body by the Jordan. He felt sure that Jesus had just spoken to him directly, and it was so vivid that, for those few seconds, he had genuinely not known whether he really had been at that camp fire or in the Lancashire chapel or somewhere else entirely. Before he could ponder this any longer, Simon rushed breathless into the encampment and Jesus turned to him, and away from Fergus, and said:

"You will be known as Peter and on you I will build my church."

The scene melted away and Fergus definitely was now very much back in the chapel and beginning a mental and spiritual wrestle with what had just occurred: he felt as though he may indeed have had an encounter with God, something that others experienced but that he had always believed would never happen to him, until now, when it miraculously had. The words *"I am in all times and in all places"* had hit him profoundly, he was amazed by how his real and imagined worlds had merged so powerfully, but most of all he was left with a clear recollection: in the moment that He had spoken and the immediate seconds thereafter, Jesus' physical presence had not been the key thing at all, because, in fact, it had felt beyond doubt that He was as much with Fergus as he sat there in the chapel as ever He had been anywhere.

Fergus spent the rest of the day contemplating this mystical experience and its intensity, doing so while walking the grounds or the labyrinth, or while sitting in one of the chapels again. He grew a little scared as doubt began to creep in. Wasn't there a prayer that went *"We should at all times and in all places give thanks unto thee"*? Is this where the words had come from rather than from some unlikely divine encounter? But Jesus had said *"I am in all times and in all places"* not *"we should at all times and in all places"* – they weren't the same. Furthermore, the answer had come instantly, without Fergus' brain having had time to conjure it up. And it wasn't just the reply, it was the feeling of presence too.

Fergus went round and round in circles, until he reached his conclusions: the experience had felt real, but he knew that with time that certainty was bound to fade, he knew that what Jesus had said was similar to the words of a common prayer but… and here was the conclusion... God wants faith, He doesn't give you certainty, you have to meet Him, if not half way, then at least somewhere in the middle... certainty requires no faith at all. Fergus had spent six days in silence listening for God, and now that he had heard Him he doubted it... in which case, why had he bothered coming at all? So, he decided to choose to believe that Jesus had spoken to him by the banks of the Jordan and, as he accepted that, it dawned on him that this meant those few seconds had therefore been the most important moments of his entire life.

The next day, he told all this to his retreat guide who listened carefully, without either sounding amazed by the miracle or disbelieving of it. Her advice was simply not to doubt it. She said that sometimes, after such an episode, you could revisit through another meditation and gain greater insight. Fergus, however, was a little reluctant to make a further attempt, he felt that what he had experienced probably could not be repeated and certainly could not be bettered. He did try though, albeit perhaps half-heartedly, but he just couldn't get into it again, at least not this soon. Nevertheless, the previous day's experience had been powerful, and it felt incredible to think that, if ever he wanted to do so in the future, he could, through silence and imagination, transport himself back there again.

What did the miracle (if that is what it indeed was) mean? Well, he hadn't gone to Lancashire in search of Justine... of course he had thought of her and prayed for her, but, however hard to admit, the truth was that he had actually felt her presence less on retreat than he had at any stage since her death. Perhaps this was because he knew he could find her at home, but he had come to Lancashire looking for God, and the 'Seek and ye shall find' promise seemed to have been fulfilled. If God existed, if, if, if... then it meant there was hope: hope for him, hope for Sylvie, hope even for Justine and hope that one day they would be reunited.

Fergus felt sure the intensity would ease over time and that ordinary life would resume, that he would tell nobody else about this experience, probably not even Sylvie; he was certain he wasn't going to metamorphosise into a Bible-thumping evangelist, but that his faith would remain a quiet one. He would continue to grieve for his daughter and he accepted that there would be moments when this would still feel almost unbearable. He was under no illusion that he was now a saint, rather (judging himself a little harshly) he knew he would still have his grumpy, impatient, anxious, lazy, antisocial personality... but he also knew (or as close to knowing as the requirement for at least some faith would allow) that, whatever his flaws, in the silence of the retreat, and contrary to his expectations, he had finally heard God.

27

North East Atlantic – Thursday 8th December 2016

Fergus was feeling a long way away from his Lancashire miracle as he lay wide awake in his bed for a second night running. It was two thirty and his head was spinning with different thoughts: nostalgic ones for Holly and how she reminded him of his daughter with her dancing, and even with how she played with her shoulder length brown hair; paternal ones for Nicole, as he worried how she had hurt her arm, whether life was cruel to her and what it was about her singing that seemed so terribly sad; and hostile ones towards the arachnid lady, that monster with whom they dined each night... most of all, he felt depressed: twice the previous evening he had succumbed to the intensity of his own emotions – so much for meditation! Eventually, he abandoned his efforts to sleep and again threw on some clothes and tiptoed out of the cabin.

The swell had got up a little and he staggered slightly as he stepped out of the door. He closed it quietly and then stopped still for a moment to regain his balance. As he stood there, he looked up the corridor stretching away into the distance and he, involuntarily, suddenly pictured it full of water, as it would be should the ship one day sink. He imagined the silence with no engines running and with debris floating around, fish too, and perhaps crabs and other crustaceans scuttling around on the floor. It was a nightmarish thought: if the ship went down quickly in the night, he and Sylvie would go with it to the seabed, and their ghosts would roam the corridors until the hull finally disintegrated, giving up their souls to the ocean. He shuddered at the idea.

He began walking down the corridor and got about half way along it when he again heard padding footsteps, many of them. People were coming. It was unnerving at this time of the morning and Fergus had an urge to hide, but there was nowhere to do so. From the next landing, the same group of hooded, orange robed monks as before appeared and, without seeing Fergus, they turned left into the corridor ahead of him, making their way silently towards the stern. He froze. After what felt an eternity, the first monk reached the same door they had used the previous night and one by one they again entered through it, the last one turning slightly, as he closed it behind him, to the extent that Fergus wondered whether he had been seen. For a moment, all was quiet and then suddenly the door re-opened and the last monk looked straight back out at him, his eyes glistening in the darkness of his hood. They stared at each other for a few seconds before the monk disappeared again, sealing the door behind him with a decisive thud.

The corridor suddenly felt extraordinarily creepy and Fergus' instinct was to rush back to the cabin. He resisted it though and, instead, quickly walked to the next landing and then up the stairs until he could get out on deck. His nerves had already been shredded from the twin experiences of dinner and the show, the monks now left him feeling as if he were on a descent into madness. As he exited, the fresh air hit him, surprising him with its coldness after nearly three weeks in the warm. He slowly re-gathered his senses and noticed a dark figure just a few yards further up the deck, leaning over the side, throwing up her extravagant dinner into the Atlantic: ugh, the arachnid lady! She disgusted him as she stood there, her limbs sprawled and flailing over the rails, retching out into the night, occasional splatters of vomit catching on the wind and dispersing towards her revolted observer cowering in the shadows by the door.

She had not seen him, and Fergus wanted to retreat inside before she did... but something deep within him felt an old familiar draw, the same one he had felt all those years ago at the train station pulling him towards the tracks, the same one he had felt just the other night calling him to throw himself off the ship – except this time the call was for nothing so self-inflicted, rather for something more malign. He took a step towards her and stopped. Then another. Then again. Then two, three, four paces more as the malevolent game of grandmother's footsteps neared its climax. She gave another enormous retch, standing on full tiptoe like a grotesque ballerina, leaning out even further as yet more of her meal poured out into the sea below. A large swell rolled the boat more extremely in the same direction and Fergus was standing right behind her...

Some five hours later and, for a second day running, he woke after his wife, who leaned down to kiss him before making her way to the bathroom. Fergus lay there, trying to piece together what from the previous few hours had been real and what just a sinister dream. They slipped into their well rehearsed routine of breakfast, returning back to the cabin for their things and then heading out on deck with their e-readers. The weather was still fine, but the wind gusted with that cold bite now, as if to remind them where they were headed, and, for the first time in a fortnight, they dressed more warmly in jumpers and coats. At noon, the Captain gave his usual update, but Fergus and Sylvie kept reading, he breaking off at one stage for his twenty minute meditation. Later, they went inside for lunch and, with the cooler weather, soup this time rather than salad – another sure sign that, although they were still on holiday, they could no longer claim it to be a summer one.

Fergus did briefly think of having a swim, but the effort of changing and then changing back, remembered from the previous day, got the better of him, especially given the deteriorating conditions. Instead, he and Sylvie completed ten laps walking around the deck (two and a half miles in total), before retreating back to their favourite sheltered haunt at the stern, where they read and dozed the afternoon away. Their relaxation was punctuated by two approaches to sell them coffee, the first by one of the wolf-like barmen, already carrying a tray with a number of pre-made, rapidly cooling lattés:

"You need a hot drink, yes?"

"No, we are OK, thank you."

"But your husband, he looks cold madam… it's very warming."

"He's fine, thank you."

"Twenty percent off madam, shall I leave them here for you?"

"I told you, we don't want coffee… but thank you," Sylvie said, controlling herself. The waiter grudgingly slouched off, balancing his tray as he climbed the stairs to the next deck where, a few moments later, they could hear him trying the same tactics with someone else.

"They don't give up easily do they?" Fergus said from behind eyes that had been kept deliberately closed during the exchange.

"At least he wasn't pointing a camera in our faces too!" Sylvie replied.

About half an hour later the approach was gentler and more genuine. The waitress, who at the start of the cruise had told them she was homesick, came up to them asking whether they would like any drinks, to which Fergus answered.

"Lattés would go down a treat! Thank you."

"How are you? I've been thinking of you, I hope you are not missing home too much?" Sylvie enquired.

"Oh madam, it is your holiday. I am OK, you mustn't worry about me. It's my job to worry about you!"

"You look after us very well, I am sure your family are extremely proud." This may have sounded a little patronising to some, but Fergus had meant it genuinely and it didn't occur to her to take offence.

"I hope so sir, it's true I do miss them and my country. But I save money, so one day I go back."

"We wish you only good things, you deserve them. And my husband is right, you do an excellent job, and you are so elegant too."

"Thank you madam… I do my best." She smiled and slipped off to get the coffees, bringing them five minutes later and placing them with precision on their table, along with two small biscuits and the chit for them to sign.

"Thank you," said Sylvie, "to tell you the truth, not all your colleagues are as professional as you." She looked across at one of the wolves.

"Oh, I'm sorry… some are a little over enthusiastic maybe…" the waitress replied, before whispering conspiratorially, "and I'm sad to say not all passengers are as nice as you!"

"Oh, I'm sorry too… perhaps we deserve each other!"

"Yes, I think so!" She reclaimed the chit from Fergus and withdrew back down the stairs, leaving them to contemplate her dignity: transcending her role through grace and good humour, despite working far from home. They hoped that they too may have made a positive impression on her, but suspected she saw so many passengers that it was hard for any to leave a lasting impact. And she had been right, of course, it wasn't their job to worry about her, nor did she want them to, nor did it serve any purpose, but somehow they still did.

They stayed out reading on deck until late afternoon when,

distractedly running her finger beneath the table edge, Sylvie caught it on something sharp, crying out at the unexpected pain.

"Are you OK?" Fergus enquired, coming up from his e-reader.

"Yes, but I've just cut myself..." She studied the wound a moment, dabbing at the blood with a tissue. "I think I should wash it. I have plasters in the cabin." And so they gathered up their things and headed back.

"You'll bleed to death if we bump into Mrs Huffington now!" Fergus joked from several steps ahead and then, as he turned the corner into their corridor, there she was again, walking slowly towards him.

"Oh, Mrs Huffington!" he called out, primarily as a warning to Sylvie who stopped dead, unsure whether her husband was serious or teasing until, still behind the corner, she heard the elderly woman's reply:

"The Captain's been up to his old tricks you know, banging on the wall of his cabin. He can't stand noise you see. He's a very bad tempered man, and universally disliked by the crew."

"Gosh, Mrs Huffington, where do you learn all this?" replied Fergus, trying to imagine the Captain stomping around his cabin in a frightful mood, while perhaps the crew conspired together in the bowels of the ship, with mutiny afoot. But she just looked knowingly at him.

"It wouldn't surprise me if he leaves the ship in Southampton and goes back to Romania... he's not popular at all, and apparently the ship's running low on whisky, that's all I'll say."

Fergus found this scenario most unlikely, the Captain sounded rather dull when making his daily announcements, but, on the few occasions he had actually glimpsed him, he had appeared genial enough, and Fergus remained in awe of his efforts at the welcome party, back at the start of the cruise. What's more, hadn't she previously told him the ship's doctor was Romanian, surely they couldn't both be? Nevertheless, he didn't like to argue with an elderly woman and, thinking of the waitress, all he managed was:

"Well, perhaps he's a little homesick for Romania…"

Mrs Huffington looked at him as if she were the one wondering whether he were crazy.

"Terrible country!" she replied, shaking her head.

"No, Mrs Huffington, I think you are being a little harsh. It's beautiful, with its mountains and woodland." Fergus was himself only drawing his knowledge from old black and white horror films he had seen in decades past, in which stage coaches broke down in the fog, stranding well-to-do passengers in the middle of deep, dark Romanian forests, only for one of them to point to a distant light, calling out in premature relief:

"A castle, we're saved!"

That, and photos of a friend's hiking holiday in Transylvania itself, on which she and her fellow walkers had been sheltered from a downpour by shepherds, who had apparently supplied them with some kind of local porridge to warm them and restore their energy levels for the journey ahead, while their ferocious sheep dogs growled menacingly outside in the rain. To Fergus, Romania had always felt a country of deep mystery and romance, but he had never been there and these were his only limited sources of information.

Mrs Huffington gave him another stare:

"I can only say it as I see it." Fearing he had upset her, he backtracked a little:

"Well, I must say you do sound a very experienced traveller."

"I am, Fergus, I am," and she gave him another knowing nod and set off again down the corridor, "have a good evening Fergus, I enjoy our little chats."

"Thank you Mrs Huffington," Fergus called after her, "so do I, and thanks again for my present too."

Once more she raised her hand in the air in acknowledgement as she trundled away, without turning round, and Fergus had a feeling that he had been dismissed. This didn't prevent a familiar wave of guilt from hitting him: here was a lonely and elderly woman, travelling on her own and, while he sought to avoid her, she had given him a gift and shared her wisdom with him. Meeting him appeared to be a minor highlight in her day, and these encounters suddenly felt like a privilege which he hadn't initially appreciated, even if her opinions were sometimes a little unexpected.

"You're a saint!" said Sylvie proudly, emerging from around the corner. "I had time to go and rinse my finger under a tap upstairs and then when I came back you were still talking!" Fergus felt a little proud of himself too, but he replied modestly:

"Actually, I like her."

After the disaster of the previous night, who knows why Fergus didn't suggest eating in the café that evening, but instead, they again made their way up to their usual restaurant. When they arrived it felt serene, quite sophisticated even, but the arachnid lady and her silent husband had yet to appear. They savoured the peace while it lasted, as did their neighbours on both sides. It was somewhere through the second course, with the serenity still intact and the table just beyond their neighbours still awaiting its occupants, that a horrible feeling began to spread through Fergus, as dream-like memories from the previous night returned to him. He began to sweat. Had he seen the arachnid lady on the ship during the course of the day? He usually did at some stage, but he couldn't recall having done so today.

"It's lovely here tonight, isn't it?" Sylvie said with a smile.

"Er, yes, yes, it is…" he replied distractedly, but Sylvie could tell something was amiss. She probed gently:

"Are you alright?"

"Yes, yes, I don't know, just a little tired I suppose… maybe I am feeling ready for home." It was another half truth. Fergus had enjoyed the cruise and could happily have stayed on board longer, but he also wasn't sorry to know that in less than forty-eight hours' time they would be safely home again. The untruthful half of what he had said to Sylvie was of course what he had not told her, the terrible dawning realisation that he may have pushed someone over board in the small hours of that morning. Sylvie knew better than to enquire further and, whilst disappointed that her husband did not appear to be enjoying this long overdue peaceful dinner, she was comfortable enough in his company to relax in it without the need for his conversation.

Afterwards, they walked on deck, Sylvie looking up at the heavens and the stars, Fergus tormenting himself with what he feared he may have done.

"It's the farewell show tonight, shall we go?"

"Yes, yes, let's," Fergus answered, without really thinking about it.

Thirty minutes later and they were in the Poseidon Theatre and, as the Cruise Director told them what a wonderful performance they were in for that night, both Fergus and Sylvie realised they had made a ghastly mistake, but, alas, by then they were committed.

"So a big welcome to the stage, ladies and gentlemen, to our wonderful comedian, Mr Wilson Wilberforce!" The audience clapped as a balding late middle aged man skipped out on stage.

"Good evening, ladies and gentlemen!"

"Good evening!" came back a self-conscious audience response.

"I said, good evening ladies and gentlemen!"

"Good evening!" the audience shouted out more loudly, with Fergus and Sylvie already sliding back in their seats.

"That's better! I'm used to people falling asleep in my act, but it's only polite to be awake at the start!" The audience roared with laughter. Sadly for Fergus and Sylvie, the comedian's first joke was his best, and the last that raised a genuine smile. Thereafter they sat – feeling increasingly awkward – while he recounted a series of lame and crude anecdotes, both of them forcing enough laughs to seek to demonstrate they weren't the prudes they were feeling, all the time wondering just how long the torture could go on.

"Wasn't he wonderful!?" The Cruise Director enthused as finally the agony was over and he left the stage. "But we have plenty more in store for you, ladies and gentlemen, yes we do! Now, most of us have seen his amazing shows during the cruise, here is one last chance to see 'Mystical Michael', our very own on board magician!"

Mystical Michael swept through the curtains, feigned a trip and immediately entered a tedious monologue which eventually ended in the worst possible way:

"So, I am looking for a volunteer!"

"Oh no!" groaned Fergus.

"A volunteer required to help me dice with death this evening, before your very eyes."

"Oh no!" The spotlight began to whirl around the audience.

"Someone with nerves of steel and the courage of a lion!"

Fergus felt disqualified on both counts and, just as the spotlight passed over him, he ran his hand anxiously through his hair.

"I saw a hand! We have our volunteer, ladies and gentlemen, let's give him a round of applause!" An eruption of clapping rose from the audience as the spotlight lingered unrelentingly on Fergus. Sylvie gave the offending hand a sympathetic squeeze, as he got up and made his way half-heartedly to the magician. His horror at what was happening to him was dominant, but, looking down from the stage, there was also in the back of his mind a curiosity that he was now seeing the theatre as seen by the singers and dancers. Sure enough, beyond the front row, faces were unrecognisable in the glare of the lights, but he consoled himself that Sylvie was out there somewhere.

"And what's your name sir?"

"Fergus."

"And where are you from Fergus?"

"Buckinghamshire."

"Ooooh, laaa de daaa!" Roars of laughter. "And are you married Fergus?"

"Yes, my wife is in the audience."

"Lovely. And do you have any children Fergus?" The question, so public with Fergus on stage and in the spotlight, was cruel... but not intentionally so. The comedian waited for the answer.

"Have you forgotten Fergus? Or perhaps you don't know!" More roars of laughter. "Come on, you can remember if you try, do you have any children?" The magician stood ready with the perfect quip for any answer but the one that finally came:

"I used to have a daughter."

The theatre fell silent and Fergus could see the panic in the magician's eyes as his response sank in.

"And where do you live Fergus?" he eventually asked.

"Buckinghamshire."

"Oh yes, we did that one. OK, so this is what we are going to do..." and the magician launched into a detailed explanation of his interminable trick. The first step was for Fergus to sign a small white cannon ball which was then loaded into a gun on one side of the stage, while, on the other, the magician made a great show of standing in exactly the right spot. Finally, opening his mouth as wide as he could, he signalled with thumbs up that everything was ready and the audience counted down:

"Three, two, one... Fire!" Fergus pulled the chord, there was a flash and a loud bang, the magician stumbled backwards, briefly putting his hands to his face and then, regaining his composure, pulled out from his mouth the small white cannon ball still marked with Fergus' name.

"Wasn't that amazing?!" The Cruise Director raved as the magician took a bow. "Ladies and gentlemen, the 'Mystical

Michael'… and a big hand for Francis too." The magician took his final bow and, glancing frostily one last time towards the man who had nearly sabotaged his wonderful act, he retreated backstage. Fergus was released and, with the spotlight now as uninterested in him as the Cruise Director who had got his name wrong, he fumbled his way back to Sylvie in the darkness and sat down. She grasped his hand again and whispered:

"I'm so sorry." He looked back at her and gave a short, resigned smile. Meanwhile, the singers and dancers had been introduced, but Fergus was still recovering and in no fit state to take them in. The truth is they were lame too, with one of the men singing a dull song, the other singers doing backing vocals, while the dancers strutted about stage in over elaborate costumes. Fergus was aware enough to know that it was pretty grim stuff, and he felt guilty towards Nicole and Holly for thinking that, whilst suspecting their hearts weren't much in this either.

"What a wonderful night, ladies and gentlemen!" concluded the Cruise Director, "one of the best that we have ever seen here in the Poseidon Theatre! Thank you for coming, enjoy the rest of the evening and, don't forget, tomorrow is our very last night and we have the crew show, you won't want to miss that!"

"The whole thing was awful, not just the last song!" Sylvie bemoaned, as she led her shell-shocked husband back to their cabin. Fergus was exhausted, as the adrenaline finally drained from his system. He had energy only to get undressed and to make a poor go of cleaning his teeth, before falling into bed.

"Are you OK?"

"Yes, I'm fine, just extremely tired." Sylvie looked across and her husband's eyes were already closed and his breathing soon grew deep. She watched him for a moment and then kissed him goodnight on the side of the head. She took her time, changing quietly and then washing slowly in the bathroom, running through the evening in her mind: her husband's quietness at dinner and his torment at the show. These thoughts were still going around her head when she turned off the light and got into bed too, but they soon dissipated as sleep overcame her and the cabin fell silent.

28

London – Monday 12th December 2016

Hannah had lived in secret with the accident for three years, only Nu had known. It had been a weight around her neck, knowing she was a killer, knowing that one day she was going to hand herself in and face the consequences, knowing that, as she went about her everyday life, there was somewhere a prison cell patiently awaiting her arrival. She deeply regretted the precious time she would have had with Nicole and Dylan, but which she would now miss in jail. She tormented herself as regards how her daughter and son would see her once they knew what she had done. She had a secret – would they still love her if they knew the truth?

"Almighty God, unto whom all hearts be open, all desires known and from whom no secrets are hid…" she prayed earnestly every Sunday, wondering for how many others in the church around her the words would be so apt?

Most of all, she kept seeing in her mind the aging couple who had been on the TV: the poor girl's parents, that hollow look in their eyes which can only stem from deeply-felt grief. Had they seen her letter? Did they understand why she had not come forward? She consoled herself that one day she would know and this torture would be over. In the meantime, whenever the despair was too great, she knew she could turn to Nu.

Only in 2013, when her daughter had safely graduated from university, did she finally confide in Nicole, looking down at the ground as she confessed, for fear of seeing horror etched across her face. When she eventually looked up, Nicole appeared stunned.

"Are you sure Mum?"

"Yes, I rewound the programme again and again… it aired on 23rd June 2010 and specifically said it was the fourth anniversary. I know that on 23rd June 2006 I side-swiped a woman walking around that corner, at the exact same time they mentioned. They even said she was a female cyclist."

"Oh, Mum, why didn't you tell me?"

"You had already lost your father. I didn't want…" She started to cry. Nicole came and sat next to her, holding her tightly. Hannah recounted her desperate visit to Nu, how she had written the letter to the police and how, once Dylan was settled, she would hand herself in.

A burden shared wasn't exactly a burden halved, but it was an immense relief to Hannah that her daughter's affections had not changed, that she wouldn't lose her. Somehow, she felt stronger for having the extra pillar of support, along with Nu. She only hoped Dylan would, one day, react the same way and that she would then have the courage to go to the police.

It took a little over three more years for both children to be safely through university and gainfully employed and then, late in 2016, Hannah finally decided the moment had come. Nicole was working on a cruise ship at the time, but had been allocated a week off just before Christmas, subsequently scheduled to rejoin the vessel again for its festive cruise. On Sunday 27th November, Hannah phoned Nicole on board the *Magdalena* to tell her that she intended to hand herself in to the police while her daughter was home. Her thinking was that they would at least have a weekend together before she did so and that, afterwards, Nicole would have a few days to understand the situation and to ensure Dylan was coping with it, before she rejoined the ship, which Hannah hoped she still might.

"Mum, please don't," Nicole begged on the phone.

"I have to... I did something terrible..."

"It was an accident..."

"I was on the pavement... a girl died..."

"Handing yourself in won't change anything..."

"Yes it will... it will give her parents some sort of justice... they may be waiting for this moment... It will give me peace."

Nicole could hear the resolution in her mother's voice.

"At least let me come with you."

"Thank you, I'd like that very much."

Hannah went on to see Nu, telling him the news too. He didn't argue, he could see that, if she had meant what she had said about giving herself up, now was as good a time as any. He promised, whatever happened, to keep an eye on Nicole and Dylan.

And so, at eleven o'clock on that Monday 12th December, Hannah and Nicole climbed the steps of Paddington Green Police Station. It felt in many ways like the most ordinary of days: grey, with a dull drizzly rain, the scene urban, with dreary buildings and busy flyovers, a nearby pneumatic drill occasionally roaring into life, drowning out the constant rush of background traffic as workmen dug another hole in the road. But, unnoticed by everyone else, the day in fact was extraordinary, it was a long anticipated date with destiny and Hannah didn't hesitate, she knew if she did her courage would desert her.

"Please can I speak to Detective Sergeant Katie Brady?"

"Er, Detective Inspector Brady... is she expecting you?"

"Kind of..." she replied, remembering the promise she had made in her letter, "My name is Hannah Webster."

The Desk Clerk looked a little unsure, but then made a phone call.

"She's on duty and will be down in a moment, please take a seat."

Mother and daughter took their places on red plastic seats opposite the front desk and waited. A clock on the wall to their right seemed to draw out time, as it stretched seconds into eternal minutes. Tick. Now and then someone, often a uniformed police officer, would emerge from a door next to the desk, cross in front of them and head out into the street. Tock. Sometimes that process would reverse and an officer would clatter in through the entrance, dripping rain water as they fumbled for a card which, with a distinct bleep, would open the door through which they would disappear into the back offices beyond, their radios crackling unintelligible messages as they went. Tick. Hannah looked around and noticed a teenage boy slouched to her left and an elderly man sitting up straight to her right, fellow human beings separated by postures and about fifty years, but both, like Hannah, waiting. Tock. The boy's eyes were glazed as he stared out in front of him, while tinny music leaked from his ear phones. Hannah watched him for a few seconds and then, afraid he would take offence, turned away – but he hadn't noticed or, if he had, he didn't care. Muffled, in the distance, she could still hear the drill as somewhere, back in the ordinary world, a hole continued to be dug.

Finally, the door opposite opened and a lady Hannah instantly recognised from the TV programme emerged. She looked around, spotted the only women waiting and asked:

"Hannah Webster?" Hannah and Nicole both stood up, "DI Brady. Come on through." They followed her through the door, Hannah wondering when she would walk back out again and, in her distraction, nearly bumping into a man bringing the desk clerk a steaming cup of tea.

"Careful there!" he said, but not angrily.

Katie, still unsure as to which of the two women might be Hannah, led them down a featureless corridor smelling of disinfectant and on to a side room, where they sat down on more red plastic chairs, these chained to the floor, either side of a table.

"So, how can I help?" Katie said, wrongly looking at the younger woman.

Hannah began to cry and Nicole held her hand tightly. She pulled herself together and spoke the lines she had rehearsed for the last six and a half years.

"On 23rd June 2006, I was riding my bicycle on the pavement along the Marylebone Road when a woman stepped out from Great Central Street. I side-swiped her with my bike, but I didn't think I had hurt her... I was wrong, I should have stopped. Four years later, on the anniversary of the accident, I saw a TV programme in which it featured, and only then did I realise I had killed her. I didn't know what to do, my husband had recently died and I had two children to take care of..." Hannah began weeping again and Nicole squeezed her hand more tightly. Composing herself quickly, before the Detective Inspector could interrupt her flow, she continued:

"... so I decided I would live with it until my children could fend for themselves, but I promised myself I'd hand myself in then. I don't know if you remember, but I wrote to you. I'm so sorry."

Katie remembered the letter well, they had tried hard to trace the sender, but there had been no clues from where it had come.

"Thank you, Mrs Webster. Please will you wait here a moment." Katie left the room, her heart racing at what she had just heard. Meanwhile, Hannah and Nicole sat there, wondering what was going to happen next. An identical clock to that by the front desk hung to one side, its second hand moving not smoothly, but marking those stretched seconds in jolts as it went around. The white walls were otherwise bare, save for a red panic strip running around the room which, just for a moment, Nicole felt an irrational urge to press. She placed her hands beneath her thighs, as if to stop herself doing so. A frosted window let in a dull light: perhaps on a brighter day sun beams could have pierced it more strongly, illuminating the wall behind them, a reminder of the outside world and a sign of remaining hope, but such was not the weather today. Nicole checked her phone – no signal.

"Well done Mum, I'm proud of you."

The die now cast, Hannah dissolved into tears again, just regaining her composure as Katie re-entered the room holding a file and some sort of machine. She placed them on the table, sat down and pulled her chair back in, scraping it along the floor in a manner which made Nicole wince.

"I do remember your letter," she said, extracting it from the file. It looked old and dog eared but Hannah recognised it immediately. "And I did try hard to find you. I'd like to ask you a few questions if I may. How do you know your accident was on 23rd June 2006?"

"Because I had an important meeting that day and I was running late, that's why. With the traffic so chaotic, I rode on the pavement," she handed over her 2006 diary with the page open at the requisite date, clearly showing the scheduled meeting. "The only thing the TV programme got wrong was saying that I was riding fast… I only wish I had been, I might have missed her. But I was riding cautiously, because I was on the pavement, that's why I didn't think I had hurt her… killed her."

"Can you remember what you were wearing that morning?"

"No, but I usually cycled in leggings, with a T-shirt and fleece, and I wore a white cycle helmet."

"Always?"

"The cycle helmet yes… the rest, well it depended on the weather, I can't remember specifically on that day."

"Can you remember the weather?"

Hannah struggled, so Katie clarified, "Was it raining for example?"

"No, no it wasn't… I remember that much."

There was a long pause while the Detective Inspector appeared to reflect on what to say next.

"Mrs Webster, we searched for you as hard as we could…" Hannah missed it, but Nicole was momentarily confused by the unexpected hint of apology in the statement. Katie opened up the machine which turned out to be a DVD player. "I should warn you, this is a little upsetting." She pressed 'Play' and CCTV footage of the corner appeared. While the image was surprisingly good, it was a little hard to see the detail because it was clearly raining quite heavily. Suddenly, a bicycle appeared at speed, heading west on the pavement along the north side of the Marylebone Road. The cyclist swerved to avoid a woman pushing a large buggy and then again to miss a street sign, but as she – and despite her dark helmet it clearly was a woman – reached the junction with Grand Central Street, she hit a pedestrian emerging from it with her head down against the rain. The cyclist just about maintained her stability, putting her foot on the ground to help her do so, but continued across the street, onto the pavement the other side and then out of shot. The woman who had been hit spun around, hopelessly sought to keep her balance and then fell, appearing to strike her head hard on the concrete as she did. She lay there motionless. Then the woman pushing the buggy appeared, rushing up and having the presence of mind to apply its brake before getting down on the ground, next to the lifeless body. She gently shook it, but seemed to know instinctively there was nothing she could do. Instead, she held her head in her hands as others quickly gathered round. Katie clicked the button marked 'Stop'.

"I don't understand," said Hannah, "that wasn't me… and it wasn't raining when I had the accident."

"She – the woman on the video I mean – was wearing a dark helmet Mrs Webster, you said yours was white. I don't know how much you have changed over the years, but she doesn't much look like you either. You say it wasn't raining when you had your accident, but it clearly is on the video. Most important though is the date. You may recall that in June 2010 a famous singer, Summer Martins, passed away, her greatest hit 'Roam' seemed to be playing everywhere for weeks, perhaps you remember that?"

Hannah nodded, but didn't understand the relevance.

"They made a tribute programme for her which aired on the 21st June... it was felt appropriate apparently, because it was Midsummer's Day... but it meant our programme went out two days later than originally scheduled, on the 23rd. It was pre-recorded and, to be honest, nobody considered, before it was shown, that the reference to the fourth anniversary would be wrong; nobody noticed that we hadn't actually specified the date. In fact, the accident was four years and two days earlier... we did try to find you Mrs Webster, honestly."

Hannah sat silently while the implication sank in. More than six years ago, a TV programme had transformed her instantly from an ordinary person into a killer, today the reverse process had been just as sudden and just as unexpected.

"Mum, it wasn't you! It wasn't you!" Nicole cried, throwing her arms around her mother. But Hannah was still trying to take it in – six and a half years of guilt and inner torment and she wasn't a killer after all. In the deepest recesses of her mind she even thought she remembered, on the day, having cycled past a yellow police sign appealing for witnesses to an accident, but she couldn't be sure and it was so long ago that she had not taken in its significance.

"Did you ever catch her?" she eventually asked.

"No, I'm afraid not." Katie replied.

"And the girl's parents... how are they?"

"They are coping... we stay in touch." She paused. "Actually, they have been worrying about you; they will be pleased you finally came forward."

"But I was riding on the pavement, how can they have been worried about me when someone doing the same thing killed their daughter?"

"Six years of torment is a heavy penalty for something hundreds of cyclists do every day in London alone. You said yourself, you were riding carefully, plus it wasn't raining. I mean I am not excusing it, you did brush against someone and, yes, you should have stopped, but perhaps it's because you were riding slowly that she wasn't hurt."

"I have wasted so much of your time, I'm sorry."

"It's OK… it really is, I knew as soon as I read the letter that it wasn't you. The dates didn't match. Also, to our surprise, we were able to find your CCTV too, from the 23rd. It should have been wiped but, by chance, it wasn't." Katie switched disks and pressed 'Play' again. Hannah saw herself pedalling, indeed fairly cautiously, along the pavement and swiping a woman who was rushing out of Grand Central Street while talking on her mobile phone. She could be seen glimpsing back briefly as the woman spun half way round with the momentum of the encounter, fleetingly looking as though she might lose her balance, but regaining it quickly, then shouting and gesturing angrily after Hannah, who by now had cycled out of sight. Katie pressed 'Stop' again and they sat in silence for a full minute, before Hannah spoke:

"I know it sounds strange, but I have spent so much time thinking about the parents… I almost feel I know them. Could you please pass on my condolences, their daughter looked a beautiful girl."

"I'll do that… time to restart your own life?"

Going in to speak with the Detective Inspector, Hannah had wondered when she would emerge again out of that door leading back to the front desk. She had feared it would be hours, days even, or worse that she wouldn't at all, instead leaving the police station from some rear exit in a prison van. It had in fact only taken a revolutionary twenty-six minutes. The teenager and the elderly man were still there, waiting patiently, almost meditatively, and the desk clerk was knocking back the last drops of tea from the same cup she had been given when they had gone through.

"All done?" she asked with a smile.

"All done," they replied in unison.

Outside, both the drilling and the rain had stopped, but the sky remained dull and the scene remorselessly urban, its soundtrack still that of city traffic and sirens... but to Hannah and Nicole it seemed that they had emerged into a completely different world and – as if on a stage before it, hugging each other on the police station steps – it felt a much better one.

29

Bay of Biscay – Friday 9ᵗʰ December 2016

For the third morning in a row, Fergus awoke in the early
hours and lay restless in bed with the events of the previous
evening spinning in his mind: yes, the waking nightmare with
the magician on stage had been bad, but worse had been his
realisation that he might be a murderer... an intended slaying,
an act more wicked, more criminal even, than the death of
Justine, as that at least had been in part an accident, even if the
cyclist hadn't had the conscience to stop. He also felt disturbed
by the idea of sinister, orange clad monks padding about the
ship in the wee small hours of the morning and he wracked his
brain in search of an explanation, but it never came.

He got dressed and put his head out of the door, looking
left then right, up and down the corridor. No sign of life.
He ventured out and began his nocturnal wanderings, his
enjoyment of the still and quiet of a deserted ship calming his
mind, temporarily freeing him from the anxiety and worries
which had been his dominating thoughts. Bars, lounges, public
rooms, all empty, save for those ghosts of passengers past. It
was eerie, but also very appealing and he was aware again that

there had to be many areas of the ship to which he did not even have access: crew quarters, kitchens, laundries, engine rooms, holds, a brig maybe – secret places passengers never saw, but from which mysterious monks could emerge when everyone else was asleep, and into which they could subsequently retreat before anyone awoke.

Fergus opened the heavy door leading outdoors, stepped through it and headed towards the windy bow from where, once more, he looked up at the stars, this time completely alone. He wanted to pray, but he didn't know what to pray for: for forgiveness for killing the arachnid lady, or for a miracle that he might not have done so? He had already experienced one miracle in Lancashire, would two in a lifetime be asking too much? Perhaps this is how the poor, anonymous woman felt who had written to Katie all those years ago, thinking she had been responsible for killing Justine. God, how had she lived with that thought in the more than six years now since the TV programme had aired? A ship's lights glimmered distantly on the horizon ahead.

Suddenly, Fergus became aware of someone approaching, startled, he quickly looked around: it was Nicole, her auburn hair blowing out in the wind.

"Can't sleep…" but she said it in a way which left him unsure as to whether it was a question or a statement. He decided to answer with a smile, after which they both stood together by the rail for a couple of minutes, gazing into the void. Eventually she said:

"I must say you looked a bit anxious in the audience the other night, when I was singing?"

"Yes," he admitted… "I suppose I got myself feeling rather intense."

"It happens," she replied philosophically.

"There were lots of reasons, it was partly your voice… along with the song of course: together they made for a powerful combination. But I also have a lot on my mind. Anyway, you seemed rather intense that night too."

"I suppose that's also why I am up at three o'clock in the morning..." she smiled, "but I think there was a compliment in what you were saying and, if so, thank you."

"Would you like me to ask why you were – still are – feeling a little uptight?" he enquired.

"Would you like me to ask you the other reasons why you are?"

"Not really," Fergus admitted.

"Me neither," she replied.

They stood in silence for a full five minutes. For a moment, Fergus worried whether Nicole might be in danger, whether he truly was mad and might in that insanity tip her overboard too. Even though he knew it wasn't true, it was a terrifying vision and he gripped the rail tightly as if to anchor his hands. After a while, it was she who spoke:

"I witnessed from backstage what happened with the magician last night..."

"I guess that is one of the other reasons I'm feeling a bit on edge."

"I'm sorry... do you mind if I ask what her name was, your daughter I mean?"

"Justine... her name was Justine."

It was a slight shock to Nicole: in three days' time she would go to a police station, accompanying her mother, who would confess her responsibility for the death of a Justine. The name wasn't common, but it was sufficiently so that she didn't think to make an actual connection.

"I think she had a very caring father... really I do, life isn't all about its length... oh God, I hope that wasn't trite..."

"It wasn't," Fergus replied reassuringly... "and thank you for saying such kind things."

She wanted to give him a hug, she wanted to tell him all

about her mother, how scared she was for her, how devastated she was to think that the woman she loved was responsible for another girl's death, that she would be going to prison. Instead, she simply said:

"Try to get some sleep."

"I will, you too… and, your singing has been…" he got stuck for an adjective that didn't sound corny.

"I'm going to choose 'wonderful'," she interjected, with another of her smiles.

"Yes, 'wonderful'. It's comforting to know that there are young people out there doing what they love… I may not see her again, so will you say goodbye to Holly for me too. She's also been very kind."

"I will, I promise," she risked a peck on his cheek and headed off into the night. Fergus waited there another ten minutes or so digesting the encounter, before heading inside himself, creeping back into the cabin so as not to disturb his sleeping wife and then falling, fully clothed, into bed.

In the morning, Sylvie woke first and was surprised to find her husband sound asleep, apparently with his clothes over his pyjamas. When he woke too, he explained that he had been unable to sleep and so had gone for a walk. He wasn't sure why, but he didn't mention Nicole.

"Wasn't it a bit creepy?" she asked.

"Atmospheric, I would say."

They got ready for their last relaxed breakfast gazing out over the Atlantic and then eventually made their way out on deck to read, wrapping themselves up thoroughly now against the growing chill. It was an 'everything for the last time' day, including the Captain's noon announcement and his standard guidance on hand washing.

"If we haven't got the 'hygiene advices' by now, then I can't help thinking it's a little late!" remarked Sylvie.

"And he could have said something to acknowledge it's our

257

last day on board…" Fergus answered. It was a fair point, but he felt weaselly saying it, remembering the Captain's kindly face.

"I suspect we are cargo to him, to be offloaded tomorrow, after which the same 'hygiene advices' will be given to the next passengers. He probably won't even notice the difference. He has kept us safe though."

"That's true," Fergus conceded appreciatively.

They ate their usual light lunch and then he went for a wander, while Sylvie retreated to the cabin to start packing. The purpose of his walk was twofold: to say a mental farewell to the ship that had been their home for nearly three weeks and also to see whether, after all, he could spot the arachnid lady. He wandered each deck in turn, but she was nowhere to be found. Eventually, he returned to the cabin where Sylvie's half-packed case lay on her bed, but she herself was absent. He decided to resume his search for the arachnid lady, whilst keeping an eye out for his wife too. Gradually, as he wandered around, the priority became his wife, where was she? In none of the usual places that was for sure: not in their alcoves out on deck, nor the Midships Lounge where the string trio were again playing softly; not in any of the other public rooms where various quizzes, karaokes and bingo games were taking place; nor either in the comfort of the Poseidon Theatre, where the criminology lecturer, draining the whisky from his glass, had just finished his presentation on *the forensics of blood splattering* and where a queue was gathering for the line dancing class to follow. Fergus began to feel a further layer of anxiety forming on top of those for the missing arachnid lady, the magician and the orange robed monks.

In his distress, he hurried down to Reception and asked if they would put a call out for Sylvie. They were reluctant at first, not liking constant announcements being broadcast across the ship, but they could see his anguish and eventually agreed.

"*Ladies and gentlemen, a passenger announcement. Please*

would Mrs Sylvie Fredricks come to Reception on Deck 6. That's Mrs Sylvie Fredricks to Reception please. Thank you."

He waited fifteen minutes, but she did not arrive and his agitation grew worse. What he didn't realise was that he was taking part in his own French farce: he twice walked into rooms his wife had only just left; as he impatiently gave up waiting for her at their usual place towards the stern of the ship so she, three minutes later, sat down there waiting for him; when the announcement for her to attend Reception rang out she was in the hubbub of the laundry room, re-ironing a blouse to wear for their final dinner.

After three hours of searching and numerous returns to the cabin, Fergus was frantic: this couldn't be happening! His head throbbed and his anxieties were overwhelming him, as he stumbled ever more desperately about the *Magdalena*. Sylvie was all he had: please God he hadn't lost her too! Please God he hadn't murdered the arachnid lady! Please God there wasn't a sinister cult prowling the ship! Please God Justine wasn't dead! His mind reeled with worry as he staggered once again past the pot plants of Millionaire's Row – the walls of which seemed to be pulsing in towards him as he went – before working his way back down to search the lower decks one last desperate time, but still no sign. He feared he was going to be sick.

"Why hello there Fergus, whatever is the matter with you?"

"I'm sorry Mrs Huffington, I'm really not feeling very well, I can't find my wife, I think I've lost her!"

"Why Fergus, calm down, you can't lose someone for long on a ship..."

"Thank you, thank you Mrs Huffington, but please I really can't stop, I have to find her." He climbed back up another set of stairs and went outside to have a further look on deck.

"Irish coffee sir!" one of the waiters commanded more than asked, as Fergus emerged out of the door...

"No, no, I'm looking for my wife..."

"Very warming sir, you can get one for her too… I have them ready here…"

"No, no, I can't stop…"

"But they are two for the price of one sir and very…" but Fergus had moved out of range as his increasingly panicked search continued and mental images of her falling overboard became ever more vivid… she and the arachnid lady, both somewhere in the Atlantic, either rolling face down on its surface or sinking down into its depths. There was nothing for it, he had to go back to Reception and get them to turn the ship around, so they could look for her and perhaps still launch a rescue…

He made his way there, but before he reached it a man rushed up to him:

"Sir, sir, good news…" Fergus saw a moment of hope and waited impatiently for the man to continue:

"You can now buy three cruise videos for the price of two… one for you, one for your family, one for your friends…"

Fergus' mind reeled in bewilderment and frustration, it was almost too much, but he quickly refocussed on his goal and, with the video man clipping at his heels and reducing the price further with every step, he staggered on to Reception. When she looked up, the smart, young woman working there was startled to see what appeared to be a man in the middle of a nervous breakdown, leaning over the counter towards her:

"It's my wife, it's my wife… I can't find her anywhere, I've been looking everywhere! I think she must have fallen overboard… I can't find her. She must have fallen overboard, you need to turn the ship round, you must turn the ship round and start looking for her. Please, you must do it now!"

From behind him: "Fergus?"

He spun around.

"Where have you been Fergus, I've been looking for you all over the ship?"

He stared for a moment in disbelief and then flung his arms around her:

"Oh Sylvie, Sylvie, I thought I had lost you. I couldn't bear it," he sobbed. She let him hug her for a few seconds, then gently pushed him back.

"I'm fine, but how have you managed to get yourself in such a state?"

"I couldn't find you anywhere... I looked and I looked all afternoon, they even put calls out for you. I thought..." hesitating because it now sounded so ridiculous, "I thought you had fallen overboard."

"I'm fine Fergus, I'm here. There's nothing to worry about." She drew him in for another hug and as she did so, over her shoulder, he saw the arachnid lady emerging from one of the little shops across the hallway. A second flow of relief cascaded through his body and his legs nearly gave way beneath him. The receptionist quickly brought round a chair and he sat down, with Sylvie kneeling in front of him and holding his hands.

"Sweetheart it's OK, everything is OK..."

"Would you like me to call the ship's doctor?" The receptionist asked as gently as she could.

"No, no, I'm sure that won't be necessary," Sylvie replied.

"Would you still like us to turn the ship around?" The video man asked sarcastically.

"No, that won't be necessary either, thank you."

She helped her husband back up and tenderly led him to the cabin, where the whole history came out: how scared he had been, and how he had also feared that he may have murdered that awful woman, that's why he had been so quiet at dinner the previous evening.

"Fergus, you are a crazy, crazy man!"

"And that's not all, there is a sinister group of hooded, orange robed monks wandering the ship at night!"

"What?" she cried in amazement at the further evidence of madness emanating from the man she loved.

"They wander the ship in the small hours before disappearing back somewhere deep in the hull, so they are out of sight when people are about… I've seen them, twice!" Sylvie thought it was time to calm things down, so she stared him solidly in the eye and said:

"Fergus, there will be an explanation, there was for the arachnid lady, there was for me… there will be for this too. I can promise you there is not some sinister cult on board this ship…"

"But…"

"No, there is no sinister cult on board the ship. There will be an explanation for the…" she could hardly bring herself to say it "… for the monks!"

Fergus again felt exhausted and lay down on his bed, falling asleep and catching up on the two hours' sleep which he had lost the previous night. When he awoke he saw Sylvie sitting in a chair, deep in her e-reader. He watched her intently for a few moments and perhaps she sensed it because she looked up.

"Back in the world of the living?"

"I made a fool of myself… sorry."

"With you it's never dull!" she smiled back.

They didn't have much time for a pre-dinner drink, so preferred instead to get ready at leisure for the meal itself. As, a little later, they entered the restaurant – the Maitre D' nonchalantly squirting hand sanitiser into their palms for a final time – the arachnid lady was already there at her table, with her husband. She appeared somehow much less spidery, even her eyes were less red, with perhaps just a tint of pink remaining.

"Sorry we weren't here last night," her husband said (so he spoke!), "but Dorothy…" (so that was her name!) "… has had a bug and a painful dose of conjunctivitis into the bargain. We decided to eat in, in fact we've been in the cabin most of the last two days… not the happiest end to a cruise."

"Oh, I'm so sorry," replied Sylvie with genuine kindness, then slightly less truthfully, "yes, we missed you," though Fergus supposed it was true in a way, at least for him.

"We were wather worwied Dorothy," Gentle Henry called across from his table, his face etched with a deep concern.

Fergus felt ashamed. As he looked at the couple now, all his animosity towards them had been punctured: they looked ordinary, slightly sad even and, to his astonishment, he felt pity. What, he wondered, was their hidden history, what difficulties and disasters in life had they overcome? While he had been despising her, how many people out there cared for her deeply, perhaps even loved her? He hoped many but, observing her husband, he knew for sure that there was at least one. He looked at Sylvie: sometimes one was enough.

"Perhaps it was me not her, perhaps I was the monster all the time?" He whispered reflectively as everyone settled down to their meals. Sylvie reached out her right hand and, placing it on his left, replied:

"Sometimes there are unseen monsters, but sometimes we see them where there are none... she's not one Fergus, and neither are you – my extraordinary husband – you are all too human: wonderfully, infuriatingly, eccentrically, uniquely human... just like the rest of us."

An uncharacteristic quiet befell the restaurant, just the clatter of cutlery on plates and, at the side of the room, the noise of a drawer opening and closing by itself to the rhythm of the rolling ship, until, after a few moments, a waiter latched it shut. Though it was the same restaurant where Fergus had worked himself up into such a state on previous nights, it felt very different now and perhaps this, their last dinner, was the one they most enjoyed: relaxing in each other's company, over good food and a final bottle of deep red Merlot. As the ship rocked them soothingly side to side, they felt at peace, both content to know that the next day they would see their home again.

At the end of the meal they had their photo taken with Angelo who hugged Sylvie fondly and shook Fergus' hand with a beaming smile.

"I hope you enjoyed your holiday?"

"Very much, thank you for taking care of us so well," Sylvie replied.

"Yes, thank you Angelo, you did a great job… we hope you enjoy your well-earned holiday when it comes too," Fergus added.

"Only 266 breakfasts, 266 lunches and 266 dinners to go!" He called after them as they left.

They headed up to the Conservatory Bar for a final Pimm's, while quietly pondering Angelo's simple, optimistic outlook on life.

"Are you too traumatised for the crew show tonight?" Sylvie asked.

"I've recovered," Fergus replied, "but let's not sit at the front, just to play safe."

And so, for one last time, they found themselves in the Poseidon Theatre as the lights went down and the show began, this time with the ship's crew the stars. It was a lively performance, done with humour and good spirit. Fergus and Sylvie felt especially touched by several acts which featured staff demonstrating traditional dances from their various distant corners of the world, including their homesick waitress who danced gracefully with five colleagues, transporting them briefly to the palm beaches of the Philippines.

"And now ladies and gentlemen… when they find time to practise I really can't imagine, but be prepared to be dazzled and amazed by the skill and athleticism of our engine room team, as we introduce… 'The Shaolin Monks of the *Magdalena*'!"

From each side of the stage burst five orange robed monks, brandishing swords which they immediately began spinning above their heads, the polished metal glistening in the stage lights, while drums beat out from deep within the orchestra. Then four of the monks dropped their weapons and proceeded to feign kung-fu fighting as, with ferocious leaps and cries, they exchanged dramatic but ultimately harmless blows. Suddenly, the remaining six took over, somersaulting and vaulting across the stage, chopping planks of wood with their bare hands and, in two cases, with their heads. The beat intensified and now all ten, facing the audience in one long line, started throwing extravagant kicks and punches until finally, with an enormous crash of drums, they all leapt high into the air and shrieked wildly, landing in a crouched position as a gong sounded.

"Ladies and gentlemen, 'The Shaolin Monks of the *Magdalena*'!" The audience roared with delight while, for a few moments, visibly catching their breath, the monks stared out intensely from the stage, before finally standing up and breaking into the broadest of smiles.

"What did I tell you?" Sylvie said to her husband as they applauded.

"You told me there would be an explanation… and you were right. Sylvie, you are always right."

"Usually, yes," she grinned.

All the performers returned to the stage to sing one last medley together, culminating in the whole theatre joining in an arm-waving rendition of a nostalgic old song. Perhaps, on any other evening, Fergus and Sylvie might have found this embarrassing, but somehow tonight they were carefree and their hands were soon high in the air, swaying side to side in time with the music, along with the forest of arms around them and, as the song reached its climax, Fergus felt a surge of elation. It wouldn't last of course, he realised that, but he did wonder whether something might finally have lifted more permanently – not entirely, but at least in some measure – something that had weighed him down ever since Thames Valley Police had unexpectedly visited them, just over a decade earlier.

It had been threatening to rain on that Midsummer's Day all those years ago, and they had both been indoors at the back of the house, so neither had heard the car approaching. Sylvie had just returned from shopping and was busy unpacking in the kitchen: vegetable lasagne was a family favourite but it involved such a lot of preparation, and so many ingredients – she felt sure she had forgotten something. It had been Fergus, therefore, who had put down his work and gone to answer the knock at the door.

"Mr Fredricks?"

Seeing the police officers there, Fergus had briefly wondered what he might have done wrong, but a far worse possibility quickly came to mind.

"May we come in?"

Given everything else that happened that terrible day, it is strange how he remembered the detail but, as he stepped aside to let them through, he distinctly recalled noticing the first heavy drops splashing on the ground, as if a prelude to the storm which followed.

It sometimes felt to him as though it had been raining ever since and, in truth, he had never much wanted it to stop. Now however, in the Poseidon Theatre, waving his arms to a nostalgic old song, Fergus, for the first time, was no longer sure that it always needed to rain quite so hard.

30

Norfolk – Late September 2015

Jones stood with his best man, Ben, at the front of the little church in Samantha's home Norfolk village, nervously waiting for her to arrive. It had felt a long road to get there, not physically, but through life... and there had been casualties along the way. He had always thought that he would have doubts about marriage and its lifelong commitment, but, now that the moment had come, he had none and he didn't think his fiancée did either, though that didn't stop him praying hard that she would turn up.

After he had met Justine's parents on his plane nearly two years earlier, he had kept his promise, visiting them in March the following year. It had felt strange to drive through the local lanes again, to turn between the hedges into the driveway and to see the familiar house ahead of him, looking just as it always had, staring back at him as if to say "where have you been?" to a returning prodigal son. He had stopped for a moment, gazing up to the woodland on the right where, the first time he had visited, Justine had made him wait patiently to see the badgers. He looked back at the house, half expecting to see the sentinel fox lingering there, washing himself nonchalantly, just as much at home as any of the Fredricks family themselves. But it wasn't. For an instant Jones had again felt overwhelmingly sad, but he quickly rallied and continued slowly down the drive, his tyres crunching on the gravel, just as they had all those years before.

He parked and stretched his legs while, high above, two red kites had danced and circled around each other in the March winds, as if in ecstasy at the turning of the seasons and the prospect of the three warmer ones ahead. The place was as magical as ever and the front door opened welcomingly before he even reached it, Justine's parents emerging to meet him as he walked up.

"It's so good to be back!" he said.

"It's good to have you back Jones," Fergus replied.

With coats on, the weather had been fine enough to sit outside while they caught up with each other's news over tea and sandwiches. Unguarded serviettes repeatedly made breaks for freedom, requiring one of the three of them to get up and chase them round the lawn, whilst the other two kept half an eye on the skies above, lest their luck ran out and they needed to make a rapid transfer indoors. Against this very English setting, Fergus and Sylvie were fascinated to hear how Jones had gained his wings and all about his life as a pilot, but he also had something else on his mind and he wondered how best to broach it with them.

"I hope you know how much I loved Freddie..." he said, rather unexpectedly changing the subject. "I didn't have another girlfriend for years. I mean, I didn't want one. But, the thing is..." he paused, contemplating how to finish the sentence, but Sylvie did it for him:

"You've found someone now?"

"Yes," he said a little sheepishly.

"Oh Jones, but that's wonderful!"

"Really? You mean it Sylvie? I can't help feeling I am betraying Freddie…"

"Jones, sometimes it feels to Sylvie and me as if she's still here, she was so much a part of this place. Of us. But we have had to come to terms with the fact that she has gone… physically at least. Having a ghost for a girlfriend wouldn't be easy and we wouldn't ask you to do it, nor would Justine, our daughter was better than that."

Fergus' words were both logical and kind, even if they alone weren't enough to relieve the guilt Jones was feeling as he sought to let go of someone he had loved. That was a process he had to work through himself, although what he had just heard would help. For a moment, he feared a tear might escape from his eye, but he was determined it wouldn't and so kept his response succinct:

"I'll never forget her."

"We know," Sylvie answered, equally decisively, "but you mustn't have so big a place for her in your heart that you don't have room for anyone else; you mustn't remember her so much that you live with her in the past rather than with…"

"Samantha."

"… with Samantha in the present and hopefully in a long, happy future. You deserve it and Justine would want it. It's for parents to dwell in the past, not young men."

They sat a while without words, the place really was as idyllic as ever it had been, surely Justine would come rushing out of the door at any moment, calling out "Surprise!" and dragging him off, rambling across her adored Chiltern countryside. But the minutes ticked by and she didn't. Then, as if to break the spell, their luck finally had run out, the clouds darkening the sky, the kites overhead wheeling against increasingly blustery gusts and the first spots of rain falling against their faces, as they packed everything up and rushed back indoors, just in time to avoid the shower which followed.

Since then, Jones had called in on them every six months or so. They never expected him to visit, but they always enjoyed it when he did, and he was amazed how easily he slipped back into being with them and by how interested they remained in his life. Sometimes, he wondered whether they were seeking a glimpse into an existence of which they might have been a part, had things been different, and he was always happy to share his news. He never took Samantha: he didn't hide them from her, she knew everything, but taking her may have been a little too painful for them. He had wondered whether they would accept the wedding invitation and their "yes" had meant a great deal. Now, as he waited at the front of the church, it felt good to know that they were there, somewhere in the crowded pews behind.

The wedding preparations had been smooth, the only hitch having been a minor incident that very morning. The ladies of the flower rota had spent most of the previous day arranging their displays on pedestals, window sills and pew ends, only for Mrs Snellgrove to tweak them on the day of the wedding itself, even removing some of the roses so that there would be space for her to show off her gladioli. The other ladies, on discovering this, had been outraged and it had been down to Samantha's mother to play the arbitrator, finding a compromise by which some of the roses were returned and some of the gladioli removed, restoring peace just before the first guests had arrived. Her daughter and future son-in-law were to remain forever oblivious of this little local drama that had briefly threatened their big day. Only Samantha fleetingly puzzled, as she stood peeking into the church from the porch, as to why Mrs Snellgrove had such a large bunch of vibrant gladioli on her lap.

However, she did not have time to ponder this long, as suddenly the organ struck up the first chords of Mendelssohn's "Wedding March", the congregation stood to their feet and, at the front, Jones and Ben instinctively turned round. Her father at her side, she stepped into the church and proceeded down the aisle, her twin six year old nieces Lucy and Catherine behind her as bridesmaids. Bringing up the rear Jones could just spot Gabriel, Samantha's five year old nephew, trailing slightly behind the others as he looked all around from beneath a disproportionately large top hat.

Hymns were sung, vows exchanged, prayers said, registers signed and forty-five minutes later they were married, with confetti raining down upon them as they left the church to the pealing of bells, in the brilliant late-summer sunshine.

Afterwards, at the reception in a nearby hotel, Jones again felt nervous as he waited to give his speech. He had wanted to include an old girlfriend in it, but somehow that had felt wrong, unfair on the woman he was marrying and whose father was now proudly concluding his own words by raising a toast to the bride and groom. And so Jones' moment finally came and, as he stood up, he sneaked a last courage bolstering sip of champagne.

"Ladies and gentlemen, I will keep this brief..."

The guests, all in their finest attire, sat in front of him around ten tables which were littered with empty plates and coffee cups. Wine glasses were also mainly drained now, but champagne flutes had been topped up and were, once again, at the ready. Everyone was looking at him, even the hotel staff standing around the sides of the room. He tried to take the scene in: it felt slightly surreal that this was his wedding. He thanked Samantha's parents for making the arrangements and Samantha herself for marrying him, spending then a few minutes recounting when they had first met and how their relationship had grown, culminating in today, the happiest of his life.

As he spoke, he realised his lungs were too full and he was in danger of shallow breathing, so he paused while he let himself exhale fully, before taking another slow, deep breath. As he did so, he looked around and, to his amazement, all eyes were still fixed on him, he was holding their attention; only one of the bridesmaids – he couldn't tell which – seemed uninterested, more focussed on finishing off with her fingers a plate of strawberry meringue left over by her father.

"Some of you may know…" he continued, *"I lost someone nine years ago, someone whose memory will always be dear to me, but then I found Samantha…"*

He noticed the bridesmaid abandoning the plate and burying her head in the lap of her mother, who gently stroked her daughter's hair whilst keeping her own focus on Jones, as he spoke from the top table. He wondered whether the little girl had perhaps overdone it on the dessert. Taking another deep breath, he continued with his speech, describing how he and Samantha both had their dream careers and had purchased a small home, how everything now finally seemed very much 'for better' rather than 'for worse', and how they felt equipped to deal with whatever life threw in their direction.

Nearly there, and Jones took a final pause before asking the whole room to be upstanding for his toast to Gabriel and the bridesmaids. This seemed to catch everyone by surprise and he waited as they rose to their feet, a process which felt as though it took forever and which was surprisingly noisy too, as his guests heaved themselves back out of their chairs. But Jones held his nerve and finally, when everybody was ready, he lifted his glass and called out:

"Ladies and gentlemen – Lucy, Catherine and Gabriel!"

"Lucy, Catherine and Gabriel!" came back a hundred voices and, as the three young children looked up at this cacophonous calling of their names, so Jones sat back down, relieved: his speech had gone well, so long as his wife had not been upset by the fleeting reference on her own wedding day to a previous love. He turned to her to try to read her expression, but, before he could do so, she kissed him.

"Was the *'someone whose memory will always be dear to me'*

line too strong?" Jones nervously asked her later, when they were briefly alone.

"It was honest, it was kind. It was a gift for her parents who were here in the room. I married a good person!"

Jones hoped so. He knew his wife and her generosity, but it had still been reckless for him to say it. However, he had wanted to do so, firstly because it was true, secondly because, if somehow she was there, he wanted Justine to hear it, and thirdly, as Samantha had insightfully spotted, it was a gift.

A short while after he and his new bride had finished their first dance, Jones noticed Fergus and Sylvie at the back of the room, in deep conversation with an earnest looking Gabriel, both of them nodding back seriously in agreement with whatever it was the little boy was saying. Eventually, he ran off, top hat in hand, leaving them very much on their own in the otherwise crowded room. Jones walked across and Fergus smiled as he saw him approaching:

"Hello there, we have just been learning all about the dinosaurs… it seems we have a young scientist in our midst!"

"Well, I suppose good weddings should also be educational!" Jones laughed in reply, "Thank you for coming."

"We wanted to."

A pregnant pause followed, all three knowing there was something important that could be said, but none of them quite sure what it was or how to say it.

"I'm sorry, I didn't feel I could mention Freddie by name…" Jones eventually apologised, aware that, having excused himself to Samantha for bringing her up at all, he was now feeling guilty for the brevity of his reference to Justine, in what had otherwise turned out to be quite a lengthy speech.

"We were so touched Jones, thank you." Sylvie brushed his cheek with the back of her hand and gave him a kiss.

"I love Samantha, but I will never ever forget Freddie… I promise."

"We know," Fergus answered, "you've told us before: on the plane, at the house, even in your wedding speech! We believe you, you don't need to say it anymore. Be happy that we are happy for you, and that Justine would be too."

"Thank you, I will." He smiled, and a few moments later, seeing an opportunity, introduced them to his nearby parents, whom they had twice met many years previously, when he and Justine had been together.

"You remember Fergus and Sylvie, Freddie's parents?"

"Of course we do…"

Their conversation seemed to take off easily and Jones let their words melt away as he surveyed his wedding scene once again. Many of the men had done away with their ties by now, a few of the women had even discarded their shoes, and everyone looked rather less pristine than they had in the church a few hours earlier – this was a good sign.

While some guests still sat at tables with their drinks, others stood around the room chatting, many were on the dance floor. Through the crowd he spotted Samantha with Gabriel: they were facing each other and holding hands, she seeking, only with limited success, to teach him to step from side to side in time with the music. He was shrieking with laughter and occasionally jumped with the excitement of it all, whereupon he would immediately lose the rhythm and they would have to start over again. She looked serene and relaxed. All had gone perfectly and Jones felt the relief sweep through him: he was happy.

Later in the evening, the celebrations still in full swing, Jones again looked for Fergus and Sylvie, but they had already slipped away.

31

Southampton – Saturday 10th December 2016

Fergus and Sylvie returned to their cabin shortly after midnight. She had already finished packing, but he, on account of his mini-breakdown, had barely begun. However, he was feeling light and relaxed: a few hours ago it had been as though his world were caving in, but all his anxieties one by one had been addressed, until now he was finally at peace.

The process was for everyone to pack and then leave their bags and cases outside their cabins. These would be picked up during the small hours and, on arrival in Southampton, transported to the baggage hall of the terminal, leaving passengers to walk off the ship with just the hand luggage they had needed for the night. Fergus threw everything into his case and put it out in the corridor with Sylvie's, then he washed, undressed and fell into bed. Within moments he was asleep and, for once, he was to slumber soundly through the night.

Sylvie was also exhausted and desperate for bed. She was mildly irritated therefore, with her husband already snoring softly, to see he had forgotten to pack some clothes he had left slung over a chair. She took them out into the corridor, stuffed them into his suitcase, without making a pretence of folding them, and then collapsed into bed herself, and into a sleep to rival that of her husband.

And so, with its human cargo dreaming contentedly, the *Magdalena* made its final journey up the English Channel, around the Isle of Wight and into the Solent, docking back in the same Southampton berth it had left three weeks previously.

Despite the occasional annoyance, the cruise company had treated them well throughout the holiday, but there was little doubting that their sole aim on disembarkation day was to get everyone off as quickly and efficiently as possible, so they could prepare to board the next passengers that afternoon. Breakfast was ninety minutes earlier than usual, between half six and half eight. Sylvie had set the alarm for seven, but she allowed Fergus to sleep on while she washed and dressed. Eventually, she drew the curtains: after so much open ocean and fresh air, it was depressing to see concrete structures, cranes and piers through the ill-lit gloom of an English early December morning. Southampton dock was quite the least inspiring of their whole itinerary, but maybe she was biased.

"Wakey wakey!" she said softly to her husband, ruffling his hair again. Slowly, like a child not wanting to get up to go to school, he came to and reluctantly heaved himself out of bed and into the bathroom, while she surveyed the cabin making sure nothing was forgotten. Fergus emerged and, looking around, appeared confused.

"Where are my clothes?"

"Probably where you left them," Sylvie retorted rather unhelpfully.

"I thought I left them on the chair," he scratched his head, opening an empty wardrobe. Suddenly it dawned on Sylvie what she had done. She rushed across to the cabin door but on opening it, whereas last night it had been lined with dozens upon dozens of bags, the corridor was completely empty.

"I think I just might have packed them last night!"

"What do you mean?"

"I was so tired, I wasn't thinking. I saw you hadn't packed some clothes and so I put them in your case before going to bed... I'm sorry."

"What am I going to do? I've got my pyjamas and..." he opened a drawer "... a pair of socks, underpants and shoes... I even packed my dressing gown. I can't leave the ship in my pyjamas!"

"It's quite a predicament..." Sylvie conceded. There were a few seconds' silence while they looked at each other wondering what to do, then she continued: "Now I'm certain this must happen all the time... I'll just go to Reception and see what they suggest. Don't worry, I'm sure we'll laugh about this." Funnily enough, Fergus did laugh and when he laughed she felt free to do so too.

"I'll be back," she said as she slipped out of the door.

Fergus sat on the bed and looked out through the picture window at the murky British morning, realising he didn't much care about his clothes: he'd happily disembark dressed like this, except for the fact it looked cold out there. Overall, it had been a good holiday, especially the sea days and the less frequented islands they had visited before the Canaries. Thereafter things had deteriorated rather, but most of the bad stuff had been, despite all his meditations, things going on only in his head. All the problems he had had the previous day had evaporated, all except for the most painful one:

"I miss you so much Justine," he said to the empty cabin.

After a moment, another guilt came upon him: Justine had died young, at twenty-four, but what an idyllic life she had led! Unbelievable though it seemed, there were greater, more recent, sometimes less mourned tragedies: drowned infants pulled out of the Mediterranean; blameless children killed in adult wars; photos of innocent, cheeky little faces staring out of newspapers, taken before some wickedness befell them. How many billions of personal tragedies had there ever been in the world, most of them untold, but all of them felt deeply by someone, somewhere, sometime? Where amongst this pantheon of disasters did Justine's accident lie? She had lived and she had lived well: happily, beautifully, surrounded by love and doing things she loved doing. She had lived: sometimes that was almost enough for Fergus, nobody could ever take that away – she had lived. And as for him and Sylvie? Well, their lives would go on, diminished yes and not the lives they had planned or hoped for, but precious none the less, and together. Walking off the ship in his pyjamas suddenly felt unimportant and he had an overpowering urge to do so, to get back to the place where, if she were anywhere, Justine was waiting for him, even if only in haunting but welcome memories.

Sylvie, meanwhile, was at Reception, having spent the short walk there considering her strategy, see-sawing between the attempted humorous *"You're never going to believe this, but…"* approach and the more direct *"My husband needs some clothes"* tactic. She found a middle way:

"I'm afraid I packed all my husband's clothes, is it possible to retrieve his bag or to lend him something, he's only got his pyjamas you see?" Even as she said it, she realised she was speaking to the sarcastic man who had tried to sell Fergus videos the previous afternoon.

"It's not a problem," he said.

"Oh, thank goodness!" Sylvie sighed with relief.

"As long as he *is* wearing his pyjamas, it is not a problem…" Sylvie wasn't quite sure what he meant.

"But you can get his clothes back, or lend him something, yes?"

"That is a problem madam, I am sorry, but leaving the ship in his pyjamas isn't."

He didn't appear sorry at all and Sylvie was wondering how to tone her answer when a female receptionist rushed across, sounding much more genuine and helpful.

"I'm so sorry madam, we can't retrieve the luggage now, it is already in the port. What I can do is arrange for you to have priority disembarkation and for you both to be escorted to your bags." Sylvie could tell that she was trying to assist and so thanked her, and they agreed that someone would come to their cabin in twenty minutes. She wondered how Fergus would take this news and was surprised to find him philosophical:

"Hey, we get to disembark first! Perhaps we should try this if we come again!"

In time, the receptionist herself knocked on their door. Carrying their hand luggage, they both took one last look at their cabin, before mentally wishing both it and its future occupants well and leaving for good. The receptionist was already heading down the corridor, but Fergus noticed as he turned to follow her that, further up towards the bow behind him, there were some paramedics assisting Mrs Huffington, who was strapped into a wheelchair. He wanted to go back and check she was alright, but he couldn't as the receptionist was by now disappearing round the next corner. He felt a real concern for this old lady with whom he had held such eccentric conversations throughout the cruise, an old lady of whom he had grown fond. Was she unwell? He concluded that he couldn't worry about everything – some things you just had to let go – and so, touching the St Jude hanging round his neck, he said a quick silent prayer for her and then rushed to catch up with his wife.

They reached Reception, where the receptionist herself briefly left them. The area was crowded with passengers, waiting their turn to disembark. Despite the hubbub, Richard and Cressida relaxed on a sofa reading their books, oblivious to the chaos around them. Fergus hoped they wouldn't look up. Replenishing her lipstick in the unlit window of a closed boutique was the lady who had worn the lurid blue dress to the Captain's Party and been so upset when he had not remembered her. For whom she was fixing her make-up now they did not know, perhaps just for herself, but Fergus wanted there to be someone, musing how alone she looked dispossessed of her finery, as she prepared to re-enter the outside world. The three Caballeros, meanwhile, were waiting grimly around a small circular table, nursing their sunburn. It was reminiscent to Fergus of how they had so often sat in the spa bath, only now they were fully dressed and without their colourful cocktails, their red faces the only brightness in the otherwise cheerless scene.

Fergus looked round for Holly or Nicole, but neither was there, he suspected they kept well out of the way on disembarkation mornings and he wouldn't have wanted them to see him like this anyway. He did, though, spot Gentle Henry and Tabitha through the crowd and they seemed to be the only ones to notice him. Completely unbothered by his attire, they smiled and waved and he and Sylvie smiled and waved back. They hadn't even taken each other's contact details and Fergus briefly wondered whether there was time still to do so; however, at that very moment, the receptionist returned. She was now accompanied by two burly port security officials, both wearing bright yellow tabards, which did little to leave Fergus feeling less conspicuous. She wished them an efficient rather than a friendly goodbye, and then the two men took over, leading him, with Sylvie in tow a few feet behind, down two flights of stairs, along a seemingly endless corridor (the length of which extra crew were on hand busily stripping bedding from cabins) and finally out on to the gangway.

So this is how it all ended, with Fergus in his pyjamas being escorted off the ship with a port security official either side, but how had it begun? It seemed both an age and but the blinking of an eye since he and his wife had left their Chiltern home, in fact it was just a few hours short of three weeks. On and on the security officials marched, with Fergus not caring who was watching, but beginning to worry about the cold which was rushing through his pyjamas, into his skin and towards his bones, welcoming him back to Britain and reminding him that he was a very long way from Cape Verde now.

Finally, they reached the baggage hall and, amongst the hundreds of other cases and bags, they quickly found their own. The security officials, who had said nothing throughout, suddenly became talkative and revealed a surprisingly warm side:

"You'll be OK from here, you know how to get back to your car?"

"Perhaps you should put a coat on first?"

"Yes, yes, thank you both. I'm so sorry to put you to this trouble…"

"No trouble at all, but do you mind if we dine out on this one for a while?"

"Not at all, feel free!" Fergus replied jovially.

With a "*Safe journey home!*", as if a double act in perfect unison, they were gone and Fergus scrambled to pull his coat out of his case, to fight off the unfamiliar temperature.

Fifteen minutes later they were driving through the port gates, Sylvie at the wheel, heading through Southampton, towards the M3. She took her hand off the controls, just for a couple of seconds, to squeeze Fergus' and he looked across at her and smiled.

"Quite an adventure!" he said.

"Quite an adventure!" she echoed.

He settled back into his seat, looking forward to seeing home again, laughing quietly to himself as he reflected back over their holiday. Sylvie heard him chuckling and she felt warm to know her husband was relaxed, happy even. There was no rewinding life, Justine was gone, that hadn't changed and it never would, but she too now felt that something else finally had, something that didn't make everything right but would make it easier to cope, bearable... better even than bearable. Or maybe it was simply the fact that they were both home birds after all, feeling as high as the kites circling above their house, to know that they would soon be back there, in the place where they most belonged.

As they accelerated on to the motorway, Fergus leaned forward and switched on the radio:

> "It's just a lifetime ago since you first held her hand,
> When you helped her to walk, helped her to stand,
> Since you travelled with her across sea and land,
> Will you join her where she's gone away?
> You cling to that hope as you breathe in and out
> Through the long years, but there's never a doubt
> That her absence in life is what life's all about.
> Will you see her? You long for that day.
> In the mountains she's absent
> And she's not out at sea,
> She's not lost in a forest,
> Nor in the city,
> And you know that you may as well roam,
> 'cos she's not coming home."

32

Post Script – Hertfordshire – early September 2017

The church was similar to the one in which Jones and Samantha had married just two years earlier – Norman and in a pretty English village – this time though, Fergus and Sylvie were there for the christening of Jones' son, Daniel. Specifically they were there because Jones had asked Fergus to be the godfather, neither he nor his wife having brothers. Ben would have been a good alternative choice, but Jones felt an important history and bond with Justine's parents and he knew Fergus had a quiet but mature faith, along with the wisdom that comes from being older.

The offer had come as a big surprise to Fergus, but he had been delighted, driving up a few days before the service to attend a meeting with the local priest, together with Jones, Samantha and the godmother-to-be, Samantha's older sister. Fergus had been impressed by the vicar, a young man who struck an easy and natural balance between the importance of the occasion and a sense of fun. They studied the healing of Blind Bartimaeus in St Mark's Gospel and to Fergus (much as he had so often experienced on his retreat) it seemed rich with imagery, not least he felt that he had only just emerged from a dark period himself, perhaps a blindness of sorts. He had arrived at the gathering with a feeling of responsibility, he left with that sense even more deeply embedded. He was determined to do a good job for little Daniel, both on the day of his baptism and throughout his childhood. Afterwards, as Jones and Samantha walked with him back to his car, she had said:

"... and we have a small surprise for you on the day. Jones persuaded me, though it didn't take much... we hope you'll like it." Fergus had briefly wondered what this might be, but then had thought no more about it and now, walking up to the church on this bright Sunday morning, he had completely forgotten the enigmatic reference.

All in all, it hadn't been a normal weekend because the previous day, after a gap of more than three years, Katie had paid them a visit. She had phoned a week or so earlier, asking to meet, but forewarning them it was not because she had any news of the accident. They had been intrigued by her call, as well as excited to meet an old friend, and so of course they had agreed.

She had been late arriving and, for a few minutes, an old foe revisited Fergus, suggesting various misfortunes that might have befallen her, as he grew increasingly anxious as to where she could be. This reminded him of the accident they had witnessed on the drive down to Southampton and he felt a sudden urge to know if it had been as bad as had appeared. He searched the internet and quickly found a local news headline referencing 19th November 2016: *"Freak Crash Closes Motorway"*... he read on apprehensively until he came to the sentence "... *miraculously, only light injuries were sustained...*"

"Another miracle!" Fergus thought with relief. Sometimes it felt as if the world were full of them. How many, he asked himself, did he miss entirely? He thought back to the little spider crawling across the Bible, oblivious to the mystical and sacred nature of its surroundings. He was rudely awoken from these spiritual daydreams by the clatter of mail being pushed through the letter box and splattering on to the hallway floor, though of course there were never actual letters anymore. Today, amidst the leaflets for autumn sales, pizza deliveries and boiler services lay one thicker envelope. Fergus opened it: another catalogue from the cruise company – sunny landscapes, smiling faces, iced drinks, show girls, sleek ships cutting across distant seas – seeking to tempt them away again. As he flicked through its glossy pages, his reflections were interrupted a second time, now by the crunching of gravel outside, betraying Katie's belated arrival. Once again he had worried for nothing.

The traffic out of London had been terrible but, as with Jones previously, memories had come flooding back to Katie the moment she turned up the drive. It felt as though she had known the house and its gardens for far longer than the eleven years she had been travelling here. And yet she hadn't known it at all in its happiest days: the near two and a half decades when Justine had lived there… Justine the child and then the young woman. She had been like a mythical figure to Katie: the centre of a long-standing investigation, someone she thought she could imagine but assumed she had never actually met… and, of course, now she never would.

It had turned out Katie had resigned from the police and the previous day had been her last in service… she was now simply Katie Brady.

"I wanted to come and tell you…" she said, after they had welcomed her and settled into the living room, "not just that I've left the police, but that I'm sorry I couldn't find out for you who was responsible for Justine's accident. I left no stone unturned, but the truth is that, after the first few days, there were no new clues and nothing much left to work on… I wanted to uncover the truth, I really did, but I couldn't."

There was a pause.

"Sylvie doesn't remember a thing of what you said on the day we first met you in St Mary's hospital," Fergus started, "but for me it's etched on my mind. I remember you spoke very clearly and said that you could not promise what the result of your enquiries would be, or that you would find the person involved, but – and I remember this very specifically – you said you *'committed personally'* to running a professional investigation, to the very best of your abilities, to give you the best chance possible. You meant it Katie, you really did... you have shown that commitment a hundred times over and you show it again by coming here today, even in your own time."

"I did mean it... but I still didn't succeed."

"You never promised to succeed, only to do your best. As Sylvie said at the time, finding who was responsible wouldn't have brought Justine back, but knowing that you were committed, that meant and still means almost as much as discovering what happened. It shows you cared about Justine's death. At least we know you did everything you could. Thank you."

"Yes, thank you," added Sylvie. There was another period of silence.

"I wish I had met her," Katie said.

"Who knows, maybe you did, or perhaps you passed in the street at least." Sylvie smiled.

"That would be nice to believe," replied Katie.

"Come with me," Sylvie said, leading her upstairs to a small room, overlooking the lawns and the woods, containing a desk, a chair and what appeared to be a sofa bed. Sprinkled across them were a handful of soft toys and, on the desk, a reading light, a vase and a framed photo of Justine. On the wall, an old pale pink baseball cap hung from a hook.

"This was her room... when a child dies, it's hard to know what to do with their bedroom: keep it intact as a museum, as if she may return unchanged at any moment, or dismantle it, like ripping off a plaster. For us this will always be her room, but gradually it has morphed into a study, or somewhere to which we can simply retreat."

Katie looked around, she had not seen it before and she imagined how wonderful it must have been growing up here and watching the seasons change through the window.

"Have this," Sylvie said, handing her the photo.

"I couldn't possibly," Katie replied.

"I'd like you to… not to put up in your own home, but to keep nevertheless. In a strange way, Justine has been a part of your life too… and anyway I have several copies, and thousands of other photos besides. So, please take it."

"Thank you. I'll look after it. I promise," and Sylvie knew that Katie's promises were good.

For the first time, her visit had been purely as a friend, rather than as a police officer, and by the time she left she had been with them a good two hours, chatting about Justine, as well as about Fergus and Sylvie themselves, their cruise and how they were going to Daniel's christening the next day. Katie had told them also about her own plans to move to Lincoln to study visual arts:

"In the Metropolitan Police you quickly learn that life can be grim, but also that goodness is out there too, sometimes hidden, sometimes, as with Justine and yourselves, shining brightly. I want to see more of that beautiful side of life, seventeen years of urban policing is enough."

They had agreed to stay in touch, but in truth all three of them suspected it might not happen, or at least not for a while. She had hugged them one last time and then had gone, leaving them alone once more, both hoping she would find the happiness they would have liked for their own daughter, who would have been only six or so years younger, had she lived.

Fergus and Sylvie entered the church and greeted Jones, Samantha and little Daniel, all three dressed smartly for the occasion. Two other babies were being baptised at the same time and Fergus surveyed them and their young parents admiringly. It was as if new life and all its promise were filling the building. When the time came, Fergus spoke his vows clearly, consciously reflecting on their meaning as he did. Finally, with little Daniel in his arms, the vicar said:

"Daniel William Freddie, I baptise you in the name of the Father, and of the Son and of the Holy Spirit. Amen."

Everyone repeated "Amen" but, as they did so, Fergus and Sylvie looked at each other in surprise at what they had just heard.

Afterwards, outside the church, Samantha laughed:

"I must be the only mother in the whole world who allows her son to be named after her husband's former girlfriend! We did think about 'Justin', but Jones told me your daughter always hated being miscalled that, and obviously we weren't going to call him 'Justine', so we settled on 'Freddie.'"

Fergus and Sylvie were temporarily lost for words, so Jones stepped in:

"Giving him her name – even if only her nickname – well, it shows that she'll never be forgotten, even though life moves on."

"Oh Jones, you don't have to prove anything," Sylvie gently chided, "we've told you before, honour Justine by being happy. But thank you."

"And thank you too," Fergus added to Samantha, touched by her extraordinary generosity.

"You're welcome," she smiled, before whispering mischievously: "and anyway, you probably didn't know it, but Daniel's father here is named after a cat!"

"Actually we did!" they both exclaimed.

As the other three laughed, Jones pretended to be exasperated at yet another recounting of this thirty-five year old anecdote, but in fact he was long immune to its embarrassment. Soon he was chuckling along with them, though, in his case, perhaps less at the oft told joke and more at his own happiness and the sight of his wife so at ease with Justine's parents.

The whole party retreated to Jones and Samantha's small but comfortable semi-detached house for a light buffet lunch, followed by tea a couple of hours later, in the garden. Fergus reacquainted himself with Gabriel but alas, now aged seven, he was rather more grown up and self-conscious than he had been two years earlier, and he neither remembered nor cared to repeat their discussion about dinosaurs, preferring to race around with his young cousins instead. By early evening, Fergus and Sylvie made their excuses. They were pleased to have come but, much like Gabriel, they both found talking to strangers rather hard work.

"One day, when he's a few years older, I'm going to bring Daniel round to show him the badgers," suggested Jones.

"Yes, do that," said Sylvie, "come sooner, you are always welcome, all three of you."

They said their final goodbyes in the hallway, Sylvie blowing a kiss across to Daniel asleep in his carrycot in the next room, oblivious that this had been his big day. Jones let them out through the front door, which then closed behind them with a louder than expected thud, decisively separating their two worlds: the one of an exciting future and the other of a nostalgic past.

"So, a godfather! How does it feel?" Sylvie asked as they strolled to the car.

"Surprisingly good, but I don't think being a godparent is easy these days."

"Perhaps not, but I have a feeling you'll do just fine."

Fergus sat behind the wheel, took off his tie and opened his collar, able to breathe unrestricted again and suddenly aware of the St Jude chain hanging hidden inside his shirt. He briefly thought back fondly to Mrs Huffington, hoping she was alright and treasuring this little gift she had given him, even if he himself no longer felt a lost cause – perhaps it had worked its magic.

No matter how happy the occasion or wonderful the holiday, outbound journeys were never natural to them, requiring more effort and resolve, as if travelling against an invisible current or an atavistic instinct. Homewards invariably felt the right direction. They loved their beautiful house, in its tranquil surroundings, where they had always been secure, where their memories were, the home they had shared with their daughter, both whose presence and whose absence they felt there every day, but perhaps less painfully now.

Forty miles away, the house was equally eager to receive them, it fairly drew Fergus and Sylvie home as they headed steadily down the motorway. Meantime, Justine and Tiger's ghosts waited patiently, playing together on its lawns, amidst the lengthening shadows, looking forward to the car pulling into the drive, to the crunching of the gravel and to knowing that all were safely home again, that all was as it should be.

Until then, brother fox sat sentinel by the front door, washing himself and occasionally swishing his tail, as dusk descended and the bats took to the deepening gloom, as the last kite sailed in to roost and a distant muntjac barked somewhere in the woods and as, from the depths of the badger sett, the first scratches and snuffles rose into the evening air.

"Roam" by Summer Martins

It's just one year ago since she went away,
It feels like forever and like yesterday,
She was so full of colour, the world has turned grey,
And feels small when it once seemed so vast.
No it doesn't seem true but her absence is real,
You're still wanting to call her to say how you feel,
But she's no longer with you and you can't conceal
How she haunts you, this ghost from your past.

It's just five years ago and you think with a sigh
How she left you that morning, no final goodbye,
And life still feels so empty, "Please why did she die?"
You ask for the ten thousandth time.
And a world rich with such beauty when she was near,
A world once filled with joy but now frozen in fear
Has lost what was precious because she's not here:
A planet that's now past its prime.

In the mountains she's absent
And she's not out at sea,
She's not lost in a forest,
Nor in the city,
And you know that you may as well roam,
'cos she's not coming home.

It's now ten years ago yet you're sensing her still
And it makes you so sad but it gives you a thrill,
You hope you might glimpse her but you never will,
She's gone and she's gone for good.
And all of those memories you hold deep inside
Are more precious than gold and you're so full of pride

That she was once yours and oh how you tried
To protect her, you thought that you could.

In the mountains she's absent
And she's not out at sea,
She's not lost in a forest,
Nor in the city,
And you know that you may as well roam,
'cos she's not coming home.

You're lying awake, can't go to sleep,
The grief too profound, the pain far too deep,
The tears that you cry the sole crop that you reap,
You were happy, but now you just weep.
Her bright light is gone and your heart starts to crack,
But your mind still returns to the love that you lack,
And all that's around in this world spun off-track
Is just darkness and blindness and black.

In the mountains she's absent
And she's not out at sea,
She's not lost in a forest,
Nor in the city,
And you know that you may as well roam,
'cos she's not coming home.

It's just a lifetime ago since you first held her hand,
When you helped her to walk, helped her to stand,
Since you travelled with her across sea and land,
Will you join her where she's gone away?
You cling to that hope as you breathe in and out
Through the long years, but there's never a doubt
That her absence in life is what life's all about.
Will you see her? You long for that day.

In the mountains she's absent
And she's not out at sea,
She's not lost in a forest,
Nor in the city,
And you know that you may as well roam,
'cos she's not coming home.